Dances of Death

by the same author:

FLY AWAY HOME
SOMEONE ELSE
THE YOUNGEST

Gillian Tindall

DANCES OF DEATH
Short Stories on a Theme

WALKER AND COMPANY
New York

First published in the United States of America in
1973 by the Walker Publishing Company, Inc.

ISBN: 0-8027-0426-3

Library of Congress Catalog Card Number: 72-96501

Printed in the United States of America.

Foreword

IT HAS BEEN said that Death has now replaced sex as the great taboo subject of our otherwise frank twentieth century society. In fact it has been said so with increasing frequency in recent years, until the observation has become something of a cliché —and, in becoming so, has rendered itself less true. To reflect upon death at all, even if only to remark that it is a pity people don't reflect on it more frankly, is, after all, to broach the topic: a start has been made, however circumspect.

Ten years ago, even five, it was probably accurate to say that the great majority of people in this country, of all ages and levels of intelligence, were reluctant to contemplate mortality realistically at all; any attempt to dwell on the topic was apt to be labelled 'morbid'. I do not think this is true now, and a number of interesting non-fiction books on various aspects of the subject have appeared. Yet the only respectable versions of death widely available in fiction are (a) untimely death as a painless conundrum in the detective story, (b) untimely death as an instant plot-mechanism in the straight novel (would anyone like to attempt a thesis on the fictional role of the fatal car crash?), and (c) more artistically 'timely' death as a means of rounding off a straight novel and endowing it with an apparent weight and poignancy not always justified by the rest of the story. Death is automatically equated with drama and/or tragedy. With a few notable exceptions there has been little modern exploration of death as a continuous and even commonplace fact of living, or of people's variegated attitudes to this incidental fact forever on the horizon of their lives.

The present collection of stories, short and long, is a partial attempt to review the universal subject over a selection of different lives and preoccupations. I have not explored very far—not, in fact, beyond today's prevailing idea that death equals extinction: I have not attempted to look below the horizon. It is not the extra-ordinary possibility of life after death which interests me at the moment but, rather, the ordinariness of death, the awkward mystery, within the context of daily life.

Gillian Tindall

Contents

1

An end in Great Russell Street

AT A QUARTER to four he left the British Museum Reading Room where he had been working that day on the Fossett papers and began to walk steadily though slowly in the direction of Oxford Circus. There was a nearer tube station— Tottenham Court Road—but getting on there would have meant going only one stop and then changing in order to get onto his own Bakerloo line, and he had spent a lifetime being the sort of man who is bored by such fiddling around. He would rather walk—even though it took him far longer than it used to and, just recently, he had had to concentrate on his feet, which occasionally behaved tiresomely.

Once, he would never have left the BM this early if he had had the papers he wanted and the work was going well. But, these days, three or four hours seemed to be about enough. After that spots began to dance before his eyes and once, last June, on rising quickly, he had keeled over, and come to his senses again lying foolishly on the floor with one of those irritating black faces that they had these days at the Central desk bending over him. Gollywogs, every one of them— amiable, of course, and just as much right as himself on earth and so forth—but as for competence... He thought, as he had thought several times, how he must say that to Kingsley, to bait him, and began rehearsing in his mind the examples of non-Caucasian incompetence he would present to his old friend. But then he remembered, again as he had done several times, that his old friend, sparring partner and literary colleague was dead. Had been for a couple of years, blast him.

After that time he had lost his balance—or 'your little fainting fit' as the Reading Room superintendent, his own doctor and Shirley all infuriatingly insisted on calling it— Shirley had started trying to make him go to bed early and eat lunch and 'take it easy' and a number of other boring things he had never done in his life and wasn't going to start now. Silly girl, who did she think she was? (In point of fact she was his eldest child, memento of a youthfully high-principled marriage with a shop-girl which had not survived the First World War and which now seemed to him as shadowy and uninteresting as an event in an outdated and long-unread novel. The stocky, anxious-to-please woman in her fifties who called herself his daughter could no more remind him of the whey-faced, over-scented, undernourished eighteen-year-old who had been her mother than she could fly—even supposing he had wanted reminding. His other two marriages, one in 1922 and one in 1940, had left more coherent traces. Had.)

Anyway poor old Shirley would be fussing if he weren't home by five eating the anchovy toast she would have ready for him. Might as well humour her. It annoyed him—as he frequently told her—to see an active young woman like herself flopping round the house all day without regular employment. It was against the principles he had held all his life and it was obviously bad for her—look how dowdy and fat she was and how she'd let herself go. No wonder her husband had walked out on her, although of course he wouldn't actually *say* that, being a kind person he thought... The fact that Shirley's childless marriage had finally come unstuck like a piece of old and grubby sticking plaster some fifteen years previously when she still had her looks, and that he himself had walked out on no less than three physically attractive wives, not to mention a number of other women, he conveniently forgot. Anyway since old Shirley didn't seem inclined to stir her stumps and do anything with her life as his other children had it was quite useful having her round the flat to do the chores, temporarily of course. And it was nice to feel that, old as he was, he could still do his bit by providing the stupid child with a home and a focus in life.

Stop. This was the place where he had to cross over. So confusing with this one way traffic. Only last week he had nearly been knocked over by a taxi—damn fool. He gripped his brief case and stood, craned forward, waiting his opportunity. As he did so he suddenly saw himself, as if from outside, a trick he had managed to perform at intervals all his life particularly when he was tired. He saw as if on a clip of film his own posture, his light tweed overcoat, youthfully brief, his long legs, his unstooped back and head of thick white hair. Still a commanding figure, thank God, not bald and run to fat or worse like so many of his contemporaries. . . Then, as he tried to concentrate appreciatively on this figure the film cut to another shot: his youngest child Merrill standing in the same posture at a pavement's edge, superintending the crossing of her two small sons, tense with the need to impart caution to them and at the same time to reassure. Splendid mother though she had married so young, splendid girl altogether, grand boys—he must get Shirley to run him down to see them again soon, they must be back from their summer holiday by now. (It was November). Then he remembered.

Blot it out. Right out. He had always done that with unpleasant things, ever since childhood. Don't think of them. When you're not thinking of them they're not there. Relativity —the-tree-in-the-quad. What is this so-called 'reality'? There are always new realities, to be sought or created. What is the use of being a gifted, creative, dynamic, compelling personality if you can't use your powers to escape from things that would otherwise bind and stifle you as they have stifled lesser men? Things like the trenches, like relationships emotional and professional which have gone stale. Like failed political enthusiasms. Like age itself... How many other men at nearly eighty are doing original research into the life and death of the enigmatic Roger Fossett, soldier, poet, pornographer and philosopher? How many other people alive today can even remember Roger Fossett?... He was another escaper, escaped alive though he was all through the trenches. Escaped as far as Greece in 1927... In his mind's eye he saw both his own life and that extended trip which he and Roger had made together to the Adriatic spread out like transparent maps, one superimposed on the other, together making a complex space-time pattern. He heard himself say, as at a cocktail party—he was still very fond of parties—'Yes, Roger Fossett was killed in a stupid car accident in Greece in 1927. I was with him on the trip but had stayed behind in Dubrovnik. Nasty things, motor cars—I've never learnt to drive myself. Fortunately for me I'm of the generation who have never thought it necessary to learn either to drive or to type. Always someone else to do it for us, you see.' And the laughter of those standing round, drinks in hand, fell pleasantly on his ears, gentle, almost deferential.

A hoot—not the first. He realised now with a painful jump that he had heard the first one without registering it. A van was impatiently stationary, the man leaning out:

'Go on then, guv', I can't wait here all night.'

He felt weak and unsteady, but:

'Thank you,' he said with dignity. 'Thank you—I was just about to cross.' He did so, slowly, as six drivers waited for him. Once on the other side he remembered that he hadn't really meant to cross there at all. He had meant to go further along, to the cigar shop, and cross at the lights. Oh well, too late now. He couldn't go back. *Never go back*. The words, the axiom of a lifetime rendered trite by their very familiarity, formed themselves in his mind and his lips moved. *Never go back*. He had never gone back to that Adriatic coast, with its endless rocks and uninhabited bays and main roads that were

mule tracks straight out of the middle ages, going from nowhere to nowhere. Though he might still go back there some-
day, he supposed, for now it was said to be quite different:
a coastal highway and the fishing villages and barren cliffs
sprouting hotels, and as for the islands... Yes. Of course.

It wasn't for fear of the past that he hadn't gone back, for
nothing really frightened him—never had. It was simply that,
to him, the past always became irrelevant. What's more, he
could never actually believe in it. The other week (it had been
three months ago) he had seen a lot of '14–'18 newsreel stuff
on the television which Shirley had wanted to watch for some
reason—she had a vicarious, morbid streak in her, he decided,
no doubt as a result of her unfulfilled life. Anyway all this
archive stock had induced in him an extreme disbelief that he
himself could ever have lived in such a quaintly remote
period. Had he *really* known a London with the streets full of
clopping, defecating horses and people in hats? Still more
unlikely, had he actually ever worn a hat in the street as a
matter of course himself? And it was the same with the
Second World War—all that *Picture Post* stuff of men with
fairisle jerseys and Brylcreem and baggy trousers and women
in drooping prints with mouths like toothy wounds: it seemed
incredible that he himself had actually been then a man in
middle life, accepting this quaint social charade with all its
naïve slang as reality, for God's sake, and even finding one of
those lipsticked houris attractive—attractive enough to marry
again and father Merrill when his other children were all
grown up. He knew intellectually that Irene, whom he had
last seen in 1954, *had* been beautiful by the standards of 1940
and that those were not the standards of today, but on the rare
occasions he thought of her now she was subtly disguised as a
girl of today—one of those impassive gipsies with long, long
legs, their tumbling hair and unpainted faces looking as if they
had just got out of bed, which no doubt was the intended
effect... He did find them quite attractive, as a matter of fact,
if a bit obvious. Thank heaven one had not remained stuck at

one point in taste like most of his aquaintances, still mumbling on about Myrna Loy or Veronica Lake like an old gramophone record while the tides of altering desire went on without them. Old fogies.

On reflection, it was only because Roger was now so utterly remote from him that he had consented to write the great biography. That tremendous quarrel they had had in Dubrovnik about which no one, living or dead, had ever known. . . He *had* felt badly about that, he was prepared to admit it. Oh, for perhaps twenty-five years he had felt vagely uncomfortable about it, when he remembered it, which was not every year. . . But, contrary to what that well-intentioned young idiot at his publishers supposed, nothing lasted forever, not even memories. They spoke to him, these raw youngsters in their forties, as if they expected his close friend the enigmatic and legendary Roger Fossett to seem as real a human being to him as ever : he did not tell them that on the contrary Roger, like everyone eventually, even his second wife or his mother, seen through the glass of memory had finally dwindled into a jerking puppet, a quaint period-doll to amuse the adults of the present, almost as unreal as the white-faced shop-girl with her scent of cheap violets, her dubious underclothes and her tinny accent which had first struck him as poignant and had later repelled him.

Then, suddenly, he saw her. She was walking a little ahead of him, her jerky walk faintly hampered by her long cotton skirt. Skirts of that length had really gone out in 1915: she ought to shorten it and show her legs in the modern way, he would tell her. He hastened a little in order to do so, feeling as he did so a pang of pity that was also sensually enjoyable at the idea that she should not be able to afford anything but cotton on this chilly afternoon. He would make her buy something better. Her dark hair hung loose as if she had just risen from their clandestine bed off Tavistock Square, and, as she turned her head (perhaps sensing his approach) he saw clearly the pinched yet flowerlike features, the short upper lip over the little teeth which at first had reminded him of a child and then finally of a rabbit.

But before he could reach her—damn these unaccountably slow legs—she had turned and was walking briskly up Gower Street. Only then did he realise he was mistaken. She was too tall for Poppy—his derisively affectionate name for her—and she was wearing long suede boots which Poppy never had and a sort of browband like one of his grandsons dressed as a Red Indian. Like a sleeper surfacing to full wakefulness through different levels of dream, he thought: no, I'm wrong about the skirt, long skirts have come back again, and the Lenglen band—of course it's 1930... No, wait, a minute: when was the New Look...? He had been caught out; the word 'modern' had presented itself to him as an image of flesh coloured silk extending above the knee and reclining against black and orange cushions. Yes, he *was* right, that had been modernity, but this was something else. 'Post-modernity'? 'Neo-modernity'? 'Posthumous'—'Post Roger'? He tried the words out in his mind and nearly bumped into a lamp-post. How odd that Poppy should have appeared just then. He wouldn't mention it to Shirley, of course. She might feel jealous of the young girl.

Noticing his cigar shop on the other side of the street he began to tack back through the traffic, which pulled up sharply to avoid him. The shop next door to the cigar shop was displaying Kitchener's recruiting poster which momentarily distracted him: he had thought the War was over. His brother was certainly dead and he'd gone west in one of the last offensives, in 1918. Yes, poor old John. One had always known that the poor old boy—His father's favourite but not gifted, not 'promising' like oneself—was destined for that sort of end. Incompetent, a born loser... But one had minded of course all the same. John, stuffy old thing, had disapproved of Poppy like anything. Fatuous simpleton.

He went into the cigar shop and there was John behind the counter, trench moustache and all. It quite threw him so that

for a moment he forgot what he'd come for. It seemed un-
friendly to say 'I'd thought you were dead' so in the end he
just bought some matches and went out again. It couldn't
really have been John. Could it? Not that John would ever
have worked behind a counter, the whole thing must be some
idiotic joke, or one of those half-baked today things like Zen
or whatever it was. Wilfully inexplicable. More dignified—
and more sane—just to ignore the whole thing.

Emerging from the shop he felt himself suddenly recovered
and in control again. Odd, and rather embarrassing these
moments of aberration. He now noticed that across the street
from where he stood they were demolishing yet another solid
Victorian building and doing it, it seemed, in the messiest
possible way. He remembered now that he had stood and
watched last week while workmen dismantled the Gothic-
gabled roof. Now he stood watching again, and became aware
that he was one of several men standing on that stretch of
pavement gazing across and up—that through their days of
work the labourers must have a constant, shifting audience.
Did people enjoy seeing destruction or did they watch it
regretfully? Last week, he remembered, he had watched
censoriously, had gone home to complain to Shirley about the
ruin of the environment and the way municiple vandalism
was subtly worse than private vandalism because it was on a
larger scale: not for nothing had he and Roger been among
the first of their generation to suggest that the then-despised
Victorian architecture had a grandeur all its own. Today half
the building was gone and the other half seemed to be lying
in shattered fragments below, really exactly like the blitz even
to the smell of the dust. A crane arm (the crane itself and the
driver were hidden from view) swung a ball and chain
slowly back and forth like some blind but menacing animal,
manoeuvring, delivering clumsy but subtly lethal blows to the
shaken walls. Now it shifted and nuzzled persistently round
some pieces of cornice, eventually sending them crashing to

their doom four floors below. It would be the turn of the whole window frame next.

As he watched his disapproval was gradually replaced by a sense of elation. The very scale of the holocaust was stimulating. A large building that, until two months ago, had been treated as serviceable, valuable even, kept clean and warm, now by an arbitrary decree lay ripped and smashed. Wasn't there something rather healthy in that? The past deliberately swept away, its fusty inner fittings consumed in purificatory fires, nothing parsimoniously saved? He watched with enjoyment for a good seven minutes as the blind monster knocked and loosened and crunched and the brick and stone clattered down.

When he set off again he found he was feeling tireder. Each step seemed to need careful planning and that damn buzzing in his head had started up again. It drove him mad sometimes when he was working. Shirley kept telling him it was 'just the blood circulating' as if she thought that knowing that helped any, silly cow. He wasn't worried by it—it just made him furious. Angry now he shuffled on... Where the hell was a taxi? ... Had he been meaning to take a taxi? Well he was now. As if in answer to his thought an empty one, its sign lit, came quickly down the street toward him. He was just about to hail it when he noticed its number plate. It said 'KRK'.

While he stood there it went past, slowing as if the driver too had expected him to hail it and then gathering speed when he did not raise his arm. Krk. An island, that was, off the northern Dalmatian coast—one of those Slav names with no vowels. Most people in England would never have heard of it, except for... And they would forget it again. In a year or two most people would have forgotten the name had ever been significant—that there had ever been an air crash there. Why even to himself the immediate impression the letters KRK left on the mind, like an image on a retina, was not that of tarmac and crushed metal and split-open suitcases of summer clothes but simply a rather bare island, one of many in the hauntingly unreal beauty of the Dalmatian archipelago. He and Roger had not gone there, he rather thought. But they had talked of going, maybe, and had visited similar ones: goats, a bell chiming flat across the flat water, peasants for whom even the trip to the mainland was a rare event. The primitive insularity (literally) of it all had begun to weigh on him after a while: that had been one of the many causes for their senseless quarrel, hadn't it?

If they had gone to Krk—if he himself had made a special trip there (but for what reason?)—would that have altered some cosmic pattern far out beyond the blue, unreal shores of rational understanding? Would his earlier visit have propitiated the gods (those gods in whom Roger affected to believe) and done something to prevent a large aeroplane crashing onto the island more than forty years later. Could he then as a young man, by some supernatural exercise of concentration and understanding have saved his future child and *her* children and husband? If so, then Merrill and his grandsons had died because all time was one and he had not cared enough, not made efforts, had quarrelled self-indulgently with Roger just because he had been bored.

All nonsense, of course. Morbid, self-important nonsense. Just the sort of thing Shirley went in for, with her blasted astrology, and which he so much despised. In reality there were no patterns, cosmic or otherwise, and one didn't necessarily 'pay' for anything and certainly not like that. But even as he said this to himself, lips moving as if he were haranguing Shirley, the fearful implications of what he was saying struck home. For if there were no retributions there were no rewards either and no promises of endeavour justified. He had also— really, all his life—believed in an unthinking, never-quite-formulated way that his own persistent good fortune owed something to his personal resilience and talents. As an outstanding boy at school he had felt there was every cause for optimism, that life would always see him right, basically, whatever it did to others. And on the whole life had. Only now, almost incidentally on a street corner in his seventy-ninth year, did the horrible truth come to him that the future was not after all preparing to make amends any more for whatever blows the present had dealt him and that there might not be much future left in any case. Whatever had happened had happened and even God—that God in whom he had not believed for the last sixty odd years—could not alter it. Merrill and the little boys were dead, and there was really nothing more to be said to anyone. In the end he had lost. The sense of oppression and failure which he had had since the summer and, not recognizing what it must be, had privately labelled 'old age' was, after all, just an unassuageable, permanent grief.

He broke into a sweat. The noise was buzzing in his ears so that he could not tell if it were that or the perpetual sound of the traffic that made his head throb. Dark spots hovered before his eyes, blotched his vision like big spots of rain on a glass, but through the spots he suddenly saw that other cars and buses in the Tottenham Court Road were also called 'KRK'— in fact they all were. Even as his eyes noticed this curious fact his common sense rejected it: this was surely phoney, a manic desire to see significance everywhere, to perceive patterns where there were really none. But a moment later he forgot this explanation as he saw that the street was filled with Johns and Poppies—lots and lots of them in different versions. It would be them, he thought resentfully; just because I don't care about them. He avoided their collective eyes.

It was then that he saw Roger, in half-profile, just getting onto a bus.

Roger!

He believed he had called the name. He thought he had begun to run. But the passers-by who fairly quickly began to gather round the slumped tweed overcoat all said that the old gentleman had just sunk to the ground there where he had been standing, his briefcase still clutched in his hand.

As a medical student knelt to undo the buttons of his tweed

coat and two policemen walked purposefully up through the growing crowd, a particularly large lump of masonry was dislodged by the crane on the far side of the street. It crashed onto the man-made rocks below, as the plane had crashed onto other rocks, as Roger's hired car had crashed into a Greek hillside, and the crashes fused in his mind with the roaring in his ears and became one.

2

The enemy

GOSH I MUST 'phone Mother some time. I was going to at Christmas but, Christ, you know what Christmas is like—absolute chaos with all the presents the kids get, and we had Auberon's brother who'd just come from St Kitts and his girl Clara *and* Lola Stein from up the road and her two because Dan had just walked out on her. (He's walked back now, incidentally, and she's having Another, she told me last week: I promised to have her children while she's in hospital, fool that I am—at least it won't happen for ages yet. I suppose.)

Yes ... where was I? Christmas. Mother. Yes. Well we did send her a present, of course. Yes, I'm almost *sure* we did. A blue scarf. Auberon wrapped it up with all the other things on Christmas Eve—he's like that, Auberon, God I should know him by now! He goes on for weeks about hating Christmas and Christmas being the annual festival of St Sales-manager and Christmas making him vomit (mainly that)—and then two days before he suddenly melts and rushes out and buys arm-fuls of things we can't afford, and discovers Love and Charity and Tolerance and gripes at me because I haven't bought a tree yet or ordered a turkey. Not having an old-fashioned Christmas is depriving the kids of roots or something—but try saying that to him before he's reached the point of psychological melt! I've learnt *not* to.

Yes I know we sent off that scarf because Clancy even did a

card to go with it. Thank goodness Clancy, at least, has got to the age of being able to organise himself a bit. In fact he'd organise the lot of us if he could—he tries. The bumps on his forehead stand out and he screams 'Mum, you're not *listening*' —or 'But you *said* we'd do that today'—or 'But we *have* to plant a bulb each, Miss said so.' And then I usually feel remorseful. Oh not specially about whatever it is he's trying to nag me into doing, but about how he's going to hate me for this more and more as he gets older, and how I'm going to fail him because I must fail him: it's the inevitability of it which saddens me. He's not like me at all—or like Auberon, much, except in the strength of his passion. He wants order, he wants rules and vetoes. He wants a household where meals are at set times every day, where people plant bulbs every spring and remember to water them, where stamps are stuck in albums and even free offer send-off coupons have their place. A household where no one ever quarrels, but when the children are naughty they are ritualistically hit—the teacher at school he's liked best so far would run a household like that. He's battling hard at the moment to change us. He doesn't know yet that it's hopeless. We shall never change now because we don't really want to, any more than Auberon himself, whatever he may say, really wants to get a better job with more administrative responsibility, or to shed completely that chip on his shoulder about being West Indian. It's got quite comfortable for him, that chip I think. He'd feel lost without it, in fact.

Auberon says Clancy's a throwback to his (Auberon's) slave ancestors—that Clancy's a natural slave, tough and resourceful but really at home under the lash, needing a harsh master, needing to feel his own unworthiness. Auberon's always going on about his race's origins—his roots—which of course is entirely right and healthy and far better than treating them as unmentionable as some other educated West Indians do, only it used to make me feel quite sick with pity and misery and not-wanting-to-know. When we were first married, when Clancy was on the way in fact, I used to lie and think about

the slave ships and the chains and the way a third of them
used to be dead by the time the crossing was over, and
particularly about that Captain who snatched a baby out of
its mother's arms and threw it far out into the sea because it
wouldn't stop crying... And then I used to cry, and Auberon
half-liked that because he found it sexy. (He finds almost anything sexy but calmness and sweet reason—me lying in bed
finishing the chapter in my book turns him right off.) But I've
got over all that years ago—that not being able to bear the
idea that my children were directly descended from such
suffering, I mean. Partly, I suppose, I've just got used to it, and
partly I no longer imagine, as I did when the children were
babies, that they are an extension of me or necessarily even
close to me. After all, once they're all grown up they might
live quite different lives from ours (Clancy I'm sure will, and
maybe Zoe too). We might never see them, in fact. And if that
is the way it is to be then I shan't fight against it or try to
get them round in unfair ways—I'm determined about that,
anyway. I mean, look at me and Mother.

Mother. That's who I suspect Clancy *really* takes after and not
after all those slave-savages of Auberon's at all. She'd never see
it herself, though—even if she saw him often enough to tell,
which she doesn't. To her, skin is everything, and she would
never grasp that her own personality traits—her own physical
traits too, for that matter—could appear within a coffee-
coloured packaging. On the few occasions when she has seen
her grandchildren I have caught her studying their mat com-
plexions, their snub noses and abundantly woolly hair, like a
person looking at creatures in a zoo: mildly curious, very
faintly squeamish, essentially disassociated from them. She is
polite to them—the nervous politeness of one who is not sure
that there mightn't be, on the other side of the cage, a notice
saying 'These Animals are Dangerous'. The only—yes, the
only things she's ever said to me about their physical appearance was years ago when Pegeen was about eight months old.
It was the first time Mother'd seen her, and she said 'She's a

little paler than the others, isn't she? That's something.'

Auberon *hates* Mother and of course it's quite proper that he should. He's a great hater and Mother's such a lovely simple target—white, elderly, Conservative, upper class, (upper middle class, actually, but Auberon doesn't realise that, his view of society being somewhat simplified)—and convention-bound to her heart. It's impossible to say what Mother 'really' thinks about anything because she doesn't actually have thoughts at all—just layers and layers of convention and prejudice and inherited assumption, all bound round and round and held together with the odd consciously enlightened maxim she's picked up somewhere. (Example: 'Of course colour of skin makes no difference to me—some of the coloured people are charming.' or 'Of course I believe children should be free to lead their own lives. I'm not going to be an interfering Grandma!')

Naturally these maxims—so transparently prefaced by 'of course'—do not represent her deeper attitudes. And when I came home from college that vac eleven years ago—God, is it really?—and said I was going to marry Auberon, she was simply horrified—and I don't mean that lightly. 'Horrified' has become a trivial word in lots of cases and therefore, I suppose inadequate to what I am trying to say, but 'horror' still has an undercurrent—of primitive fear and abhorrence—*that's* a better word, perhaps—and that's what I'm trying to express. Lots of parents might have been 'a bit horrified', I should think, in the chatty sense, but Mother... It wasn't just that Auberon was a trainee social worker with a minimal grant and no prospects. It wasn't just that he was foreign (which West Indians are, poor them, whatever they or other people may say) and that he was, for all his airs, pretty badly educated. Nor was it his admittedly deplorable personality. I could well understand—could even then have understood—any prospective parent-in-law who really got to know Auberon being put off by his excitability, his moodiness, his compulsive exhibitionism, his tendency to lie, his self pity, his lack of

brains, his boring bloody chip—But Mother didn't know
Auberon at all. She'd only met him once and had said
restrainedly afterwards how charming he was (true) and What
Lovely Teeth These People Have. No—she was just absolutely
and profoundly horrified at the idea of my marrying what I'm
sure she really thought of as 'a nigger'. She quite lost her head,
and stammered, and went white and red and used the most
extraordinary words I'd never heard from her before—words
like 'nasty, dirty physical appetites', and a lot about how I
must be 'sex mad' and was 'letting myself down' and being
'like a young man with a barmaid, only worse', and then a lot
about it being 'the primrose path' and how (if I got her meaning straight, which I've never been sure) once I'd got used to
being embraced by someone like Auberon I'd never be able
to go back to a more 'suitable' man.

So what, you may say, I might have expected it; this is just
the language of blind prejudice, transparently Freudian and
common enough. Why was I in my turn so shocked?

Well but it was *Mother*, not just some female of similar age
and background I'd met on a bus. And she'd always seemed,
however irritating, at least more or less rational before,
according to her own view of life. More rational than me, in
fact. She was always telling me that I'd have to organise myself
a bit more or I'd never get anywhere. And she was absolutely
right—I never have.

Take Christmas now! Well, Christmas with her wasn't
chaos, wasn't a saturnalia gone wrong, wasn't a time when the
accumulated mute reproach of all the people unwritten to, the
presents unsent or unthanked-for—all the things left undone
in the last twelve months—threatened to become overwhelm-
ing. Christmas with her was a sustained campaign, a challenge
proudly met. Even the vocabulary for describing it is martial:
the day in early November when she drew up the first list, the
buying of the cards, the planned sorties 'to town' for presents,
the wrapping and labelling and despatching. The first part of
the campaign used to be regularly won a good fortnight before

The Day, when she would, with justifiable pride in her own
efficiency and generosity, line up all the bought, wrapped,
labelled and sealed presents before taking them down to the
post office. There was no risk either that she had forgotten
anyone, or embarrassingly bestowed the same oven glove or
box of candied apricots on anyone that she had done the year
before. She kept a card-index to avoid such mistakes—like the
other card-index she had in the kitchen with the names of
people who'd been to meals and what they'd eaten. 'It just
makes it easier,' she used to say with off-hand pride. 'You'll do
the same when you're grown-up and have a home of your own.
It's just common sense.'

After the expedition to the post office ('I could hardly carry
them all!' she would cry gaily: excess made permissible, kept
within bounds)—After that, the only other major hurdle (apart
from the mass of cooking) was the noting down of all givers'
names on the appropriate list at Parcel Opening on The Day.
She would have four lists ready prepared on the mantlepiece,
with four pencils, one for herself, one for Dad, one for me and
one for Charlie, and as each parcel was opened the recipient
had to note down the gift and the giver on his own list
(Mother herself did Charlie's and mine until we were old
enough.) Till that was done, no one was allowed to open
another present: Mother, in her gay Christmasy way, was
quite firm about that. Otherwise, she said, it would be Chaos.
A terrible thought, chaos, to Mother. I have sometimes thought
that the tabloid press direct their headlines straight at Mother,
knowing just how to rouse her—though she wouldn't thank
me for the thought: she reads the *Telegraph* herself. At any
rate whenever I see a placard saying 'Frost and snow bring
chaos' or ' "It was chaos" says Ministry spokesman', I think of
Mother and her gay, unremitting battle against such forces of
death and night.

It would be easy to pretend—in fact I rather think I was
about to—that I always loathed these family Christmases and
similar over-organised events (half-terms, the annual holiday

to the Isle of Wight) and squirmed at such regimentation even at the age of six. But the truth of the matter is, of course, that, like all children, I loved Christmas, and my Mother, and took her fetish of order and control as being just one of those things grown ups are supposed to go in for, not personal to her at all. We were a fairly-well, close-knit family, I suppose you'd call it, we didn't go to other people's houses much, or have many visitors, in spite of that careful card-index, and it was years before it began to dawn on me that not everyone's mother found it necessary to go on like mine. By that time I was in my teens when it is natural to criticise your parents any-way—Mother herself had certainly heard that 'adolescents' (the word seemed newish then, and Mother rather liked using it) were supposed to go on like that. Thus she pre-empted any complaint I made, justified or unjustified, by putting it all down to 'my age'. She seemed to have my age on the brain. She kept dropping jolly, casual references to 'awkward feel-ings' and spots and 'the curse' and 'tiresome moods', and how lovely it was going to be for me when I was grown up and could 'go out with young men in cars—to dances and so on'. She thought it would be nice for me to go to college because there were 'lots of young men there', some of whom would, hopefully, be 'my own sort'. She meant brainy, since she believed I had brains, and also upper middle class, from Public Schools, with homes like mine in Esher, East Grinstead or Basingstoke. She was, and is, so completely snobbish, so obsessed by class in all its aspects, that she manages not to realise her own obsession at all, like a fish not knowing its in water, or a person not knowing he is breathing air. She believed herself to be splendidly modern and democratic, and used to refer laughingly to her 'best friends', the milkman, the baker and the ingratiating character who delivered vegetables. It was as if she thought that still, somewhere in England in the mid-fifties, were members of the upper classes who had old-fashioned servants and ill-treated them, and she enjoyed the implicit contrast with her own egalitarian kindness.

Because she also believed herself to be enlightened and modern about sex she confused me for a while into believing that she was. 'You can always ask me anything you want to' she used to say. So one day when I was sixteen I asked her where one bought contraceptives because I had read about them in a book and they sounded useful. I wasn't planning to rush off and buy any of course: none of the 'nice boys' in whose company I was allowed to go to Pony Club dances had so far got any further than clutching at my rather obvious breasts. I just thought it would be useful to know. Her neck flushed a surprising red; her chin jerked up. 'Good heavens!' she said, 'What a question! I don't really think you need know that *yet*, do you? . . . And anyway, girls—women, that is, of our sort—they simply don't go buying such things. I—I simply can't think where you get such sordid ideas from.'

Later in the day, when she had had time to mass her forces for the attack, she gave me a little, understanding, motherly lecture on not moping around on my own having unhealthy thoughts, and how much better I'd feel if I tidied up the awful mess in my room and then went for a bicycle ride with Charlie. She was always telling me how I would feel, either in the short or the long term, and of course I resented it—wouldn't anyone? She was also given to asserting that I would do so-and-so when I was older—see the social point of playing tennis, or take to wearing a roll-on-suspender belt, or even to keeping a card-index of guests' eating habits in my own kitchen. 'I won't!' I would cry, and she would nod and smile till my fingers itched to slap that smirking pink visage of maternal conceit and supremacy, pink pancake make-up and all. 'Oh, but you will,' she would say. 'You will. You'll see.'

Christ, it was enough to drive anyone to Auberon, wasn't it? Well, yes, that's just the trouble. . . You see, when I really think about Mother and get worked up about her all over again (which is only once in a blue moon these days, I must

admit) I pretty quickly convince myself that my marrying
Auberon the moment I was twenty-one was just the inevitable
end-product of all Mother's controlling and needling—the
grand gesture of defiance. But do I really want to think of
Auberon, after eleven years, five—well, four—kids, and innumerable shattering rows, as just my adolescent gesture of
defiance? To think that seems really capitulating to Mother
—seeing everything in her terms, even if it *does* enable me to
go on blaming her forever. No, oh God no—I'd much rather
see myself as just myself: a freak, a throwback, fundamentally
unsuited to the family and the way of life into which I was
born; a black sheep who knew what she was and cut free as
soon as possible to do her own thing, lead her own sort of
life with her own black ram—how pat the image falls! And
most of the time I do genuinely manage to think of myself like
that—someone just alien to Mother, someone whose present
way of life has nothing whatsoever to do with her childhood.
Someone to whom Mother is no longer relevant.

Auberon is a pretty ghastly social worker really—I mean, he's
always working his clients up when he's supposed to be sooth-
ing them down (working them up in silly ways, I mean—not
political ones which might have some point to them)—and
then when more senior people in the Agency criticise him he
gets huffy about it and says they just want him there as a
show-case nigger etc. etc. But in spite of being like that, and
in spite of hating my Mother, he has vague social worker-
cum-homespun West Indian principles about families being a
Good Thing. So in fact it's usually been him over the years
who has said 'We ought to go and see your Ma,' or, more
commonly 'What about that fucking cow of a mother of yours
then, have you rung her yet like you said you would—eh?
eh?' This suits me, I suppose, because it lets me out of taking
any initiative unprodded which might look as if I actually
liked Mother or something. And it lets him feel momentarily,
while he's nagging me into doing my daughterly duty, like the

more 'mature' one (social workers' cant for 'more amenable to low reasoning'). And it's nice for the poor old thing to feel like that once in a while, because mostly I treat him like one of the children, screaming at him to take his horrible feet off the table and stop picking his nose for God's sake and stop teasing Zoe about being fat.

But I suppose he hasn't been doing much nagging lately, or else I just haven't listened, because even I have to admit we haven't seen Mother for *ages*, not for—gosh: well over a year, it must be. I didn't realise it was quite that long. I've seen Dad and Charlie once on my own: I had an expensive but rather dingy lunch with them in November at Dad's club—I suppose I should say 'their' club now that Charlie himself is an accountant and rising thirty with a pregnant wife in Aldershot. It was so that they could explain to me about some Trust that's ripened or fallen in or whatever Trusts do... God knows, Auberon and I need the money, but for so long I've got into the habit of never listening when anyone starts on about Trusts or Wills or legacies or any other form of unearned family loot, that I couldn't bring myself to listen hard about this one. Anyway I seem to remember Dad saying Mother was well but had been having—what was it now? Headaches? Stomach upsets? No: 'dizzy spells', that was the phrase. She sent me her love, he said. I sent mine back, I suppose. I don't remember, actually, but I never, when confronted with poor old Dad in his office clothes, *quite* have the nerve not to. He must know now, as Mother herself surely does, that love 'sent' is a meaningless counter, just a piece of nickel passed dutifully from hand to hand.

But Mother herself I haven't seen or spoken to since—well, since last winter anyway. And now this winter's over: it's March already. Heavens. Oh I don't mean, heavens what a long time since I've seen Mother (as if I care—) but just—Oh heavens, time! Time. It's true, the children are all growing and growing as if they'd eaten Time and it was packed inside their expanding torsos and gangling legs... Only Auberon and I stay the same, unexpanding, not advancing, fixed in our postures facing each other with drawn knives. I expect we'll still be standing there, like fighters in a frieze, when they've all grown bigger than us at last and gone away. Whatever shall I do?

August. In August I know we had a card from Mother. (Well ostensibly from Dad as well of course, but Mother wrote it.) It was from Majorca or Torremolinos or some such synthetic haven outside time and geography, and it said the things cards say, I suppose. You might think it a little irrational that Mother should have to go all the way to southern Spain in order to communicate with me: after all, you might think, for the rest of the year Esher, Surrey, and Holloway, London N7., are not really so far from one another... You would be wrong.

Mother sent the children things for Christmas, of course—jigsaws (they've none of them ever liked jigsaws) and a printing set which lost bits of itself at once. And Dad sent us his usual cheque. Of course we thanked them... We *must* have.

Yes, we did. I've just remembered! We opened the presents as soon as they arrived: we always do. And it was after that that Clancy wrote the card to go with the scarf and I put our thanks on it: that'll kill two birds with one stone, I thought.

Suppose that card didn't get sent?

... Oh Christ. I've just been upstairs to look. And I found the bloody thing with several others, lying under a lot of papers and balloons I'd got for the kids and forgotten to give them, under the wellies in the big wardrobe. I knew there was a lot of guck down there but I just hadn't looked at it. Oh hell. And I'm not even sure now that the scarf got sent either. I have a ghastly feeling I saw it recently, in the boys' room, under the bunk beds with a lot of old paper hankies I suppose I ought to clean out before they start walking out on their own... Come to think of it, Mother didn't ring me up to thank me for it and almost certainly she would have, if she'd had it. I know she's completely lost interest in me these days—just given me up as a bad job, I'm happy to say!—but she does observe the proprieties, of course. She would have phoned.

Oh hell.

Too late now. I feel very low. I've just remembered that row. I once had with Dan Stein—oh, ages ago, and I was bloody angry about it and suppressed it, I think. It was one day when Pegeen was a baby and I'd taken her to the clinic and had been listening to all those women yacking idiotically on about how nicely they'd got their babies organised with feeds at regular hours and sleeping at regular hours and shitting in the pot and so on. And I think I was saying to Dan what a lot of bloody ball-breaking cows they were, thinking he'd be sympathetic because Lola is as disorganised as me, jolly nearly —but he suddenly got furious. Yes, furious with *me*. He started on about gastro-enteritis (which admittedly Zoe did have once) and when I said 'But antibiotics' he said 'Yeah, Yeah, antibiotics, doctors, the sewage system, all that—people like you just rely on all that to prop you up so that you can go on being as bloody childish and irresponsible as you like. You're sort of parasites,' he said, 'parasites on other people's common sense and effort. You can only afford the luxury of squalor because you live in an affluent and well-organised society which takes care of you nevertheless. In any other place and time, he said, your children would just die because you're incapable of looking after them properly. Too busy striking attitudes.'

Well of course I was simply *furious*. Who wouldn't be? And I still think it was frightfully unfair of him. But the awful thing was, *I'd* used that word 'parasite' myself, often—about Mother and people like her. I mean, middle class women whose children have all grown up and who do nothing all day but shop and play golf and drink coffee with their friends *are* parasites, aren't they? Well, you know what I mean. And about Mother I meant the word more specifically, too: I meant that she was an emotional parasite—on me. It was Auberon who first said this about her, actually. It was before we were

married, when this frightful family row about us was going on,
and I used to cry a lot, particularly after we'd made love.
(Can't *think* why, now.) And Auberon used to say 'That Ma of
yours is sucking your blood, man. She means to gobble you up.
She's feeding on you. You get out from under her.'

Funny thing is, I've gone on thinking about her in those
terms all these years, and that's been my reason for avoiding
her—and a pretty good one, surely? But I have to admit,
thinking about it, in strict truth, that this has become a bit
out of date. I mean, it's actually been years since Mother's
tried to *feed* off me. Or take a nibble, even. As I said, she's
lost interest.

Anyway, to return to Dan Stein, as far as I remember, I
told him that my kids were growing up without me on their
necks: that at any rate *they* didn't have someone making
them tidy up their things pointlessly and telling them lies
about life and interfering with them—And he said nastily:
(he was really nasty that day) 'Yeah, and no one looking after
their interests either. No one making sure they're warm enough
or have their dinner money on Monday or remembering to
take them to the dentist.' Bloody hell, how could he have
known Rory's teeth were rotten just then and our doctor was
saying I should have noticed?

There was a lot more he said I don't remember—but anyway
I kept telling him that he didn't understand; that Auberon and
I *like* living in this muddle—that surely it was our business
and just a matter of taste? And then he shouted 'Sure you like
it, and why? Because it makes you feel bloody superior, that's
why? Because you're so damn conceited that you think your
squalor proves you're someone—that it makes you free or
spontaneous or life-loving or creative or some such fucking
cant! You can't see, can you, that all these broken toys'—we
were in our place and he started kicking things on the floor—
'all those appointments you don't keep, all those letters I bet
you don't answer and bills you don't pay—aren't grand, free
gestures; they're just *failures*. You can't carry anything

through. You and Auberon spoil and ruin everything you touch: clients, kids, possessions, this house—everything. What about those rabbits of Clancy's that starved to death because he forgot to feed them, being a kid, and you didn't remind him? Yeah—and come to that what about that other baby—'

It was at that point I hit him. I can hit hard when I try, having had practice with Auberon, and the discussion ended there. The next day he apologised. He said he'd been drunk, and furious really with Lola because she'd let the kids pick up impetigo—he'd just displaced his fury onto me, he was sure I'd understand. He hadn't meant any of it really and particularly about the baby, he was really sorry at having mentioned that, he knew how cut up about it Auberon and I had been at the time... And I, pained but dignified you know, said sure, sure, I understand: we all have our hang-ups, I'm prepared to forget the whole thing.

But he did mean it. Every word of it.

I really ought to phone Mother some time. If we go *too* long without speaking (is over a year too long?) it'll get embarrassing. I'll do it tomorrow. I really will.

I haven't phoned Mother after all. I was going to, I really was, I'd just get set to do it... And then, two days ago, I had this telegram from Charlie.

Mother died yesterday, it said. *Please ring me.*

In the end I rang him, and his wife answered. Hallo, I said, how's it going—meaning her pregnancy—and it turned out of course that she'd had the baby weeks ago. It's a boy—they're calling it Claud. 'Charlie did try to ring you several times,' she said, in her stupid little schoolmistress's voice, carefully not reproachful. 'We knew you wouldn't have seen it in *The Times*. But we could never get you. Perhaps you were away?'

We weren't, but I just remembered then that I'd gone through a phase of not answering the phone—I do sometimes, it makes me feel good to hear it ringing stupidly away to itself and finally giving up. I feel quite cunning for at least half an hour after. No doubt some of those ignored rings were Charlie. Or Mother, come to that. I'll never know.

'That's why Charlie sent you a telegram this time,' she said, modulating her voice now to a suitably repressed note. 'I'm sorry about your Mother,' she said awkwardly, and I said, 'Good heavens—why?' Which was really ruder than I'd meant to be.

She started telling me that Mother had had high blood pressure and had died suddenly of a coronary—which I'd always thought was something only sexy old men got, not golf-playing housewives in their fifties. Then she moved onto when the funeral is and how Dad (she calls him Dad too) will be going to live with them in Aldershot 'for the moment'. What a lot they seem to have fixed up in two days. I feel for once quite admiring at their energy.

If she'd said 'Will you be coming to the funeral?' I think I might have said No. I mean, what is the point? But she just sort of assumed I was, so I suppose I shall. I suppose it's just as well, really. I mean, not going to someone's funeral (however pointless)—well, it's a bit of a gesture, isn't it? A bit of a grand repudiation. And there wasn't ever anything grand between Mother and me—just nothing left at all.

... It's funny. I've just been thinking about it. Charlie's wife said 'I'm sorry if the telegram was a shock to you—so sudden, I mean.' But how can you be shocked by something that's completely meaningless to you, in personal terms, a non-event? Because that's what Mother dying is to me. But for Charlie and Dad being dutiful, she could have been dead for months before I'd even have known about it, and then it wouldn't have *meant* anything. It makes not the faintest difference to me these days whether she's alive or not: I shouldn't think we've seen each other more than half a dozen times in as many years, I don't believe we've even exchanged anything as meaningful as anger for the last ten. Mother died *years* ago for me, man—years and years. This death of hers is just a footnote. It isn't relevant.

Then why do I feel so damn shocked by it?

. . . I know why. I've known for a while, really. Mother's dead, and I'm left alone.

—Well, I don't mean *alone*, for God's sake—not in this house, with Auberon and the kids all screaming for their tea. No, I suppose what I really mean is—isolated. No one there on the other side. No figure opposite me. For perhaps the other fighter hasn't really been Auberon standing opposite me all these years but Mother—Mother in frozen, smiling immobility, a permanent punch-ball at which I jabbed and thwacked. Take that Mum, I thought. And *that*. She was the one I was showing up, all the time, whatever I did. Dan Stein would say showing off to. Well, alright, showing off to as well. And now, suddenly, she just isn't there any more.

. . . But in what sense has she been there for years? We had no communication, everything had withered away, love, anger —even a lot of the resentment. She really was a *dummy* for me, not the real person at all. The real person may have changed a bit in ten years—have become humbler or something. I wouldn't know.

Perhaps as a dummy, an effigy for me to make my childish faces at, she can still go on existing? Perhaps I'll soon be able to forget she's dead and go back to thinking of her in the same vague, warm, resentful way I always have, doing things to shock her, doing things *my* way because it isn't hers and she might be watching.

Perhaps I'll even feel she's watching me *more* now she's dead?

Perhaps. But meanwhile what I feel is—lonely.

3

Daddy

DADDY ALWAYS WANTED to go to Israel, but somehow it had never happened.

Long ago before the War, when he was a young man, he thought seriously about making his home there—or so he used to say. Mother always looked as if she didn't entirely believe him, and perhaps she was right: Daddy did exaggerate a bit, and nostalgia and 'if only' regrets became something of a harmless self-indulgence with him as time went by. As I grew up I came to understand that Mother didn't think Daddy had it in him to take a big step like emigrating. Apparently at one time he had talked about Canada, also, but that came to nothing either. Not that Daddy was weak, mind you. He was a good businessman, and Mother was proud of that and of the way *he* took a pride in giving her a nice home and everything she wanted. (Except a son. But that was hardly his fault.) But he was a man who stuck to what he knew. He inherited the business, he didn't start it. He liked to live where he knew people and people knew him—'living centrally' meant, to him, living in or near Edgware. It meant a lot to him to feel loved and respected. He was unhappy away from home. When holidays in Spain came in in the 1950s and we all wanted to go, he took us, and told all his friends about it, and how much it had cost, but secretly, I knew, he didn't really enjoy it. The sun was too bright, it hurt his eyes and his bald head; he felt

silly in the shorts Mother had made him buy, and he couldn't
get the sort of nice, tempting little meals his poor stomach
liked. Mother said to us afterwards that she thought the sight
of all that shellfish upset him. Not that he had to eat any of it
himself—naturally Mother had made sure of that before he
went—but he just didn't like the *look* of it. Though Mother
hasn't kept kosher seriously since the War, when food was so
impossible that you felt like kissing a ham—if you ever saw it;
and Daddy'd become quite partial to a nice bit of bacon for
breakfast, still he had a sort of sentimental attachment to the
idea of kosher: shellfish just didn't seem to him a very nice
thought.

To tease him, we used to tell him that Israel was just as hot
as Spain and hotter, and that everyone wore shorts there. And
he used to put on a dignified, pained look because, though he
didn't mind being teased about other things, Israel was
different. Even the sun in Israel, he somehow gave us to understand, was different too—it was beneficial, and didn't blister
you—and the food there was good, wholesome stuff, produce
of the land: Jewish eggs and Jewish vegetables and yoghurt
from Jewish cows—he'd read all about it. Somehow I don't
think Daddy ever quite believed, though on one level he
knew it quite well, that Israel is hot and dusty with large,
barren tracts. In spite of all those books about pioneers in
kibbutzim lifting rocks off the ground with their bare hands,
I think he secretly went on seeing Israel, with some childlike
inner eye, as a green and shaded land, a kind of rural England
only hotter and more mountainous, with streams bubbling
beneath trees, and milk and honey just sitting about in bowls
for the taking.

Mother always said she had hoped Daddy would get sent to
Israel (or Palestine as it was then) in the War, as—though she
didn't add this bit in so many unkind words—that would have
put paid to his nonsense. But in 1940 he was already a bit old
for active service, and what with his history of stomach ulcers
it was a desk job for him on Salisbury Plain. He never got

abroad at all until the War ended when he and his desk were sent out to Germany because he spoke the language. I believe Daddy was very unhappy during the six months he spent out there. He never said much about it afterwards, or not to me, but Mother hinted to us once that the things Daddy had seen and heard then had marked him for good. It was only quite a while after he had come back to England again and been demobbed that he began to try to talk to people about it, and by that time of course we all knew about the camps, and the Nuremberg Trials were over, and everyone was sick of the subject. He tried to express himself—just to speak of it was something—but what was there to say that had not already been said? There was—is—nothing you can adequately say about all that, no way of taking hold of it. He fell silent and was unhappy, and was not well for a while. Presently, though, aided by Mother who maintains in all circumstances that it's simply no use being more sensitive than other people—that it gets you nowhere and makes others take advantage of you— he revived, and he and the business began to thrive again. And now, too, there was the State of Israel for him to take an interest in, and that was nice for him.

It should have been nice for Mother too. In fact, she comes from a far more Zionist family than Daddy, and has relations out there. But Mother is odd about Israel. Secretly, I think, though she would never admit it, she disapproves of the place. She never let on about this when my sister Rose and I were children, and we always had to put our sixpences in the JNF box regularly, but once I grew up I began to grasp the—the reticence, is really the only word—with which Mother views the Jewish National Homeland. Not, mind you, that this is due to any intellectual scruples on her part about the rightness of Jewish nationalism: that sort of misgiving isn't Mother's line at all. No, I believe it is rather that Mother has always mistrusted Israel *socially*. She thinks that once all those Jews get together out there, particularly the younger ones, they'll lose their standards because they'll be no Others to keep them up to the mark. They'll stop going to *shule* and they'll get uppity with their parents, and they won't keep kosher properly (not, as I say, that she does herself, but apparently that's different, and it's the principle that counts anyway. . .) All that riding around on tractors and doing things with animals and crops (Mother has looked at Daddy's books) is no life for educated people, thinks Mother, you can say what you like about pioneers and spiritual regeneration, it doesn't make any difference. And, what's more, she suspects that half the people in Israel today aren't nice, educated people at all, but a very low lot from Morocco and the Yemen and such places—not what she calls real Jews at all, they're bound to drag the tone of the place down. About all of which, of course, Mother, in her usual infuriating way, is absolutely right.

'But they're all friends there,' Daddy used to say wistfully when they argued about going there for a trip, and she reminded him he didn't like going among strangers. 'You'd like it, Hettie. All our sort. Think of it!'

Mother thought of it, and I could see from the expression on her face she didn't entirely like it. Mother likes to feel just the smallest bit exclusive.

As for Daddy, bless him, I believe he really did see Israel in his mind's eye as one big Edgware on a summer's day: all friends there. It was almost as if, toward the end of his life, he felt they were waiting for him there on the shore at Haifa with open arms. So perhaps, after all, it was just as well in a way that the dream was never put to the test.

In 1965, when I had been to Israel twice myself, Daddy finally got very restive. Why *shouldn't* he go there, he kept asking anyone who'd listen, as if they were the ones telling him he couldn't? He was half retired now that his nephews were in the business, he could manage the money, in a few years he would be an old man and it would be too late. What was stopping him he enquired plaintively? We all said Nothing Daddy, absolutely nothing, but somehow that wasn't entirely the answer he wanted. Mother listened, but remained silent. Daddy went on talking but did nothing. Eventually a tentative plan emerged that *I* should go with Daddy to look after him, but that was shelved because it looked for a while as if I might be going to get engaged. Then, when that was all over, Mother had her Operation, which absorbed all our energies for a further nine months. Then the Six Day War happened, and Mother took a considerable pride in pointing out how fortunate it was that Daddy and I had not, after all, followed our crack-brained scheme of going to Israel that year. She spoke as if we would have faced certain death from an Arab bullet, whereas all that would have happened was that we would have been flown home by the tourist agency in a hurry—a little drama he would certainly have enjoyed, and which would have given him much food for pleasant reminiscence and participation in the fighting that followed.

At last, the year after, it was agreed: Daddy and I would fly to Israel for Passover, and Mother would spend it with Rose and Des because, since her operation, she hasn't really fancied going away from home.

Daddy bought a lot of new, thin underwear and a beach shirt, though I kept on telling him that it wasn't really beach weather yet, even in Israel. I bought several frocks and wondered how short skirts were being worn in Israel now, and got quite excited myself.

Daddy's stomach hadn't been too good in the last two years, and I knew I was going to have to watch what he ate, but the high blood pressure was a new thing. Mother swears, and will always swear, that it was brought on by the unsuitable upheaval of the trip. Myself, I suspect that he'd had it quietly for years and we'd none of us known about it till Mother made him go to the doctor for a check-up.

Three weeks before we were due to leave Daddy had a 'little attack' and was in bed for two days. We none of us said anything. Then, thirty-six hours before he should have stepped onto the plane, he had another, more serious one. The message was clear. Mother and the doctor were both, for once, in adamant agreement. There would be no Israel for him this time.

He was *so* disappointed. I couldn't bear to look at his little face, all pinched and puckered above the new, brightly coloured pyjamas which should have been going into his suitcase and which Mother put on him to cheer him up. 'You must go, Ruthie,' he kept saying, and at last I saw that he really meant it, and that if I cancelled my own flight too he would mind still more. He wanted to think of me going there, seeing people there, even if he couldn't; it made the place seem more accessible to him, not less. 'You mustn't disappoint your friends out there,' he kept saying obsessively—as if it really mattered, as if they really were waiting for me on the beach with open arms. I think he secretly still hoped I might, perhaps, marry an Israeli and give him Israeli grandchildren. In the end, I agreed to go.

I had been there nearly a week when Mother's cable came. It was a muggy day in Jerusalem, the clouds kept coming up, a touch of hot, stuffy *hramsin* was blowing from Jordan, and I knew now that there was no Israeli husband for me this year and probably never. When I got back to the hotel before lunch it was almost a relief, in a desolate way, to read that Mother was worried and wanted me to call her, on reverse charges.

I 'phoned—not Mother, but the airport at Lod, and then cabled Mother that I would be on the afternoon plane. I couldn't stand the thought of talking to her about Daddy over all that distance.

As the plane climbed I felt sick. I suppose it was because of all the hurry and no lunch, but it seemed to me that the air-conditioning was not all that it might be. I wondered whether to faint. The person sitting beside me called a hostess, and she gave me a breathing mask and cold towels, but I thought, as I obediently sucked and breathed, that all her attention was not on me: something was going on further down the gangway. Most of the hostesses and the chief steward were standing round there, and someone brought what I suppose was a portable oxygen cylinder and began to pump it. It looked rather like the gas-and-air thing Rose had when she had Vicky at home. I was so interested I forgot about being ill myself, but I couldn't see very well, the high backs of the seats hid from me the person being treated. I wondered if it was a rather pregnant girl I had noticed getting on at Lod, but the plane had started its journey at Delhi, it could have been anyone.

When the announcement was given out that we had a sick passenger on board and were going to turn back, people sitting near me craned their necks and looked expectantly at me, but by then of course I was disappointingly well again— disappointing for them, I mean—and I just flapped my hands and pointed to the huddle further down. I felt immensely angry—not with the unseen person, who presumably couldn't help being ill, but with the pilot for turning back. We'd waste at least two hours that way, two hours more away from Daddy, and I strongly suspected that it was unnecessary. The hostesses' expressions gave nothing away, they gave their usual bright, vague smiles at passengers in their to-ing and fro-ing between the sick passenger and the pilot's cabin, but I sensed something—not tension, as you might think, but its absence, almost an unwillingness on their part, as if they, too, thought turning back to Lod unnecessarily dramatic. There is, presumably, a drill laid down for these things, and I supposed a pilot would always want to ditch someone ill as quickly as possible in case they get worse, but I thought that we could have gone on to Rome, at least, since we were on the way.

A solid, hairy man in tortoiseshell spectacles was standing with the in-group, and people who had been craning their necks discreetly to see were whispering that he was a doctor who had just happened to be sitting near the sick man— apparently it was a man—and wasn't that lucky? This thought seemed to soothe everyone, and we all settled down for the half-hour it took to get back to Lod. There was nothing to see, except for fuel being wastefully jettisoned from somewhere in the middle of the plane, and nothing to hear—the patient was silent, the doctor and the cabin staff were being very quiet among themselves—except for the swish-swish of the breathing pump, at which the hostesses seemed to be taking turns.

On the tarmac was an ambulance with its doors ready open that said it belonged to the Red Star of David Hadassah Fleet, and a large number of people—ambulance men, airport mechanics came to look, several BOAC and El Al men, and a fat woman in a white coat with a stethoscope in the pocket who came up the steps of the plane as soon as they were in place.

For people who had turned back the plane specially, they seemed in surprisingly little hurry to rush the man off now we had arrived. The woman doctor and two men in green overalls joined the group in the gangway, and there was a considerable conversation carried on in undertones. The rest of us sat like good children pretending not to want to listen; the woman next to me, who kept rummaging in her two handbags, said comfortably 'There—he can't be that bad.'

Someone else said officiously: 'They're wondering how to get him down the gangway, you see. . .'—and then, suddenly, there was a stir making itself felt down the lines of seats. The huddled group was breaking up and the two men in overalls began to move in awkward unison, like the component parts of a pantomime horse, with the sick man, still silent, between them.

They were carrying him face downwards. And one of them had his arms over the man's face, so that you could not see the mouth or nose but just a strip of forehead, bluish-mottled as if with cold, and a glimpse of lids not quite closed beneath. Only the top of the head, an old, balding head, rather sunburnt, with sparse grey hair just like Daddy's, was fully visible and reassuringly normal. At the other end the conventional black shoes were, like Daddy's too, highly polished.

Even then it took me a minute to understand: you do not carry a living man that way. Yet it wasn't till I saw from the porthole that they had covered his face with a blanket as soon as he was outside on the stretcher, that I realised why we had really come back to Lod. The cabin staff must have known it all the time and that was why their appearance of urgency had been a bit perfunctory: all that pumping of oxygen had been an optimistic formality, a keeping up of appearances with us, the rest of the passengers, rather than a genuine attempt to save a 'life' that was already over. Even then I don't think most of the people on the plane realised what had, in fact, taken place—which I suppose was the way the crew wanted it. People today are, through unfamiliarity, very innocent about death; I was myself till that moment when the two men shuffled out with their awkward load. Or perhaps, like me, quite a lot of people *did* realise but, through reticience and that docility in the face of superior forces that overcomes passengers in transit, did not like to say anything. Or perhaps they were, for some deeper reason, afraid to. We hung around for ages at Lod, in Israel again and yet not in Israel, while the plane refuelled, and quite a lot of people got out to stretch their legs, but not me because I was afraid of crying, in public, about Daddy. You see, I knew by then that he was surely dead. And as it turned out, illogically yet inevitably, like one of Mother's own predictions, I was absolutely right.

Several days afterwards I caught myself consoling myself with the dotty thought that Daddy has, after all, been buried in Israel. Of course he hasn't. He never made it. But the man on the plane has become him in my mind and I go on believing it. And who is to say it is not, in some fundamental sense, true? Spiritually, Daddy *was* with me in Israel that week, *did* die that afternoon. What more can I say?

Only much later did it occur to me that the man on the plane might not have been a Jew or even been visiting Israel intentionally at all: he might have come from Delhi that morning. How ironic to land up as a corpse in Israel, of all places, just by chance—like going to Mecca by mistake. How distressing and embarrassing for all his relations in Britain and India! But yet I go on being certain, no doubt because I want to be, that the man had left Israel only that lunchtime, unwillingly, feeling sad and tired, not knowing yet to give that sick-feeling the name of dying, but sick to leave the country where everyone was his own sort. I even like to think, stupid, unmarried female that I am becoming, that had he known of his impending fate, he would have been pleased.

4

A true story

MORRIS FENNER WAS trying to 'phone his wife, Ruth.

There was something wrong with their 'phone at home, had been all the week. When anyone tried to 'phone them it rang, but often only once and then would lapse into silence again so that they weren't sure if they had even heard that one ring. Sometimes it would ring two or three times before losing its voice, but sometimes apparently it didn't ring at all—people complained of having rung and rung and not been answered: they had heard rings but Morris and Ruth had heard nothing. It was, said Morris sourly, great for him professionally; for a freelance journalist there's nothing quite like a 'phone which sounds to the caller as if you're away or dead or something.

They had been trying to get something done about it for days, but it hadn't been a good week for getting things done. Since Ruth was out at work all day it was normally Morris who managed to be in for the 'phone, gas or delivery van. But Morris had been out every day, hanging round waiting for Seamus Lannion to die.

To his numerous acquaintances and contacts, who didn't know Seamus, Morris simply murmured something about it being one of his oldest friends. But, though that was in a way true, he wouldn't have said it to a real friend or to anyone who actually knew Seamus or had known him long ago. To these, he had been saying for a long time that Seamus Lannion had gotten to be a pain in the arse these days, a schmuck, an inadequate, a soak, a menace, a sponger—a psychopath. Yes, to Ruth he had said 'psychopath', and meant it. But then Ruth knew how much he had once cared for Seamus. She was also the only person among his immediate circle who knew how he had spent the week. Morris was like that.

In point of fact, when their 'phone had first begun playing up, they had said to one another 'I bet that's Seamus again'. About five years ago, when Seamus' first wife Jean had finally left him, sick of lies and whisky bottles and lachrymose scenes, Seamus had gone right off beam and had taken to ringing Morris and Ruth up at any hour, either to pour out his heart to them or to lambast them for 'taking Jean's side'. At first they had been fairly sympathetic and consciously patient and understanding. But gradually, as Seamus' demands increased and his temper seemed to grow more and more uncertain, first their sympathy and then their patience had been eroded. Presently they stopped treating him as an equal (a fellow journalist and once, long ago on the *Highgate Echo*, Morris' father-figure) and began treating him like a tiresome three-year-old. Gradually, first abusive and tearful, then patronisingly off-hand, he had drifted away from them. The calls had ceased, and they had been left feeling relieved but vaguely guilty, as if they had failed to rise to an occasion or make an effort they really might have made. Somehow, Seamus always managed to make people feel like that. But though he disappeared out of their life for a while he came back again at intervals, making calls or visits which were sometimes ebulliently gay, in his best old style, sometimes openly distressed, and sometimes veiledly hostile and threatening—as if, said Ruth acidly, he had been testing them and finding them wanting yet again. And once—this, they had discovered eventually was after a girl had left him, fed up at last as Jean had been, as so many others had been—he had taken to ringing them up and putting the 'phone down after a couple of rings or when they answered. For a long time they

had not known it was him, but then Morris developed a hunch
—said he could smell the whisky-laden breath down the 'phone
—and had said when he picked the 'phone up for the fourth
time that evening: 'Seamus you old buggar, if you do this
again I'll set the rozzers on you. Straight up, I mean it.' And
after a brief pause Seamus had answered back in a quite
normal voice, and had eventually agreed to come round for
coffee and apfelstrudel, and had sat for hours, eating, and
telling them quietly all about what a cunning, paranoid bitch
his last girl had been. It had been sad, Ruth had said afterwards to Morris, to see the poor thing looking so aged, his
hair quite grizzled and his suit hanging on his big, rangy
frame: he probably, she said with professional concern, didn't
get enough to eat these days: most drunks didn't, and it was
that, rather than the alcohol in itself, which ruined their
health. After that evening any shred of respect or awe they
had left over for him was quite gone and they were no longer
believing a word he said. But they felt more kindly towards
him again, and protective for the ruin of a gifted man that he
now was. They no longer avoided him with contempt, and
they even rang him up from time to time to suggest dinner or
a movie. By and by, he had got himself a new girl, as he
always did—though the girls were half his age now—and life
went on. They never did discover what he used for money.
The girls, perhaps?—not cynically, but childishly, a man who
must be supported in every sense. He tended to go for upper
class girls, as he always had, and most of them seemed to
love him, at least for a while. He was hardly working at all
these days, hadn't seriously for years, but he still, in his gay
moments, retained the most inflated idea of his own talents
and market price. Intermittently, in his own eyes, he was still
the 'brilliant professional' whose big features on gambling,
strip-clubs and horse-doping had wowed the readers of the
Dispatch, Sunday Pic, and *People* long ago in the 'fifties.

Morris wouldn't lend him money (Seamus tried him a
couple of times), because Morris never lent anybody money:

it was his one practical principle. Oh, the odd quid here and there, of course, but that was just casual, on the pretext of cash for a taxi or sharing a bill. But, at the beginning of that year, he had, unknown to Ruth, relaxed his principle because of two things Seamus had told him. One was that Seamus was getting married again and the other was that Seamus had lung cancer.

At first Morris had been disinclined to believe either of these pieces of information. As far as he knew Seamus had never got a divorce from Jean. He was, it was true, living with his latest girl, a whey-faced and near-silent twenty-two year old with a Greek name and large breasts (Seamus had always had a greedy thing about breasts). But Morris thought that all this about their getting married was probably just Seamus' habitual romancing, extending itself now further and further as a dangerous flowering growth upon reality. And as for that *other* growth—well Seamus had always been a roaring hypochondriac, demanding attention even in the days when he had been as strong and fit as a horse: six foot two of blue-eyed, black-haired stage Irishman.

But both things turned out to be true. Jean was apparently letting Seamus divorce her—indeed positively urging him to —because Melina was expecting a baby, and Jean was a very conscientious person at heart. And as for lung cancer, two weeks after telling Morris about it Seamus was in the Royal Northern having part of his left lung removed.

Morris visited him there and found him very cheerful. The surgeon had used a marvellous new method on him, he said, and had become a great friend too. He was going to be alright and his life was going to be quite different from now on: No more cigarettes, no Scotch, just wine with meals, no more rows, no more nervous tension—it would all be completely changed. Morris felt sad hearing his old friend, who had once been so lovably cynical, talking like this, but when Seamus went on to ask him earnestly if, on the strength of his new and different life, he could borrow several hundred pounds,

Morris could not refuse. To be broke as well as doomed seemed too hard a fate for anyone—and then there was Melina and that baby to think of.

In due course they were married in Marylebone Town Hall, with Morris and Ruth as witnesses. Seamus was very grey, but gay. Melina, portly by now, was dressed as the Madonna and still hardly said a word; Morris tried not to feel irritated by her. If she was really the placid, bovine creature she seemed, she was certainly going to need her reserves of placidity in the months ahead—though there might not be many months, at that. Seamus insisted on taking them to lunch at Wheeler's, and Ruth said, almost too acidly for a wedding guest, 'Seamus, no wonder you never have any money!' Morris felt uncomfortable and wondered if she had guessed about the 'loan'.

Walking back afterwards to where their car was parked, they said to one another with sad nostalgia 'Do you remember the biscuits?' The biscuits had been when it all began. Morris, as a young reporter trying to leap the gulf between Highgate and Fleet Street ('It's called Hampstead Heath, mate,' Seamus had mocked) had managed to get himself commissioned by a dull quality magazine to do some articles on provincial towns. He had picked Reading as a suitably drab example and had slogged off there to look at local industry. On his return, brain-washed, he had begun his piece *'If all the biscuits manufactured in Reading in a single year were laid end to end, they would—'* He was just trying to read his own short-hand to find out how far they would stretch (the statistic had been eagerly fed to him by Huntley and Palmer's PR man, along with Buttered Specials) when Seamus had leaned over his shoulder and typed with one finger: *'they would get very wet'*. He 'happened to know', as he said jauntily, that Reading had one of the heaviest rainfalls in the South, and he turned out to be right, damn him—in those days he always was. In fact, the editor of the dull quality magazine didn't like Seamus' version—said it was 'journalistic'—but for years Morris used to quote it as an example of Seamus' flair. That, and the time when Seamus had, with a poker face, told the Salvation Army girl in the pub that he was worried she might not find Heaven all that she expected it to be: it wasn't, he said, full of old gold and William Morris wrought iron these days; it had been modernised, with synthetics—more durable of course—and the perpetual sound of harps was all canned these days, like the nectar: the old place had changed, just as the Mediterranean and the Spanish coast had—he just thought he ought to warn her. . .

'You can say what you like,' said Morris to Ruth, 'but he really was witty in those days. In his way. He had style.'

'Oh he still does,' said Ruth, 'in his way. Poor old thing. I'm sure he really is awfully ill, Morry. That look—those mauvish rings round his eyes. Like a lemur. You can't mistake it.'

Morris, who had met the surgeon in hospital—a cold, energetic man to whom Seamus was clearly just another case —knew that Seamus was dying, but he had not said so to Ruth in so many words. Morris was like that, and besides, he was mortally afraid of death himself.

Three months later Melina had her baby, also in the Royal Northern. Ruth took her a towelling baby-suit and some daffodils, and reported that Melina didn't seem that keen on the baby really—she just wanted to leave hospital early to get home to Seamus who was, she said, 'in bed most of the time, now. She asked Ruth for some money, just like that—she was, Ruth decided, an odd girl, with more to her than they had at first thought, and so Ruth took out her cheque book there and then and wrote Melina a cheque for fifty pounds from her own account. There was always, as she said to Morris when she got home, Social Security—though Seamus, being technically still self-employed, might be having difficulty claiming it, and anyway what that paid would hardly keep him in whisky, let alone anything else—assuming that he was still hitting the whisky, in his decrepit state.

And now, barely a month later, Seamus' life was truly end-

ing. Morris had been at their flat most of the day. Melina was
there, and the baby, and it cried a lot in a weak, insistent way
because it had something Melina called 'colic'. She kept offering it her white, veined breast, and sometimes it took it and
seemed pacified for a while, but then the crying would begin
again. Morris kept averting his eyes from that white breast:
it attracted him too much—not sexually, but in some other
way. He wanted to lay his heavy cheek against it, as if to weep.

Most of the time there was a girl cousin of Melina's there
too, a heavy and coarse version of Melina with a disappointed
face, who kept washing up cups and saucers. And a district
nurse came and went several times: she was worried because
she thought Seamus ought to be in hospital, tidy and alone
with screens round him, not in a cramped studio-flat with a
crying baby and a workman calling at midday to cut off the
telephone because the bill hadn't been paid—Yes, really.
Morris had been able to deal with that one, fortunately. Doing
something, like that, had made him feel marginally better
about the whole thing.

Towards the end of the afternoon he went out to try to
'phone Ruth from a public box. She had rung him earlier at
the flat, but how could he talk to her there, against the baby
crying, against the slow, perpetual rasp of Seamus' breathing?
Seamus was dying of gradual suffocation while his wife and
his oldest remaining friend and one or two extras looked on.
They called it 'cancer' to make it sound known and permissible, Morris thought, but it was really, when you came down
to it, suffocation pure and simple. He was appalled.

At last, after much trouble, he got through to Ruth. 'Are you
coming home to supper, do you think?' she asked in a
sympathetic voice, and he answered angrily 'Of course I'm
not—you've no idea what it's like here, or you wouldn't ask
such a silly question.' He had rung her because he wanted to
tell her what it was like, but found he couldn't.

But when he got back to the flat the scene had changed.
Everything was quiet. The baby was asleep, the cousin had

retreated to the kitchen and had shut the door. The nurse was
packing up her case. The rasping noise had ceased and
Seamus' lemurian face was neatly covered with the sheet.
Melina sat composedly beside him.

'Doctor will be here very soon,' said the Nurse consolingly,
adding in response to Morris' uncomprehending look: 'To
certify death. He has to, you see. I didn't want to leave Mrs
Lannion, but now you're back. . .' Obviously she had a higher
opinion of him than of the Greek cousin, and he felt vaguely
flattered. At the front door she said to him:

'Do keep an eye on Mrs Lannion, won't you? She's been too
calm—hasn't broken down at all. It isn't natural.'

'Maybe I should take her and the baby home with me
tonight—that is, home to my wife,' said Morris, blushing at
what he at once perceived to be a Freudian slip.

'Yes, I'm sure that would be best. They can't all stay here. . .'
He understood the delicate 'all' to include the object on the
bed, and shuddered inwardly. 'Usually,' the nurse went on,
'when someone passes on in a small flat like this we get the
undertaker to remove them within a few hours. But Mrs
Lannion seems very determined that the body should stay here
till the funeral. I said to her "It's different in a house, where
you can set a whole room aside, but really, here. . ." As I said,
though, she seems very determined.'

'Yes. I see. She's quite a strong-minded girl, I think.'

'Poor thing,' said the Nurse with mechanical regret. She
added: 'Anyway, I've sent for Mrs Bovey. She does all the
home laying-out in this district.'

'I see. Goodness.' He hadn't realised that still went on. It
sounded Dickensian. But then hadn't the whole day been like
that? Fantastic, lugubrious—unlike everything else.

Two hours later Mrs Bovey had completed her work to her
satisfaction. In a neat, tightly-made bed Seamus Lannion lay,
hands clasped, jaw bound, eyes closed, other orifices all
(Morris had gathered) discreetly dealt with. When he, Melina
and the cousin were suffered to emerge from the kitchen the

main room was filled with a smell of unfamiliar hygiene
—Ether? Formaldelyde?—although the window had been
opened wide.

Mrs Bovey was so small a woman that she almost missed
being stunted and seemed to belong, simply, to another,
squatter race than the normal one. There were other mysteries
about her. She might have been anything between thirty-nine
and sixty-nine: she looked faintly raddled but that might have
been just from the excess of make-up she used, particularly
the pale-pink lipstick with which she enhanced her small,
puckered lips. Her clothes were ladylike, almost girlish in an
old-fashioned way—pink suit, white gloves, hat of a different
pink with a scrap of veiling: everything was very faintly
grubby, but only her run-over high-heeled shoes were notice-
ably shabby; her slightly bowed legs seemed older than the
rest of her. She looked to Morris like someone dressed to go
to a nearly but not entirely respectable wedding.

'What do we owe you?' he asked her awkwardly. He had no
idea if the answer would be one pound or twenty. Her task
had been trivial, menial—yet how many people were prepared to perform it? Could it possibly be a full-time job, and,
if not, what did she do the rest of the time? Work in a
launderette? ... Visit betting shops? ... Care for an invalid
mother? ... Somehow, in spite of the 'Mrs', he didn't feel
there was a Mr Bovey.

'We discuss the fee outside, dear, if you don't mind,' she
said firmly, 'I never talk of money by the side of the dead.
Brings bad luck.'

At that moment, such a concern seemed redundant, but perhaps Mrs Bovey meant bad luck to *her*. Suppressing a smile
he followed her down the stairs and out of the street door.
Once on the pavement she turned to him and said in a
wheedling voice:

'I tell you what, dear. There's a nice little café just opposite.
They do a nice cuppa. Let's you and me pop in there and we
can discuss terms in comfort.'

Telling himself he must harden his heart to this preposterous little creature, who probably was supposed to charge a fixed rate for the job anyway, he followed her unwillingly across the street and into the workman's café. He ordered two teas— 'Would you like anything else?'

'Well thank you, dear. Since you're so kind I won't say no. I'll have a poached egg on toast.'

What a nerve, he thought, amused in spite of himself. But then someone doing that job would have to have a nerve, wouldn't they? And why shouldn't she try to exploit him: it was right and natural. He wasn't Melina.

While they were waiting for the poached egg he tried to find out what she did with the rest of her time, but she was evasive. 'I love my job,' she said happily.

'*Really?*' He began to think about necrophilia, but she went on:

'Yes. I like to help people, you see. And my job—well, that's really helping them in their hour of need, isn't it?'

Fair enough, he thought, absolutely fair. The poached egg arrived and she attacked it with appetite.

'There is just one thing, though,' she said between mouthfuls —her pearly false teeth fitted badly, they were giving her trouble he saw, and sympathised.

'What's that?'

'Well ... it's like this, you see.' She slid a coy look at him from under her blue-smeared lids. 'When I've laid out a poor soul I always like to drive death out—with life, you might say. It's a principle of mine. A bit of fun afterwards. Clears the system. If you take my meaning.'

He still had not done so completely—or rather could hardly believe he was getting the message right. Hoping wildly that by 'a bit of fun' she might, improbably, be meaning no more than a poached egg and a cup of tea, he said:

'Was—was that why you wanted me to come over here with you?'

'Well yes, dear.' She surveyed him with her pale blue eyes,

which he now saw to be surrounded by a million tiny lines. She seemed to be faintly amused at his discomfort, but also dubious herself, on the edge of disappointment: 'But you don't want to come with me, do you dear? I thought at first you might—but now I think I was mistaken?'

'I—I'm afraid you were.'

'Pity. I like a well-set-up man like you... I got a nice room. Homelike.'

'I'm sure you have. But—I just don't feel like it, just now.'

'Oh yes you do, dear.' She spoke now not to persuade him but with an off-hand authority. Returning to her egg with the air of one briskly shrugging off a mild set-back, she explained: 'Everyone does, after a death. It's Nature, you see. Like I said, death has to be driven out... Never mind, dear, I expect you'll find someone tonight you fancy more... Are you taking that poor young girl home with you? She didn't ought to stay in the flat with the body, you know—' 'Tisn't healthy. There's vapours.'

Feeling himself blushing again as he had with the nurse, he said:

'Look. I'm married. If I want to do—what you suggest—I can.'

'Oh well that's alright then, isn't it dear.' She sounded generously pleased for him, and he was filled with remorse. Now the poor little woman would have to find someone else.

'I'm going back to the flat,' he said. 'Are you—that is, are you staying here?'

'Yes dear, might as well.' The innuendo in her voice was unmistakeable. 'I usually do. If not, I'll try Lyon's.'

'I see,' he said. 'Well—good luck.' He was already making his way to the door when he suddenly remembered that he hadn't after all paid her. He had to go back and ask her how much he owed her.

'Oh—just two pounds, dear.' Obviously there was a fixed tariff, and anyway she had lost interest in him. Her eyes were wandering over the other, sparsely populated tables. He slipped two pound notes into her lap, feeling exactly as if they *were* payment for quite other services, then asked on impulse:

'Suppose I had gone home with you? Would that have been another two pounds?'

'Oh *no*, dear.' She sounded quite shocked, and at once he was sorry if he had hurt her. 'No, that would have been quite free—my treat. Didn't I make that clear?'

'Yes. I'm sorry. I shouldn't have asked.'

'Oh that's all right, dear. Of course, if you want to know, I do have my usual rates... But what we were discussing was a bit special, wasn't it?'

That evening he took Melina and her baby and a suitcase that seemed to be full of heavy knitting and packets of cotton wool home to Ruth. They dropped the Greek cousin off in Neasden on the way. He felt that Melina, though she still said little, minded very much leaving Seamus alone in his tightly made bed, and so did he. Poor old Seamus had always needed company so much.

For the first time in years he missed his old friend bitterly —oh not the whining, fibbing, drink-sodden Seamus of the last half-dozen years (no one with any sense would miss that) —but his *old* friend, of long ago, when he and Ruth were young. He missed the Seamus of the *Highgate Echo*, of the Reading biscuits and the Heaven where the William Morris angels were all being put into more up-to-date uniforms, like air hostesses... Oh, there had been a style and originality about the boy, you couldn't get away from it.

Perhaps, after all, his dying hadn't been such a squalid dissolution. Not so entirely out-of-character with his better days... Mrs Bovey had certainly given it something, had rounded it off, you might say. How Seamus would have relished her! Through his sudden, crushing sense of tiredness and apathy, Morris felt particularly sorry Seamus was never destined to hear about Mrs Bovey. He would have made such a good story of it.

5

The loss

WHEN TOM HATCHER's wife Susan died it was pretty bad for him, and yet not—he realised in queer, grey moments of lucidity—quite as bad as he had thought it might be. He had expected the pain and loneliness to be unbearable—or, rather, bearable only in the sense that he would bear it because he had to. Instead, the very fact that he had had the time and the knowledge to envisage beforehand just what it would be like, seemed, when the time came, to make the experience subtly different. The pain was already familiar. He had begun to get used to it even before it happened.

It was pretty bad at times, all the same. Not just at first, when all he felt was the sheer relief that it was at last *over,* that she was no longer suffering and that there would be no more visits to that side-ward which had become as familiar to him as the lounge at home. Also, people were very kind. They had all been expecting it too, of course, he and Susan had let their closest friends know pretty much how things stood, everyone had therefore been poised ready on the side-lines, so to speak, with cautious words of comfort and tumblers of whisky. People offered to help him pack up her things, invited him to 'drop in any time' for the good hot meals they felt he wouldn't be bothering to cook himself: some of them almost overdid it, he felt. After all, by the time the end came he had been to all intents living alone for the best part of two months already, and for most of the year he had been the one doing the cooking, the shopping, the cleaning even, because of course Susan hadn't felt up to it. He was used to the routine. As a schoolmaster, his working day outside his home ended at four, he had time to do after that what another man might not have been able to. And then, later, when he'd had a bite to eat while watching that news round-up programme, at the moment when the blank evening ahead might have menaced him with despair, there were always books to correct and tomorrow's lessons to think about. He was, he greyly reckoned, more fortunate than many men in that his life fell naturally into this particular healing shape. He was under no illusions about the need just to keep going, the way in which 'keeping busy' did actually help even though it seemed a bit mechanical, a bolt-hole from pain rather than any real solution... 'Solution'? There were ultimately no solutions to intractable facts. He knew that, he was a grown-up. There would be no solution to Susan's dying or to his missing her, any more than there had been a solution to the fact of their childlessness, which had cost them so many fruitless tests and hopes, and Susan, at one time, so many tears. But she—they— had got over it. The last five years, before the wretched kidney business started, had been really happy for both of them. And he told himself he was adult enough to believe—dourly, for the moment, on trust, as an act of faith—that it was quite possible that one day he himself would be happy again too.

Later, when their friends had realised that he could after all manage, that loss had not transformed him into some haggard and incompetent travesty of his former self, the pressing invitations did fall off a bit. Actually, that time, about four months after, was the worst time—not because of anything his friends did or didn't do, but simply because it was. He began to sleep an alarming amount, as if sleep itself were a drug, and even feared, for a week or two, that he wasn't going to be able to hold his own at work—that he was going to have to give in, ask for time off, get tranquillisers or pep pills or

something from his doctor—play the role, in fact, after all, of
the grief-stricken widower. But he managed to get through
this time without anybody realising, chiefly, he thought,
thanks to Jess.

Jess had been Susan's dog, bought only the year before she
died, when they still clung to the idea that she was just run
down and needed the fresh air and exercise which a young
dog would inevitably provide. After the first few months, however, it had been Tom who had taken the bouncing, girlish
creature out, early morning and evening, for runs on
Parliament Hill. But Jess still loved Susan best because Susan
had fed her, right up to when she went into hospital for the
last time, and anyway Tom had always referred to her as
'Susan's dog'—or, jokingly—'that silly bitch of yours' because
he had never particularly liked dogs, as a matter of fact, and
was very down on what he had always called 'sentimentality'
about animals. When he got fond of Jess it was in spite of
himself, he thought, a matter of propinquity, like an un-
maternal woman coming to love a child simply through the
necessity of looking after it.

Jess was a golden cocker spaniel with a long plumey tail
which picked up dead leaves on every outing and huge pink-
padded paws on which she liked to race through mud. She
was enchantingly affectionate and maddeningly indiscriminate. She would fawn on anyone; Tom growled that she was
hopeless as a watchdog. Susan had replied laughingly that
they hadn't *got* her as a watchdog and that Jess's friendliness
ought to be an example to both of them. She had said that they
had both been getting too selfish and set in their ways: it
was good for them to have a young thing like Jess tearing
around, savaging slippers, stealing chops, making shame-
faced puddles, or worse, in the middle of the night when they
hadn't heard her scratching and whining. After this had
happened several times they left their bedroom door open to
hear better, and then of course Jess took to creeping up from
her basket in the hall once they were both asleep. Once she

tried to get into bed with them, as if she believed herself the size of a kitten who might easily escape detection—she was always trying to get on people's laps, it seemed a long time before she realised that she had become quite a large dog. Tom had taken her sternly downstairs and told her to stay there, but the next night she had been up again. Finally they compromised: Jess might creep in and sleep on the rug by the dressing table—they were prepared to pretend they didn't know she was there—but if, said Tom firmly, there were whinings or tail thumpings or other attempts to join them in bed out she must go. He was not going to share his married life with a dog. Evidently Jess must have understood the situation because the compromise worked, and she never leapt joyously onto the eiderdown till Tom was up at 7.30 and putting his dressing gown on.

When Susan was no longer there she did not at once insinuate herself into the bed in her place—no, not at once. For a week, she was clearly puzzled. But Susan had been away before and come back—Jess was fairly confident this time, looking for her mistress on the side nearest the wall each morning. But because he hated to see her look, and to see the disappointment in her foolish, toffee-brown eyes, Tom took to calling her briskly the moment he got out of bed and urging her downstairs ahead of him. Gradually she got into the new routine and seemed to forget the old. By and by she even ceased looking round, faintly puzzled, for another person when Tom gave her her plate of food. She was, thought Tom, with the painful realism of which he made a perverse solace, beginning to forget.

It was not till one night about a fortnight after Susan had died that she—Jess—first came while he was lying awake and wretched, and pushed her nose into his hand outstretched on the pillow. He thought afterwards that she must have heard him tossing about and surmised, with some canine cunning beyond organised reason, that this was an opportunity not to be missed. But perhaps, too, she had understood at some level that he was miserable and was, simply, trying to comfort him, as people were always telling one dogs did... In any case at that moment he neither knew nor cared what her true motives and understanding were, but simply gathered her large, exuberant body onto the bed with a groan and buried his face in the clean, feathery undergrowth round her neck.

After that, of course, she slept on his bed every night, there was no stopping her. He still went through the ritual of making her sit down on the rug and telling her to stay there. But it was perfectly well understood between them that she climbed onto the bed after he was asleep and often before... After a while he began to wait to hear the soft rustle and pad, to feel the slight lurch of the bed as she sprung delicately over his legs and settled herself comfortably within touching distance. Then, reassured by her presence, he would drift off.

On those mornings in the Bad Patch when it seemed as if he could not face shaving and breakfasting and going to school that day, or indeed life at all, it was for Jess that he heaved himself out of bed, since she had to be let out. It was for Jess that he went into the kitchen and while he fed her he automatically fed himself. Then, since Jess had to have her early morning run he got dressed anyway, and so one thing lead to another and he got to school after all. One day, he had the idea of taking her with him, and that helped enormously. Why, he wondered, had he not thought of it before? She had undoubtedly been lonely in the house all day, she had begun to make messes before he could get home to her, and to whine, the neighbour said. Now she came with him to school, sat behind the blackboard and was much happier. So was he. His classes made much of her. She made much of them in return. The Head didn't object, merely warning Tom to keep on the right side of the school-keeper and not to let an inspector see her. For the first time in nearly twenty-five years of variegated teaching he found himself becoming A Character. Lovable Old Mr Hatcher with his dog. Well, well. It wasn't perhaps the image he would have wanted to present—had ever

thought he would present, for that matter, in the days when
he was young and unscarred by things and known for energy
and tough discipline—a bit of a bastard, in fact. But it helped
for the moment to find himself Lovable Old Mr Hatcher and
his dog. Oh yes, it helped.

In the playground she would bound around retrieving a
tennis ball again and again for a knot of admirers, while he
himself kept an eye open from a safe vantage point to make
sure no one mistreated her. There were one or two boys—
just one or two, mind, and not in any of his sets—whom he
didn't entirely trust. Other boys used to gather round him telling him about *their* dogs, real, imaginary or longed for, the
Alsatians their brothers were going to give them when they
were sixteen or the champion greyhounds their uncles were
breeding. He found he had joined, unawares, a new club
which transcended age, intelligence or status. At midday Jess
used to skedaddle down to the kitchens, where the dinner-
ladies soon learnt to have something tasty for her. Tom used
to go down too, apparently casually, to thank them, but in
fact to check that they weren't giving her pastry or cake or
God knows what. Women always overfed dogs, even Susan
had tended to, worrying because Jess's scatty, pubescent
form was so thin... She had filled out now and was beautiful.
She had already been in season, twice, with the maximum of
mess, inconvenience and noisily optimistic barking. Later, he
must think about getting her mated to someone worthy of her,
try to plan it so that the puppies would come near the end of
the summer term... But not yet. He did not want to share
her with puppies yet.

One fine March day, when it was nearly six months since
Susan had died, he drove out to spend a Saturday in the
Hertfordshire countryside where they had often picknicked.
He looked at a couple of churches, took Jess for a good long
walk and sat in a cleared copse to eat his sandwiches while
she chased imaginary rabbits enthusiastically through the
stumps. Here, as everywhere, he was reminded of former

occasions, when Susan had been with him, but he had become quite used to this perpetual undercurrent of memory, it no longer ruined his day for him. He took pleasure in Jess's almost hysterical appreciation of the outing, and had considerable difficulty in luring her back into the car again when it was time to turn for home.

Two days later, she went.

He had taken her out onto Parliament Hill after school and had got into casual conversation with a neighbour, owner of a badly behaved poodle. When they called and whistled for their respective dogs, the poodle reappeared readily enough but there was no sign of Jess.

For ten minutes or so he did not worry seriously. She had done this several times before, it was her way of teasing, and he kept expecting that she would, from one moment to the next, be there, flying across the darkening grass from a great distance, ears and tail streaming, tongue flapping, mouth agape as if she was laughing. Not till almost half an hour had gone by, and he could no longer see beyond the nearer clumps of trees, did real dread suddenly strike home to him. She had never been gone nearly as long as this before.

Wretched, he made his way back home. It was not far, she would no doubt follow him in her own good time; she was hardly likely to get lost in her familiar streets, and if she did she had her collar on, someone would bring her back. . . But he could swallow no supper and soon he was out again, tramping the Hill and then the whole Heath in case she had wandered further there and lost herself among unfamiliar scrub, calling and calling in the darkness. At one point a keeper with a flashlight joined him, stood by him a few minutes while he called, feeling a fool. The man listened to a description of Jess and promised to look out for her. Dogs, he said, sounding kind and experienced, often lost themselves on the Heath: they went after something that smelt interesting, see, and then wandered in circles, but they nearly always turned up next morning looking pretty ashamed and sorry for themselves. Tom wasn't to worry too much. For a few minutes, after the man had gone on his way, Tom did feel fatuously cheered by the keeper's calm. Only gradually, as loneliness and fear settled on him once more, did he realise that of course the man was calm because he didn't care—why should he care? It wasn't his dog.

In the end he went home because what else could he do? He left the gate open and the side door wedged ajar. Lying alone in bed he felt cold, and tried his hardest to fix on an image of Jess, cold too of course, but basically *safe*, huddled under some bush, waiting for the morning light to trot home, tail between legs. For a long time he couldn't sleep, but at last got off by telling himself that if he did so he would be wakened by the soft pad of Jess's feet on the stairs, the thump and lurch as she sprang onto the bed, and the night past would seem like a bad dream. . .

He woke. There was no Jess. Cold seemed to have settled in his stomach and his feet. He huddled on some warm clothes and went out into the piercing early morning. Almost no one was about on the Hill. He met another keeper and gave him Jess's description too, and this one took out his notebook and wrote it down. The gesture should have reassured Tom, but instead he felt worse. Now Jess was officially Missing. He called and called all round their usual haunts, still expecting to hear her flying feet on the turf, her excited bark, yet knowing at the same time that he was not likely to, that wherever Jess was it was unlikely now to be here. As he walked slowly home again to swallow a cup of coffee before leaving for work, he had a very complete image of her, in last night's darkness, not huddled beneath a bush as in his earlier fancy, but looking for her way home, running head down with a ghastly precision right into the path of a lorry.

The police would know. Run-over dogs were supposed to be reported to them, weren't they? He gulped his coffee and rushed to call at the police station on his way to school. The young policeman was quite kind, said no accident of any kind had been reported in the area last night and that dogs often turned up again as right as rain—he shouldn't worry too much. They would call him at once if any lost dog answering to Jess's description were brought in. Once again he was illogically comforted, and once again the comfort evaporated ten minutes later.

He came home again in the dinner hour, possessed by an image of Jess returning wet and draggled in his absence and wandering dejectedly off again because she was not there. There was no sign of her. He made sure the side door was open, put down meat, dog-biscuits... He had told no one at school that she was missing. His B-stream maths thought that he hadn't brought her today because they had played up a bit last week when she was there.

That evening, realising that he had had nothing but coffee for twenty-four hours, he forced himself to swallow a tin of soup before setting out again for the Hill. It was twenty-four hours since she had disappeared. Illogically, he convinced himself that this was therefore the moment when she would reappear, racing down the wind toward him just as if today were yesterday, the last twenty-four hours wiped out... She didn't.

When at last darkness drove him home again he rang the vet, who said had she been coming into heat by any chance?

'I didn't see any sign of it. But it's possible, isn't it?' Particularly at this time of year.' It wasn't actually, likely. Her last heat had been just before Christmas. But he seized on the hope, elaborating it in his mind. Of course, Jess would be ranging north London in a ferment of desire looking for a mate. Had found one, no doubt, if not several. But when her desire was satiated she would turn for home.

'She had her collar on of course—?' said the vet. 'Well then. Let's just hope for the best. You've tried Battersea Dogs' Home, I expect? ... Yes, they'll let you know. But in another day or two she may very well come trotting in as cool as you please.'

He saw her doing it. He saw her constantly, whenever he closed his eyes. Only it just did not happen.

On Friday, at dinner-time, he packed up his books and left for home on the pretext of a sick headache. He had indeed slept so little the last three nights that 'a headache' was as good a phrase as any for the sense of shivering unreality which possessed him. That afternoon on the Heath as he walked and called and called again—people who passed were beginning to look at him oddly, he thought, but that didn't matter, nothing mattered—he met the black poodle owner and told her what had happened. She expressed shocked concern and wondered if perhaps Jess had gone off on her own looking for those rabbit-haunted woods where she had so enjoyed herself the weekend before.

It was a long shot, but what else could he do? At least to drive out there passed the time, provided the illusion of doing something. But there once again in the empty copse he felt, this time, terribly alone, and his visit of the preceding week-end might have been an idyllic memory from years before, long gone beyond recall. He could hardly believe now, that he had not then been perfectly happy. The time when Jess had been his constant companion was already, in the space of a few days, beginning to acquire for him the fabulous quality of a lost golden era, such as youth or liberty.

On Sunday he busied himself by typing out a score of neat notices on cardboard, covering them with polythene, and going round the neighbourhood fixing them to posts and trees. He was not sure if one was allowed to do this but did not care. He also had cards posted in half a dozen local newsagents. 'Missing since Tuesday 7 March, cocker spaniel bitch, 18 months, light brown colour...' He thought humbly of the times when, glancing over boards in the past, he himself had seen such notices and had not registered any particular emotion, had not been arrested in pity and sympathy... He had not understood what pain such a notice represented.

The woman in one newsagent was particularly kind, creasing her face and clicking her tongue. She'd lost her doggie, she said—getting on for four years ago, now, that would be. She still thought she saw him in the street sometimes and called out his name, but of course it was never him. Those people must be really wicked, mustn't they, to do such a thing and cause such unhappiness?

He murmured some vague assent and promised to let her know 'if he had any luck'. Only when he got outside the shop did he realise that she had been referring to the possibility of Jess having been stolen, for one of several purposes.

The thought had already occurred to him. But he pushed it from his mind again. He spent the afternoon ranging systematically over the Heath, taking it in sections, searching every patch of trees. Tomorrow he would ring Battersea Dog's Home again, see if any new spaniel had been brought in.

The first person to mention the word 'laboratory' to him was Wrighty, the fat old science master at school. Wrighty had a dog himself, a wheezing dachshund of great antiquity: in another, happier life Tom had seen it waddling round last Open Day and had faintly despised it. It transpired that Wrighty had a morbid dread of his dog being stolen and subjected to nameless experiments and had had it tattooed with a special number on the inside leg—'so that any lab. would see it, and know this is someone's pet all they have to do is return it to a certain address and there'll be no questions asked.' Wrighty represented the business of stealing pets and selling them to laboratories for vivisection as a vast, highly organised and satanic conspiracy. Tom's heart quailed within him though his reason tried to resist Wrighty's pessimism.

'But good heavens surely any lab. would know that a dog like Jess isn't likely to be an unwanted stray?'

Wrighty shook his head dubiously. These people were pretty unscrupulous. Heartless—they'd have to be, wouldn't they? If they thought they could get away with it. . .

'In that case,' snapped Tom, 'why should a tattooed number help?' But he was cursing himself that he'd never thought of it himself, never realised that any such system existed. In his mind Jess's smooth inner flank was extended before him, *there*, safe and receptive, and the vet was there too with an inky punch in his hand saying: 'Just hold her firmly, would you? It'll just be a bit of a prick for her, over in a moment...' And then there, on the milk-caramel skin, were the identifying, saving numbers.

When he got home that evening, after his usual painful session on the Hill—the ritual of calling and whistling her each night dreaded yet felt compelled to perform—he sat down and concocted a short, careful but (he hoped) pungent letter for circulation to laboratories. It was a long shot, perhaps, but Tom was not the man to leave undone anything that possibly could be done. In the letter he wrote, after describing Jess, that he was not interested in legal proceedings, that he simply wanted her back—'and so does my little boy, who is crying for her'. He was normally a truthful man, almost pedantically so, but this lie seemed to flow naturally from him without making the smallest dent in his conscience. The truth: '*I* am crying for her, every night' would have been impossible to write. But children were allowed to cry, and surely even a vivisectionist's heart would be softened by this? Vivisectionists always justified their unpleasant trade, he understood, by saying that they placed ultimate human welfare above that of animals. That had been his own viewpoint too. In the past, before he had understood anything.

Normally, when he had any duplicating to be done—test papers and so forth—he asked the school secretary to do it for him. But, with the exception of Wrighty who kept himself to himself, Tom had told no one at school yet that Jess was lost, and quailed so far from doing so: every time he mentioned the fact to anyone the admission of it seemed to make it more real and potentially permanent. So he waited after four till the secretary had gone home and then worked the machine himself. He ran off four hundred copies. Surely that would be enough? Then he went down to central London to an antivivisectionist league whom he had rung earlier in the day, and picked up from them a list of licensed laboratories. There were well over four hundred places listed. He would have to do another batch of copies.

For the next week all his spare time was spent addressing envelopes. At least this was something to do. It even felt constructive. When he carted yet another basketful to the post box he almost felt as if all those letters despatched represented something achieved, something solid. Surely, he felt illogically, such endeavour should eventually produce some result? He had grown up in a world of study, of exams and scholarships, a world in which efforts made with sufficient application and intensity of purpose normally produced results. It was hard to shed the habit of rational optimism.

Sooner than he expected, the replies began to come, thudding through his letter boxes in batches each morning, gaily littering the mat when he got home in the afternoons. After the first few he no longer opened them with much hope, but he still opened them. Some of them were mere formal notes, regretting to inform him. Others seemed to have a slightly indignant note 'would wish to assure you that this laboratory never purchases animals from dealers...' Others wrote with what seemed both kindness and real concern. Sometimes the letter would be from the top man himself, in his own writing '—wanted to let you know without delay that we are, alas, unable to help you in your search... Do hope most sincerely that it may prove fruitful ... quite understand what you and your family must be going through.' One lab. even sent a multi-colour ball pen stamped with their name 'as a small gift for your little boy. I know how hard such an experience must hit a child...' He used the pen for marking. As it could write both red and blue according to how you twisted it, it was most useful. Not that he did any more marking than he could help that week, and his lessons went unprepared. There was always old stuff to fall back on, and he was not capable of more...

The letters were, oddly, for all their lack of concrete help, some sort of solace. They also reminded him of something. After a while he realised that it was a little like it had been receiving letters after Susan had died: 'So very sorry to hear your sad news ... if there is anything we can do ... our thoughts are with you.' Letters of condolence, the formal recognition that a loss demands. He did not throw them away, but kept them altogether in an old box file. A record of his endeavours, hence of the strength of his feeling. A testament of love.

He ate little, moved abstractedly through the days working the minimum, vague and testy when anyone spoke to him. He felt as if his body were made of some strange substance, heavier than usual. He experienced pains in his stomach and supposed that these must be due to his continual tension. For he was constantly on the alert, even at school, constantly listening. In counterbalance to his lethargic, vague body his hearing seemed to have become abnormally acute. He heard, even from up in the bathroom, the soft chink and flap of a letter arriving, or the creak of the gate outside, or the tiny vibration the phone makes before it even begins to ring. He heard boards shift and furniture expand and curtains move in the breeze. He could almost hear the bulbs pushing their way through the soil outside. And every time a dog barked anywhere within half a mile outside he started to his feet, listening intently.

All this awareness made him very tired. At night, his loneliness was soon blotted out in an exhausted sleep. In sleep, she was waiting for him. Not—oh not—in the dreadful mangled shapes of his rational day-time fears, brown eyes glazed with death, soft fur mangled and bloodied by the wheels of cars, but in her own shape, whole and real. She leapt onto the bed and licked his face so that he started up crying 'Jess—at last—' And then he awoke. She came running up the small garden to him and he knew beyond any doubt that all the last two weeks had been a bad dream, nothing more. And then he awoke. He caressed her smooth head, played with her collar, told a friend at his side how he had had this frightful, damn stupid dream about losing her. . . And then he awoke.

When term ended he knew that he could, in any case, have held out for only a very few more days. The world of narrowed intensity in which he was living was almost incompatible with ordinary existence. In any case he had just inserted advertisements in several papers, both local and national—cursing himself for not having thought of this before. He needed all his time for driving out to inaccessible points on the perimeter of London, various places where a trickle of telephone callers were all sure that they had seen Jess. In response to one particularly emphatic and encouraging woman he even went to see a dog in Gloucestershire. But it turned out to be brown and white, and not a bitch anyway.

He didn't, in fact, find these fruitless journeys, after the first one, so desperately disappointing. He had begun to arm himself against disappointment, he did not undertake each one really expecting that Jess would be at the end of it. It was almost as if the journeys were some sort of end in themselves. Something to do—a further testament of his love.

By and by there were no more phone calls. But he still continued every day, driving round London, its suburbs and the country beyond, always looking, searching, peering forward, skidding to sudden stops a few times when an arching back, a plumey tail bobbing by the kerb had convinced him for a half a second that it was her, truly her—

It was at the fourth or fifth of these sudden stops that a heavy lorry ran into the back of him. It had been entirely his fault: he recognised that blearily and immediately, even through the pain that lacerated his back and took his breath away. A crowd gathered and the clamorously competing sirens of police and ambulance vehicles seemed to fill the air surprisingly quickly. People were pretty efficient, really; he felt vaguely grateful to them. The steering wheel was pressed into his chest, the door had buckled in on him and they had to

cut the metal away to get him out. Quite soon he was in
hospital and likely to be there, he realised with a dawning
sense of relief and relaxation, for a good long while. Really,
what with the way he had been feeling, it seemed the best
place for him at the moment. He even wondered, between
the waves of morphia and the intermittent stabs of pain, if
he had gone and had the accident on purpose to get himself
here.

Over the next six weeks his body gradually repaired itself, and
people endlessly told him what a lucky man he was that he
was not, after all it seemed, going to be left with a crippled
back, paralysed legs or a neck he couldn't turn. He came to
believe them, and learnt to smile at them. It was, after all,
rather nice being lucky. He didn't seem to have played that
role for a long time.

After the hospital, they sent him to a convalescent home for
a month, near Brighton, and he played chess and chatted and
was gently bored and went for rather careful walks along the
shore. He felt luckier than ever here, among so many people
who would never be entirely whole again, and at times was
tempted to show off, rather.

By the time he was passed fit for work again the summer
term was the best part over. The Head, who had visited him in
Brighton, said 'Don't think of getting back into harness till
September, old man—I'll make it OK with the Office. Why
don't you pop off abroad or somewhere on a really nice long
holiday? Make the most of it?'

As a matter of fact that was just what he intended. He'd
made a good friend in the convalescent home—chap called
Jo, in a wheel-chair now, he'd never be able to get back into
harness himself, but he was getting a pension from his firm
and had just had a good fat sum in compensation from the
firm of the stupid bugger who'd done for him... Anyway Jo
was an old hand at foreign travel, knew half a dozen
languages, and was just looking for someone to team up with

this summer on a trip to Italy—someone to push the wheel-chair and lend a bit of a hand in the bathroom and so on. . . Tom agreed with alacrity to Jo's proposal. Not that Jo was the most exciting person in the world, but Tom was tired of excitement—tired to death of it, as a matter of fact, and Jo was a really good sort. It would be grand, anyway, to have a really long trip abroad without worrying too much about the expense and to feel at the same time that he was doing someone else a good turn.

He went back home for a few days first just to make sure everything was alright and to arrange about having letters forwarded and so on. The house, with all the windows and doors carefully locked by a neighbour in his absence, felt oddly unfamiliar. He wasn't entirely sure, as a matter of fact, if he wanted to keep it. Mightn't it be better for him to get some smaller place, a flat perhaps? He might even think of teaming up with someone. . . With Jo, perhaps, if this summer's trip went well.

There was a good film on locally he wanted to see. He was on his way out when the phone rang. He almost didn't answer it. When he did so he nearly put the receiver down again because the fool on the end was using a pay box and didn't know how to get through, then—

' 'Allo-oo?' said a woman's voice at last, loud and aggrieved.

'Hallo. This is 094-9269.'

'It's about your dog. See, we've just seen the bit in the paper —In an old bit of paper that was round the shopping—'

With the greatest reluctance he asked, after a pause:

'Where do you live?'

' 'Oundslow. Well we found her by the edge of the M4, see, and we did put a notice in the pet shop at the time, but no one claimed her—'

'When was this?'

'March. She's a brown cocker spaniel see—just like it says.'

With a sinking heart he heard himself say:

'I'll be over first thing tomorrow morning. No—not first

thing, because I'll have to come by public transport, I've just remembered. But I'll be there by eleven. If you'd just give me your address—'

A tudor villa in a run-down residential district. Too near the motorway now, probably, for comfort: he could hear the stationary, continuous sound of the unseen traffic as he stood by the gate. A bald lawn with a broken bicycle. A heavy motor-bike parked by the front door. Milk bottles on the step and a banging window. When he rang the bell barking began, and he turned his head sharply, but it was only two collies who rounded the corner from the back of the house and bore down on him, all noisy self-advertisement. Behind them came a boy of about ten in shrunk jeans and heavy boots. He stopped short on seeing Tom and retreated shouting 'Mum. Mu-um.' Tom waited resignedly. Long experience of boys had made him familiar with homes like this, with everything any-how and the basic parental good nature too sloppy and un-focussed to be worthy of the name. If that boy got into trouble ever and was asked by some well-meaning social worker how he got on with his family he would hunch his shoulders and say vaguely, as if he did not understand the question 'Awright'. . .

He had known before she in turn appeared that Mum would be a blowsy woman with slippers and bare legs, and he was right. For a moment she seemed to have forgotten all about his coming. Then she remembered and became friendly.

'Oh come in do. Just step over—yes, that's right. Do excuse the mess won't you, we're a bit upside down. Trev—my husband, that is, and my eldest boy—they're doing a bit of decorating, see.'

The littered hall smelt strongly of dog, and contained a large number of things which could have had nothing to do with decorating. Through the open door of the kitchen ahead he caught sight of mounds of dirty crockery and plates on the floor. As if following his eye she said, laughing defensively:

'If I don't put our dishes on the floor see, they just jump up and lick them on the tables. Proper devils they are—fair wearing me out. I tell you, I shan't be sorry to see the back of yours —if she *is* yours. That's five of 'em I've had on my hands for the last two months; the two collies, my husband's prize greyhound what's out in the shed, another puppy this fellow here brought in—' aiming a vaguely affectionate blow at her younger son—'and yours. Driving me mad, they are.'

He murmured what was intended to be both thanks in advance and disclaimers in case 'his' should prove after all not to be... How much real hope had he? He did not know. He felt confused. He was straining his ears for a known bark, a known scutter of feet on the smeary lino-tiles—and yet this was not like it had been before. The intensity, the sense of personal effort and involvement, were lacking. He felt disorientated, as if he were playing a part. Playing himself, perhaps, of months ago. Was it really so long? Yes. Time had passed, in hospital, at Brighton. Nothing it seemed had remained exactly the same. He was cured. But there was still that slight stiffness in his back, now and probably forever, which would prevent him from taking games at school any more. And perhaps a new kind of stiffness ... weakness ... elsewhere too...

They went through the kitchen, past the reek of cooking horsemeat and lights, out into a squalid back yard. 'There,' said the woman, pointing unnecessarily, 'there tied up by the fence.'

She had been whining and snuffling as they emerged from the kitchen, but for some reason he had not registered the fact. Now, at the sight of them, she let forth a spate of high-pitched barking that did not stop.

'There,' said the woman fatuously, 'seems to know you, doesn't she?'

'She barks at everyone like that,' said a man who had just joined them from nowhere, adding dourly to Tom, 'On heat, she is. Goes on like that at everyone just now. That's why she's tied up. Kev, don't you let those collies out here again, or I'll give you what-for.'

Brown. Indubitably the same breed as Jess. Much heavier, and in need of a bath. Fat, foolish, barking hysterically. Limping a bit, he noticed. A hind leg.

'Yeah, she was like that when we found her,' said the man, 'Lame, I mean. Was she before?'

'No. Mine isn't. Wasn't... I mean...' Trying to collect his slithering thoughts, he said: 'Did she have a collar on?'

'No. Reckon someone pinched it maybe. Pinched her, perhaps, and then couldn't keep her. Wouldn't wonder—right nuisance, she is, even when she isn't in season. Meaning no offence to you, of course,' the man added hastily.

Swallowing, he stepped forward, caressed her head. She fawned on him, trying to rub herself against him. Then she turned her attention with equal enthusiasm to the boy.

For something to say, he said:

'It's funny that the police never connected her with my description... You did say you'd reported her to them, didn't you?'

'That's right,' said the woman. 'The kid went down there to tell 'em... Didn't you Kev?'

They all looked at him. He looked away. Abruptly his mother cried:

'Kev—*did you*?'

'I meant to,' he said sullenly after a silence.

His mother hit out at him with hasty and perfunctory aim. He dodged and began to whine: 'I did mean to Mum, honest, I jus' forgot...'

'Forgot. I'll see you don't forget another time,' said his father grimly, as if it were no surprise to him and the whole family were simply going through some sort of charade for the visitor's benefit.

'I'm ever so sorry,' said the woman turning to Tom with fulsome insincerity. 'I did think he 'ad. I *told* him to but you know what boys are, and this one's potty on dogs, I think he's mental or something, I really do...'

He didn't listen to them. He went on staring at the dog as she squirmed before them in an ecstasy of undirected anticipation. And he simply didn't know.

It *could* be Jess. She was the right colour and size, and the changes *could* be accounted for by the lapse of time, by idiotic over-feeding, by several things... He simply did not know. He who had thought once he would know Jess out of millions, simply could not now be sure if this were her or not. He had carried an image of her in his heart every moment day and night for weeks: every time he had closed his eyes for a second she had been there, gambolling behind his aching lids, flying, ears flapping, down the wind on the Hill... But perhaps that was the trouble. He had carried this image with him for so long that the picture had begun to wear itself out like a film incessantly being run. And he had beome confused. The Jess he was now trying desperately to recall was not perhaps even the real, original Jess but Jess at second-hand, the quintessential, ideal, golden Jess who had lived behind his eyelids, the shadow he had pursued so obsession-ally, with such desire and pain. That shadow had gone, suddenly and completely, at the moment when the lorry had rammed into the back of his car. She had not accompanied him in the ambulance to hospital, had never visited him there. It was as if the accident that had miraculously spared him for a further extension of life had killed her, for good.

The noisy, indiscriminate, flesh and blood spaniel before him now seemed to have nothing to do with the golden shadow, or with the dead past at all. It might well be Jess, he told himself again; he didn't think so but that was just prejudice, it was perfectly possible... He simply did not know.

What's more, he felt that he would never know. He was under no illusions any more. If this brown bitch were not Jess then this was the end, he would never find her anywhere else. This was his chance. If he took it—?

If he took it he *might* be taking a completely strange dog, a dog who might, even with proper food and discipline, remain fat and stupid and almost certainly lame, a dog who would only come to represent to him, as time went by, a cruel disappointment and a daily regret and resentment. He knew in that moment that he wanted Jess and he wanted absolute certainty, no second best would do.

Perhaps, even if this dog were not Jess, sufficient love and effort could transform her into a living image of the original. . . Perhaps. But so much of his love and effort had been expended in the search for her that he felt he had not that much to offer any more. An intensity within himself was worn out too.

And, in any case, with Jess or any other dog on his hands, he would not be able to go abroad with Joe. He was particularly unwilling to let Jo down, he thought. . .

Turning to the boy, he said:

'So you're fond of dogs? You fond of this one now? Is that why you didn't want to report her to the police?'

The child nodded wordlessly, one eye on his mother. Perhaps he was afraid of her. It wasn't a very convincing nod. But Tom decided to take it for what it was. He faced the parents squarely.

'It's not my dog,' he said.

Their faces fell. But they looked resigned. Perhaps they had really expected this.

'Oh. Not yours then?'

'No. Not mine.' And he added, not just politely but as if apologising for himself:

'I'm sorry. . . But there it is.'

6

The secret of a joyful life

GEORGE AND THE children call it my blacking factory. Like Dickens.

Of course, in my case, this is intended ironically. Unlike Dickens I did not have hopelessly unreliable parents, but very stable, predictable ones, and nor did anyone ever force me into a factory at the age of thirteen to stick labels on blacking bottles thereby engendering a lasting social neurosis. On the contrary, I had what passed for a secure, middle class up-bringing period circa 1950, amply garnished—in the holidays —with such suitable appurtenances as riding lessons, swim-ming lessons and trips 'to Town' for the dentist, the theatre and more school uniform from Marshall's. My parents loved me; I had a bedroom of my own with 'The Boyhood of Raleigh' and some Chinese horses framed in passe-partout, I had a glass animal collection and a carved bear collection, I had a bicycle and—for the Christmas when I was thirteen—a really grown-up party frock, ballet length, in taffeta and tulle, and cuban-heeled silver shoes to wear with it. Such things girls wanted, long ago, before there were jeans and pop music and sex for them.

It was just that I was sent to this boarding school. To explain why would, I suspect, require a detailed and tedious study of the prejudices, hopes and delusions of the class and generation to which my parents belonged. Their forty-year-old lives had been sandwiched between war and peace in alternate jerks, like a clock running fast and then slow and then fast again with at least one attempt to 'put it back' altogether. That was the point that had been reached—or reached again—by the late 1940s. It was odd, and unnerving. Children automatically think in terms of progress, of life becoming bigger and better and freer, but it seemed to me that between 1948 and 1950 I got younger, my life more circumscribed and old-fashioned. During my first term at the school clothes rationing was still on, and you were allowed to wear whatever shoes you had and your own skirts and jerseys at evenings and weekend. But two years later all shoes had to be strapped, with buttons, and the school revived the pre-war regulation supper-wear, in 'neutral' shantung. I remember wondering if that was the prevailing colour of Switzerland, also neutral in my experience. The word 'pre-war' was much on people's lips, and it was used to mean, not that which has gone irrevocably, but a norm that would soon return. It felt to me as if we were moving steadily backwards— that within a few years more we would find ourselves in frilled pantelettes being waited on by a host of submissive servants. Yes, it was confidently expected, even by my own moderately rational, fairly kind parents, that the working classes would soon be driven back into their places, as they had been in 1926: once again housemaids would become normal property, Socialism would be vanquished, private education would triumph—in short, that they should be rearing their children for a world as like as possible to that of their own youth.

That, at least, is the only possible explanation I can find for their sending me to the blacking factory; such a small, 'select' boarding school was simply part of their received image of a suitable middle class upbringing. That I could have been educated better, cheaper and more happily in the country town two miles from where we lived, did not, apparently, enter into their calculations: 'people like us', once past ten or eleven, went to boarding school. There was apparently a virtue in the very fact of being exiled from home, irrespective of the objective advantages of the place of exile. Had I had a brother, he would have been despatched to a similar establishment at an even younger age. For children from homes like mine, the average prison sentence was six years for a girl and ten years for a boy.

Prison, did I say? Yes—I recognise that the emotive language is already getting out of hand. Of course my parents didn't think of it as a prison and nor, reared by them, did I, or not in so many words. I accepted that the recurrent and inevitable home-sickness, the sense of desolation, the estrangement from family and friends, the loss of freedom and privacy for eight or nine months of the year, were simply the way life was for children 'like me'. Nor did I even—or at least not for several years—perceive that the blacking factory was a particularly third-rate example of its kind. Children have not the experience to judge these things. It was not, after all, like the school in *Jane Eyre*, the only ready-made example I had of an Awful School. We did not die of typhus—though it was true you had to have something worse than a cold before Matron, who had nursed wounded soldiers in the War and did not forget the fact, would take any notice of you. Nobody forced us to eat burnt porridge. Nobody whipped us. The food and heating were both inadequate and the hot water supply a disgrace, but after all we were children of the 1940s, our standards were not high. Our Sunday letters home were read, but I cannot honestly remember anyone being punished explicitly for what she had written in hers—though, if the spelling were bad, one was made to copy it out again, thus missing the Sunday story. And after all, unlike poor Jane Eyre and her fellows, we were *not* orphans but fortunate beings with individual homes—however distant and forbidden—which could be relied on to keep us supplied with sweets, cakes, jams, fruit, extra blankets, hot water bottles, talcum powder, reading matter and the various other articles which prisoners require in order to make their sojourn tolerable.

Some of the more thoughtful among us might possibly have wondered what the advantages were supposed to be. We might have asked ourselves—and, more to the point, our parents—what were the supposed cultural benefits of incarceration in an enclosed community without access to theatres, films, concerts or many books? (The school's 'library' consisted of six shelves of novels by Monica Dickens, C. S. Forrester and Baroness Orczy, with *Just William* and Enid Blyton for the little ones.) We might also have enquired what sort of preparation we were supposed to be receiving for life, taught by an ill-assorted band of unattached, middle-aged women of various eccentricities and neuroses, presumably none of them equal in qualifications or personality to a post in a school offering respectable facilities and salaries. Much of their meagre energy was expended in governess work—policing us out of lesson hours and particularly at weekends. (We were forbidden to set foot outside the school gates, except in a crocodile, denied the elementary right to do our own shopping, make telephone calls, choose our own dress, speak or write to members of the opposite sex.) We might also have asked our elders how the enforced and continual company only of others of the same sex, background and age-range, was supposed to teach us how to 'mix'—a lesson such schools were considered peculiarly equipped to inculcate.

But few of us asked any of these questions, or at any rate did not ask them soon enough, loudly enough or in a clearly formulated way. Where schools have the edge over other institutions—hotels, hospitals, even prisons themselves—is that, in their very nature, they breed children incapable of coherent criticism. We accepted it as normal that school should be boring, futile and degrading. We were silly, ignorant, gauche, badly educated, profoundly uncultured. The few precious, cosily indulged weeks of holiday three times a year could hardly remedy the fruitless, mediocre expanses of the rest of the year. We knew little, had few ambitions beyond leaving school at seventeen and getting engaged on our eighteenth birthdays. We giggled a lot, we quarrelled a lot, we were sentimental and sadistic, we victimised certain girls. We complained a lot in an unfocused, whining way; when not complaining we showed off to one another about what we had done in the previous holidays, jealousy competing, quick with the squashing comment. We were, I suppose, deeply bored and frustrated, intellectually and emotionally. In short we were the products of a third-rate private boarding school.

One of the victims was Daphne Cattley. I don't know why she was despised particularly—it may just have been her dank name, or the fact that her khaki-coloured hair hung drably down on either side of her regulation hair-band, making her look sulky behind her pink-rimmed glasses. Or it may have been that she wouldn't share her jam at tea one day, or that she claimed to have an Auntie in Scotland who spoke Scotch, or simply that her family lived in Ilkley and had (presumably) sent her south to acquire a desirable accent. I don't remember that she had any perceptible northern accent, so that couldn't have been it... It might have been anything. In that community without outside interests any pretext would do for scorn and apartheid. Anyway it was soon established—though only intermittently remembered—that no one wanted to walk in crocodile with Cattley, no one wanted to sit next to her in prep. It was said that she smelt—but then this was said of all unpopular people, whether they did or not, and the washing and laundry facilities were such that I imagine we must all have smelt, more or less. Cattley crept mournfully around, looking sourer and sourer, but still occasionally trying to make friends, fulsomely and insincerely—she was indeed an unattractive child—with those who laughed at her. On Sundays, I suppose, she wrote neat letters home saying that they were starting Biology that term and that the school had won its last netball match 7–3 against St Michaels of Bexley Heath.

That persecuted, flat-chested child is, at any rate, one image of Daphne Cattley. After that, she disappears for a year or two. When I next see her a change has taken place.

Her khaki hair has been frizzily permed at the ends, and she has grown a bust in a tight, grubby pink brassière. Her face has the odd spot on it—pus-white, so that your fingers itch to squeeze it. Though still technically unpopular, she has become mutinous, and therefore has acquired a small and sycophantic following.

The staff do not like Daphne Cattley at all now. They use words like 'bad influence' and 'letting the school down'—as if there were any audience within its narrow walls to notice whether the school is being let up, down or has simply expired altogether. She hums the Harry Lyme theme in Needlework. She takes ages changing for Games. She hangs out of the dormitory window in the evening and giggles and whistles when the choirboys go past—the only ones that ever go up that quiet, country road. When she sniggers in Bible Class, the Head lectures her afterwards for half an hour on dirty-mindedness and being a Tainted Person, and Daphne emerges looking red-eyed and swollen. She is a soft thing really, and not clever.

At the time I was squeamish and scornful about the choir-boys. I accepted that to try to attract their attention in this way was being 'boy-mad' and 'vulgar'. Now, it strikes me as infinitely pathetic. Like half-grown cats on heat, not fully understanding what Nature wanted of them, Daphne Cattley and her group hung over the parapet outside the dormitory window, yowling vainly and innocently into the night towards toms they could not hope to reach, yearning for simple freedom.

The Head, whom we referred to as Mother P, liked to lecture us on the virtues of independence and clear-sightedness. It was important, she told us, not to Be Sheep. We should act for ourselves and not be afraid of the opinion of others. See Kipling's 'If', parts of which she read out in her special, contralto, reading-aloud voice. Her text one end of term was that The Secret of a Joyful Life is to Live Dangerously. The sophistication of this impressed parents when they were told of it, as no doubt it was meant to. 'You're so lucky, darling, to have such an amusing, intelligent Head—not a dried up old school-marm,' my mother said complacently. Mother P had once been married—much was made of this. Her husband had died of some tropical disease in Burma and each year on the anniversary we had special prayers in Assembly while Mother P clutched a lace handkerchief and breathed deeply. Unlike her drab staff she wore noticeable clothes, rings and a lot of very red lipstick. She talked French to the depressed French teacher in our hearing. She staged scenes occasionally, making girls beg her pardon for the grief her misdemeanours had caused her. When, to fill the long weekend hours, I started a novel in a school exercise book, and the English teacher found it and showed it to Mother P, Mother P threw it away and lectured me on being Underhand. We knew that she was a liar and a fraud but we did not really appreciate to what an extent. We were, after all, just misguided sheep.

Aren't I taking it all too seriously? Haven't thousands of women of my age been through similar mills—and don't they just regard it as a bit of a joke, St Trinians and all that?

No doubt. But isn't that the ultimate indictment? Either one's childhood matters or it doesn't. If it doesn't, if it's all just a bit of a joke, a bore, not frightfully interesting really—then nothing matters, ever. Everything is dead anyway.

In any case, when I do try to pretend that the blacking factory was just something quaintly period that didn't happen to *me*, as I am now, reality stops me in the shape of my mother's face. In spite of the glass animals and the Chinese horses she was *real* and individual, and thought of me as real too. She would have been sincerely shocked and upset had I managed to convey to her what the school was actually like. She may have been naïve and a bad judge of character (Mother P) but never would she have wanted the latter half of my childhood to be just something I had to tear up and throw away—as Mother P threw away my novel. If I throw the blacking factory away I have to throw Mum away as well.

Would you? (I guess this was Dickens' problem with his father, too.)

But I had better come to the point, hadn't I?—Or to what many people would consider the point of it all, the pay-off line, the only real horror and the reason for my trauma. Though personally I'm not convinced.

As I said, Daphne Cattley and her followers had this habit of hanging out of the dormitory window at night. Running past that window—it was on the top floor of a mid-Victorian mansion—was a long parapet. On summer evenings, if you felt like it, you could crawl along the inside of that parapet to visit other dormitories on the same floor. You could also, if you were brave, walk along the top of the parapet itself, high, high above the paved front terrace, silhouetted against the pink sunset.

Daphne Cattley, I suppose, was brave. Or, more likely, she was neither intelligent enough nor imaginative enough to be aware of the danger. The first time she did it her followers oo-ed and ah-ed and wondered how she dared, so she began to do it every evening, in her rubbed Wincyette pyjamas that made her bottom look big and unappetisingly low-slung. It was a spell of particularly fine weather, and at least Cattley's exploit provided some entertainment during the long, light time—'lights out' was a good hour and a half before most of us could reasonably have been expected to sleep.

One or two others tried imitating Cattley, but they were more cautious and people were less impressed by them, even taking the view that they were just copy-cats. One or two older girls also wondered, with self-righteous consciousness of their own positions rather than with genuine concern, if they 'ought' to tell someone about Cattley—Matron, or even Mother P. They hesitated, savouring the horrific row that would ensue without really being able to envisage it. What punishment could possibly be considered bad enough for parapet-walking, and would Mother P go white round her reddened lips and pretend to cry?

One particularly beautiful evening, when a yawning and yet nervously cackling ennui possessed the inhabitants of the front dormitories, Daphne Cattley, who was not particularly neat in her movements, executed a clumsy side-step while showing off on the parapet, and over-balanced.

Sitting up in bed myself, straining my eyes to read *Forever Amber* in the dying light, I did not see it happen. But I heard the small scream, a few yards from the window where my bed was, and heard the other screams from other windows as if in answer to it. By the time I got my own head out of the window and over the parapet, Daphne Cattley was lying in an odd position on the flag-stones about sixty feet below, and Mother P—past whose drawing room window she had fallen —was approaching her at a run on staccato high heels.

For a long moment she stooped, prodded, shook. From second to second I expected to hear her voice in its tones of familiar, pained outrage—or coldly vicious, which was reserved for the worst offences of all, like writing a novel in a school exercise book: *Daphne Cattley get up this instant and stop shamming. Do you imagine that all your sheeplike friends up there are admiring you, you dirty, stupid, sex-mad little girl.* Absurdly, in spite of being quite old enough to know better, I expected and hoped to hear it.

Instead, Mother P raised to us a face that was white but like a potato, greyish and somehow lumpy, and shrieked: 'Go back in! Get to bed *at once. All* of you.'

And, like sheep, we did.

The next day, in Assembly, she had her orange lipstick, and quite a lot of rouge and the dress she had last worn on Parents' Day, as if she expected visitors. She was cold, but calm. She announced that Daphne Cattley had been taken to hospital where she would have to stay 'some time'. We all said a prayer for the recovery of Those Amongst us in Sickness or Distress, and then Mother P announced that Daphne Cattley would not, in any case, be returning to the school, since unfortunately she could not now be Trusted.

We knew, or at any rate some of us knew, that she was lying. I had seen Cattley sprawled with her neck broken—her poor body all broken, for that matter—and although I had never seen such a sight before (or since, for that matter) I knew that she must have been killed on the instant. Even had I not been certain of that the night before, I knew now: Mother P's attitude of distaste and rejection had told me clearly. Death was, simply, taboo—too disgusting to mention, when it really happened, in spite of Beloved Husband and the ritual of the Anniversary Day. I could see it myself, actually. A dead, elderly husband was permissible, placeable, but Daphne Cattley of all people, obscenely and suddenly dead at one's feet in her Wincyette pyjamas, was really too awful to acknowledge. Even among ourselves we did not really dare to, speculating in euphemisms, hushing one another ostentatiously when Juniors came round the corner, avoiding one another's eyes.

There was, of course, a more calculated reason for the headmistress's calm denial of the truth. As I see it now, she was boldly hoping to keep the death a secret not only from all of us but from our parents as well, who might otherwise have lost their faith in an institution where such things could happen. Daphne Cattley's own parents had to be told about it, presumably... But Ilkley was (how fortunate!) a nice long way off: no other families with girls at the school lived in Yorkshire. With an impressive resolution Mother P embarked on subterfuge: the following Sunday we were told what to say in our letters home, about poor Daphne who had had a silly accident doing something she had been told many times not to do, but was now getting better. It was dictated to us, with punctuation.

Now I think about it, there must have been an inquest, mustn't there? But I suppose the bald fact of an accident was insufficiently interesting to be taken up by the national press, and, if a report did appear in the local paper, no parent was likely to see it, since the parents of boarding school children do not live locally. I do not know, I can only speculate—we never saw newspapers anyway. At the time, in the school, the conspiracy of silence did not seem incredible but merely in keeping.

A rule was added to the substantial list of them on all the notice boards, saying that no one was allowed to climb roofs, walls or trees. One day soon after that, when we came in to change from Games, the windows which looked out onto the parapet had all had blocks put in them so that they would only open a couple of inches top and bottom. Life went on as before, with hoarded fragments of peppermints in dirty pockets, with queues for lavatories, with slack boredom and then sudden fierce, arbitrary punishments for talking on the way to tea. Daphne Cattley's name was never mentioned.

About half a year later, home for the Christmas holidays, I began having such nightmares that I became afraid to sleep at night, and moaned and clung to my mother like a six-year-old. She, alarmed at such an unprecedented display of emotion in what she had hoped was a carefree schoolgirl, sent me to the doctor, who, on hearing that my nightmares were 'mainly about blood'—I kept seeing Cattley walking round, grinning, and bleeding copiously from eyes and finger ends—asked a series of embarrassing and, to me, irrelevant questions. I had been menstruating for a year already and it had never bothered me anyway. In reality, no blood had been visible when that body had lain sixty feet beneath me, but my imagination, clumsily questing for understanding, had supplied it.

The nightmares gradually faded, but so did I. I drooped, lost my appetite, became neurotic about trifles, bit my nails, had tics. My school work deteriorated. Meanwhile I think whispers must have been abroad. The headmistress sent round a bullying roneo-ed letter to all the parents, which made my father laugh, about how adolescent girls should not be allowed to give way to 'morbid fantasies'; the school doctor, a vague, unseen authority trotted out on a variety of occasions to lend

weight to otherwise dubious assertions, had apparently said
so. But some parents, uneasy, were taking their girls away.
The educational standards really weren't all that high, were
they? Uncertain, unwilling to admit they might have made a
mistake and wasted good money for nothing, or worse, my
mother and her best friend conferred. Eventually, at fifteen,
I was removed.

For years, I was unable to think of Daphne Cattley at all—
not because I was filled with horror at such a tragic death but
because Daphne Cattley patently did not have the stature to
rate tragedy at all, and the whole thing embarrassed me
dreadfully. Reluctantly I concluded that Mother P had, in a
way, been right: Cattley falling off the parapet like that had
just been grotesque and a bit revolting, as if she'd had a baby
or wet her knickers in Assembly.

Only as the years went by, and the capacities of charity,
understanding and pity which had been atrophied in the
blacking factory gradually expanded themselves, did I
become capable of recognising that Daphne Cattley, though
a spotty, fat-bottomed clown to me and evidently to Mother P
too, had been as real to her parents as I was to mine. For them,
the event *was* tragedy, *was* horror, in the highest degree, no
question of their shuffling it off or dissembling it. Mother P
couldn't make *them* do that, could she? And only through an
adult perception of their suffering and loss did I come to realise that, far from Daphne Cattley being an inadequate figure
for the tragedy which had befallen her, the event itself
had been provoked by the all-pervading inadequacy of the
situation. Covered over and lied about, it was in itself the
fruit of ignorance and evasions, the product of frustration,
boredom and poisonous affectations... *The secret of a joyful
life is to live dangerously.* That colourful and vicious quarter-
truth, and not the event, was the real horror.

Though the nightmares were of short duration, I continued
to dream of the school intermittently through the years—
whenever, in fact life was being difficult or depressing. 'I was

back in the damn place again last night,' I would announce—
to George's amusement and, presently, the children's too. It
became a signal for George to take me out to dinner or buy
me a little present.

Then, about three years ago, I heard by chance from a
friend living in the area where the school was, that it was
closing. Evidently my sub-conscious took note of this very
satisfactory piece of news, for the dreams promptly ceased.

Till last month. Then I had one more. We had happened to
be passing near the place, driving from somewhere to somewhere on holiday, and I, morbidly, wanted to go and have a
look at it. For the first time in twenty years I saw again that
high roof, those evergreens in the front, that paved terrace.
The evergreens had got much taller, darkening the lower
windows, and the top ones, above the parapet from which
Daphne Cattley had plummeted, had one or two broken
panes. The house was derelict.

A few nights later I had this other dream. I was not, now,
back in time, but secure in the present, safely adult. We were
driving past the place, as we had done in reality. Only it
wasn't there. The whole building, roofs, evergreens, parapet
and all, had been completely swept away. Beyond the gates it
was an empty site, like those you often see in towns now.
And, lashed to the gatepost, was one of those agent's boards.
It said: 'This important redevelopment site for sale. Suitable
for erection of blacking factory or similar'.

George thinks it a great joke, and I suppose it is.

7

One of the family

WILLIE AND ELLA had come from a large family themselves, so
in principle Willie was all for Ella and her husband adopting
another child. They had had one born to them, a pretty, polite
little girl with her father's plump features and Ella's dark eyes,
but after that apparently Ella's tubes had blocked or swollen
or got kinked or something; Willie was not quite sure what,
and it would have seemed indelicate to ask. He and Ella,
though fond of one another, had never been that close ever
since their enforced separation when he had been six and
Ella nine. A break in the continuity of a relationship at that
stage destroyed real intimacy for good, he supposed; with all
the good will in the world you couldn't re-establish it.

You might suppose that Willie's own wife, Jill, would have
heard all about Ella's tubes or whatever in the course of a cosy
feminine chat, but Jill wasn't like that. She had never wanted
children herself, and said frankly that she wasn't much
interested in other people's, or in their gynaey problems
either. Gynaey and paediatrics weren't her subjects. She was
a pathologist at the North London—what she liked to describe
as one of those vital backroom jobs in medicine.

Nor had Jill come from a large family herself, and she was
politely unimpressed by Ella and Ivor's desire for lots of
children and by their image of the good life as being full of
uncles, aunts and cousins. She couldn't be expected to under-

stand, thought Willie: he had never made any attempt to convey to her what their early childhood in Vienna had been like. Uncles, aunts and cousins indeed! They had had, all living within the same city or within a radius of a hundred miles, fourteen uncles and uncles-by-marriage, eighteen aunts and great-aunts and a number of first cousins which was continually augmenting—as far as Willie remembered, it had been thirty-three by 1939. And, of course, there had been grandparents too, and a great-grandmother, and second and third cousins, and an unnumbered and shifting host of in-laws —not to mention their own elder brothers by their father's first marriage: Johann and Jacob. Father, who was a goldsmith, had been a widower when he had married Mother, and *her* father was a goldsmith too: it had been, said all the family comfortably, a nice match. But then the family had been lucky that way, they went in for nice matches; jewellers' daughters marrying other jewellers, wholesale furriers marrying dealers in silks, and there was one big family of first cousins-once-removed all in the wine-trade. They didn't have any lawyers or doctors in that generation, which hadn't quite reached that elevated level, but it had been obvious around 1930—the date of Ella's birth—that they were going to: Mother's eldest brother had gone into banking and was doing well, and later Johann went to medical school. True, Ella and Willie had one big cousin who was studying to become a rabbi, but Father and Mother and most of the family were a bit cool about that: keeping up social customs was one thing, but none of them had ever gone in for making a show of their religion; after all, this was Austria in the twentieth century, not Poland or Russia in the nineteenth. When they spoke of Hymie, the aspirant rabbi, whom nobody liked much because his hands were damp and he couldn't sing (so unfortunate in that job!) and was no fun on Sunday picnics in the country, Mother and Father used to sound deprecating; almost as if he were a black sheep like the legendary Uncle Adolf, who had gone to Israel in 1920 and changed his name from Katowski to Bar-

Ackbar and had never been heard of since. It wasn't, as Mother had explained to Ella and Willie, very nice to drop your whole family like that: after all, they *were* your family.

So they were kind to Hymie, in spite of what they thought of him, and went on including him on huge Sunday outings to the river or the forests, just as they did Aunt Rosa, who was fat and querulous and smelt of cold cure pastilles, and old Uncle Baba who was so deaf that talking to him was agony, but who insisted on being talked to just the same. There were pictures of those Sundays in the fat brown photograph albums Ella still had; fading snapshots of plump cushions, tableclothes shadowed under trees, faces shadowed under cloche hats, stiff collars, braces, boaters and parasols: great-grandmother beached hugely in a wheeled chair with four generations grouped round her; Ella and some girl cousins all grinning in floppy sunhats, Willie at four looking mournful in a sailor suit with huge, bare knees too close to the camera— that was one of the last pictures in that album: 1937. After that, they didn't seem to have gone on picnics any more. After that—Willie now knew—the uncles and cousins began to disappear. Johann disappeared.

Gone, all gone! Every last one of them. All those faces and hats and braces and drooping skirts and sailor suits, not to mention all those huge picnic meals, all gone and nothing left at all—no sequel. It was almost incredible. Of that whole enormous family of sixty or seventy people, most of them stout and fertile, the *only* direct living descendant was Rachel, Ella and Ivor's little daughter. Willie had tried repeating this remarkable fact to himself many times, but he still couldn't make it mean much. It was uncanny, but ultimately meaningless—just as it was meaningless, or at any rate not meaningful in any present sense, when you tried repeating to yourself 'Aunt Rosa is a handful of ashes in the earth at Treblinka', 'Cousin Hymie fueled the ovens at Madjanek'. Just because these dimly remembered people happened to be related to you, it didn't make them special or any different from all the millions of others who were now ash too. In any case it was only conjecture—or a shorthand way of expressing the inexpressible. Really, he and Ella had no means of knowing which of several possible places had been the ultimate destinations of what members of the family. They did not even know where Father and Mother had met their end. Yes, you could even try saying, as you gazed at those photographs—those *other* photos, in books, of piled-up corpses being shovelled into pits by bulldozers: 'One of these is Mother'—Willie had tried it. But it just didn't, when you came down to it, *convey* very much—not much of perceivable, all-time truth or reality. Perhaps it did to Ella, he thought, but not to him.

To him, everything that his adult self knew about the War and the fate of the people from whom he had sprung, was so irrelevant to the happy, comfortable life he dimly remembered and the people as he had known them, that he could make no imaginative connection from the one thing to the other. It was as if, by their unimaginable sufferings, all those people he had known and taken for granted had become somehow *different* from himself and alien precisely because of what they had undergone and he had not. Intellectually, he was aware of the absurdity of this—or, as Jill would have put it, aware of the defences he had carefully erected to protect himself from having to face the unbearable. But to know something was not to feel. He recognised—he fully admitted, to himself at any rate—that his present attitude to his family simply would not do; such a reluctant half-interest was a quite inadequate acknowledgement of their cumulative fate and his own and Ella's miraculous escape. But to know that you *ought* to feel grateful, humble and appalled does not automatically supply the emotion to do so.

Once, half hoping and half dreading that he might stumble there on some genuine fragment of the past, sharp beneath the foot, he had even gone to Vienna. Jill had been attending a medical conference there, one parched July, and he had gone

along for the ride. During the three days she had been con-
ferring with other pathologists, he had had plenty of time to
conduct a little experiment in morbid anatomy himself—a
joke he had been about to retail to Jill and then, for some
reason, had decided not to. But, although he had found the
quarter where he had lived for the first six years of his life, it
had been totally rebuilt, presumably as a result of War
damage. Even the street pattern round there was different
from the plan of Vienna in the pre-war Baedeker he had
secreted in his own suitcase, and the trams which had been
the delight of his infancy were gone too. He seemed to think
that they had sometimes set off for picnics by tram, the grown-
ups clutching great baskets on their capacious laps, but presumably these routes which had then run quickly out into
open country would now run only through interminable
post-war suburbs. The very sites would have disappeared.

He wandered for a while among the square yellow blocks,
through a newly laid out public garden where thirsty saplings
drooped over landscaped mounds which might—mightn't
they?—indicate heaps of concentrated, irreducible rubble:
the blackened bricks and mortar of his own earliest days, now
ground to dust, a handful of ashes... But it was no good. The
sheer physical changes were too great. There was no point in
standing around on a cement pavement laid in 1957 thinking
'here, it happened', if 'here' were an utterly different sort of
place. The scent was obliterated.

Back in England, when he told Ella he'd been to look round
Vienna, she said, almost reproachfully, 'I don't know how you
could. I couldn't.' But then Ella, besides having been three
years older when they had left home, was 'like that'—by
which phrase he supposed he really meant, if he were honest,
that she was not only emotional but also a bit given to self-
dramatisation, and to thinking herself more sensitive than the
next person. Not in any nasty or snooty way, of course. No one
would ever have called Ella's warm, quiveringly responsive,
rather demanding personality, 'snooty'.

He had sometimes wondered if she had known, at nine, that she was leaving home and parents forever, when they had stood together in a group of forty children on the mainline railway station that day in what he now knew must have been August 1939. She always maintained now, almost hysterically, that she had had *no idea at all*, and that, had she had, Mother and Father would have had to drag her screaming to the station. But he wasn't convinced. Why, if she had genuinely thought she was coming back again, had she weighted down her suitcase with two heavy photograph albums—he could see her struggling now under the weight of it, her narrow shoulders bowed, her beret askew, gripping him firmly with the other hand. She had been a bright child, quick to pick up undercurrents, and a reader of newspapers. Surely she must have had some idea that she and her little brother were being sent away simply to save their lives, and that therefore it was highly possible that nothing and no one else would be saved at all? But perhaps even the grown-ups, in spite of their pathetic willingness to despatch their children via an agency to total strangers in a far-off country, had not really thought the thing through? Perhaps they half-believed their own verbal assurances to one another that the children's 'visit' to England would be just for 'a year or two'—till the Nazis were beaten and they themselves could stop being afraid, and life could go on just as it had before.

As a sturdy six-year-old, illiterate as yet, most of the agitation had passed over his head. He had simply been excited at going on a long train journey, and unperturbed by the information that he and Ella would be staying in England with strangers who might not speak German, since none of these concepts meant anything to him. He remembered packing his toy soldiers in his own satchel, and being puzzled because his mother insisted on cramming in his winter coat. He remembered that he was one of the smallest children in the group and that they had all had labels tied to them. But he didn't remember kissing his parents goodbye: too many

other exciting and interesting things had probably been going
on.

Years later Ella told him that she and he had been in one of
the last groups of children to get out of Vienna. Right up till
3 September the Jewish Agency there had been bargaining
with the British Foreign Office, trying to get papers through
in time for more children... You had, she said knowledgeably,
to have a written invitation with a guarantee of support from
a family in England, besides masses of other things. But quite
a lot of the families in Vienna who applied under the scheme
were worried about the idea of sending their children off into
the void to foster parents who were not only foreign but might
not even be good Jews—they didn't, of course, she said pity-
ingly and bitterly—appreciate the true desperateness of the
situation. And in fact a lot of the families in England who
were prepared to take these children weren't Jews at all, but
just decent *New Statesman* types who *were* aware of the
gravity of the situation—like the Prescotts in Northampton
who eventually took Willie. Also most of them only wanted to
take one child, while many families were sending two or more
and pleaded that they should not be split up. What were the
Jewish Agency officials to do? In fact, said Ella, what they did
was make use of a few public spirited orthodox Jewish
families over and over again for official invitations, like the
Loewes in Hendon to whom she herself had actually gone—
and then, once the kids were in England, sorted matters out
as best they could. They did the very best they could, said
Ella passionately, as if permanently defending the Jewish
Agency against some never-voiced charge.

That was how he and Ella were separated, abruptly on
Victoria Station, and why (he thought) their subsequent lives
and character developments had been quite different. Ella
had gone to the Loewes, who were actually far more religious
than any of the family at home. *All* their relations seemed to
be rabbis, and Mrs Loewe wore a wig and had, said Ella
humorously, started repairing the gaps in Ella's education (in

fluent German) about what tea towels to use for what, before
she had been in the house an hour. Not that Ella seemed to
have minded this. She had apparently taken to orthodoxy like
a duck at last finding its natural element. She had become very
fond of the Loewes, had stayed with them for the next fifteen
years till her marriage, regarding them as her family, and
Rachel now called them Auntie and Uncle and was taken to
visit them every Saturday.

Meanwhile Willie had been sent to Northampton where he
was kindly if uncomprehendingly received into the family of
a Methodist minister. He didn't see Ella again for over a year.
It wasn't really the Prescotts' fault. The allocation of the
various children at Victoria had, of necessity, been hurried
and arbitrary. Unable to speak German themselves, they had
not understood that one of the people Willie cried for in the
early days was there in England too; they were not aware that
he *had* a sister. And by the time Willie had stopped crying
and learnt to speak English he had already begun to forget
Ella—and Mother, and Father, and Johann and Jacob and all
the uncles and aunts and cousins, and Vienna, and German
itself. The change for him was so complete that inevitably it
forged a new identity for him. And when it finally was realised
that he had a sister in Hendon, and elaborate and difficult
wartime plans were made for the children to meet, the new
Willie—with a proper English double-you sound now instead
of a vee—was half-reluctant. He and Ella had become
strangers to one another. The infrequent, artificial meetings
which the grown-ups went on arranging for them, evidently
feeling it their duty to do so, were strained affairs; they made
Ella cry because she remembered things, while Willie sat there
stolidly *not* remembering and feeling embarrassed.

When the Loewes invited him to spend a week with them in
1946 it was even worse. He was a big boy by then and
resented being despatched like a child to an alien house and
a busty teenage sister he hardly recognised. Half the time he
didn't even know what she and the Loewes were talking

about. Friday night supper was a disaster: well, how was *he* to know that those candles weren't meant to be blown out? At home in Northampton you didn't waste candles like that for no reason—you saved them for power cuts. He picked up the fact that the Loewes were disappointed—even grieved—at the idea of his being at the Prescotts' (though you could say it was partly their fault for not wanting to take a boy), and that Ella would not be allowed to visit him there because there was something wrong about the food. He resented this aspersion cast on his foster-mother's cooking, as any other English boy would have done. To heavily delicate enquiries about whether he ever attended synagogue and if a bar-mitzvah was planned for him, he answered in negative monosyllables that were puzzled as well as resentful. He had all but lost sight of the fact that he was supposed to be Jewish. Mr Prescott had mentioned it to him once or twice as though he thought it was his duty to, but he had sounded slightly reluctant, as if he were referring to some minor but embarrassing disability or base personal habit which in general it was wiser to disregard. Without probably meaning to, he conveyed to Willie the impression that 'Jewish' was a slightly dirty word (like 'working class' or 'common', or even 'dirty') which he, Mr Prescott, regretted having to use. If, Willie now thought, he had been black instead, the good, simple Prescotts would have ignored the fact entirely except for rare, tactful references—probably followed by the brisk assurance that not many people noticed and that he had got much lighter recently anyway!

Years later, when he had read Koestler's *Thieves in the Night*, he had laughed derisively at the scene in which an upper class English girl rejects a would-be lover when she sees that he is circumcised. Odd of Koestler, of all people, to be so naïve—growing up with the Prescotts Willie knew that to be circumcised, as he himself was and as Johnny and Mike Prescott were too, was just a nice, middle class thing to be, like being fond of dogs and wearing old clothes on Sunday afternoon. When, at London University, he first heard a Jewish acquaintance of his say that, on religious principle, he would have his own sons circumcised, he felt amazed and rather scornful: fancy any intelligent person setting store by such a thing. He was now meeting, for almost the first time, Jews with a corporate sense of their own race, and on the whole he steered clear of them. They seemed to him a bit like Catholics—members of some exclusive private club which he didn't want to join but which made him feel left out and somehow deficient in one dimension. As for his relationship with Ella, now that he was in London too, that gradually burgeoned —but poor old Ella had to make most of the running. And at that he doubted if he would ever have got onto terms of real friendship with her again if she hadn't eventually married Ivor, who was such a nice chap in his unassuming way that no one could help liking him.

So, what with one thing and another, Willie felt himself pretty well qualified to have views on the subject of adoption. Weren't both he and Ella (but particularly him because he had been younger) both examples of successful adoptions in their way? He spared a brief thought to wonder how each of them would have turned out had they gone to the other family—he to the devout and intense Loewes, Ella to the milder, cooler Prescotts—but abandoned that line of conjecture as too confusing. Imagining yourself quite different from what you actually were was really too difficult. . . Basically his attitude to adopted children was straightforward. He believed that people's personalities were mostly determined by the environment in which they were reared. Any child you brought up would therefore resemble—at least in a number of important ways—your own children. Even intelligence, he understood, was not a fixed quotient (as psychologists had originally thought) but was modified by the environment. That, apparently, was why working class children—now, as a social worker he felt able to say 'working class'—tended to do less well at school than middle class ones. It wasn't because they were intrinsically stupid but just because their mothers brought them up differently and talked to them differently—or didn't talk to them. It was quite obvious, to him at any rate, that any child brought up by Ella would be fairly articulate, as Ella was herself. Not that Rachel was a particularly chatty little girl. But then she took after Ivor more... He hesitated, a little confused, and then dropped this line of thought.

He was surprised, even a little shocked, when he discovered that it was a specifically Jewish child Ella and Ivor were hoping to adopt. On reflection, he realised that this was not out of character, with Ella at any rate. 'But what the hell *is* being a Jew except thinking of yourself as one?' he asked them.

There was a slight pause round the table where they were all having supper. Then it was Ivor who said:

'Well Willie—you're right, of course. But Ella and I don't feel we'd have the right to impose our—uh—Jewishness on a child that wasn't born that way.'

'You mean like a black family adopting a white child and painting its skin?' said Jill, amused. 'Rather a good idea!'

Ella, who (Willie could see) thought Jill was being flippant and not very funny, said in a too-creamy voice:

'Jill, dear, I *know* religion doesn't mean anything to you. But it does to us—'

'And anyway,' put in Ivor quickly, 'I don't think Ella and I'd ever be offered a non-Jewish child. Most adoption societies simply won't take Jewish couples on their books—they say that by the terms of their charter they're supposed to be placing babies in Christian homes and that if they gave one to the likes of us they wouldn't be fulfilling their duty to the mothers.'

'How monstrous,' said Jill vaguely, 'So what do you do? *Are* there many Jewish babies going a-begging?'

'Hardly any—' Ivor began, but Ella rushed in:

'But we think we've got one! A friend of Ivor's father's daughter—I mean, the daughter belongs to Ivor's father's friend—came back pregnant from Israel last month and apparently it's too late for her to have an abortion. We're simply *thrilled*—'

'Poor her,' said Jill shortly. Willie glanced at her: she could be a bit hard sometimes. Just because all this maternal bit meant nothing to her, she ought to acknowledge that it meant a lot to others: it was so like Jill to express pity for the girl giving birth, as though childbirth itself were a misfortune, rather than pleasure for Ella. But fortunately Ella didn't seem to have noticed. She was sweeping on:

'It's so marvellous to think that this baby—if we do get it, it isn't born yet—won't be a complete alien. I mean, in a sense he will be of course—or she—but in another way I think, well, he *is* a little Jew—or she is. In a way part of the family already. I could never take a child from just anywhere.'

Jill was looking annoyed. Willie sensed that she was getting ready to talk about coloured children and handicapped ones and how badly they needed homes—Jill had this priggish streak in her. He thought that he must stop her, but he felt angry himself.

'For heavens' sake, Ella,' he said, 'surely this is just sentimental? I mean, I don't blame you for *feeling* it, but surely you're not seriously telling us that there's any special reason beyond pure expediency why this particular baby should come to you?'

'Well you see his family—his grandfather's family, that is, did come from Austria too, like ours,' said Ella, as if that explained matters.

'So what? Even if we turned out to be related to them six generations back—so *what?* Honestly Ella, it's all just in the mind.'

'So are a lot of things,' put in Ivor quietly, but Willie was launched now:

'I don't get all this stuff about being "one big family",' he said loudly and truculently. 'I certainly don't get it when you just mean all Jews—and I don't even get it when it's an actual family. What are "family links"?—Chains, half the time, artificially clamped on people who'd rather just be themselves, without being kidded that they "take after" this or that senile old relative. As if you could genuinely take after anyone but the people who've brought you up and influenced you, and that's all. People talk as if there's something special and different and interesting about their blood relatives—"blood is thicker than water" and so on. Well, it just isn't true. It's a subjective conceit. Remember that awful old judge—'

'Oh yes, the blood tie case and those poor foster parents,' said Jill, and they talked about that for a bit. But Willie could see that Ella was pinkly harbouring something, and in a break in the conversation she leant forward to say, too sweetly:

'Willie, we *know* you don't like or approve of families very much, you and Jill. But Ivor and I happen to feel very deeply—'

'Hey, who says I don't like families?' He felt slightly hurt, as if she had accused him of not liking music, or food. 'I like some families very much. The Prescotts, now—Jill and I visited them only last month when we were driving to Edinburgh.'

'The Prescotts! But Willie, they aren't even—Anyway you hardly ever *do* see them these days, do you?'

'No. And that seems to me as it should be—after all, I'm grown up now. But because they brought me up I regard them as—'

'Exactly! You regard them as your own family, but that means you hardly ever see them. You've really very little in common with them these days, Willie, you know you haven't.'

Don't nag so, he thought irritably: I don't like being told what I feel. She was in fact right about him finding Mr and Mrs Prescott and their sons rather dim and provincial these days. Methodism undoubtedly had a limiting effect on their social life, and their food, he now realised, was rock-bottom:

give him Ella's abundant Loewe-trained cooking any time, now. But, he said, to bait her:

'I don't know *why* you should think I don't have much in common with them, Ella?'

'Why, because they *aren't* your real family, Willie, that's why. Poor boy, you don't know what the word really means, that's why you don't understand it—'

'Oh, come *on*, Ella! Don't you preach to me. It's exactly the same with you and the Loewes.'

'No it isn't! I mean, No—it isn't, because they're much, *much* more like our own family were. I know, I can remember —you can't... Well, alright—Auntie and Uncle aren't *exactly* like Mother and Father were, of course, no one's exactly like your own parents, but they were a pretty close match and I was so frightfully lucky to go to them. That's why I'm so keen that this baby we've heard of should come *here*, where there's a good chance of it fitting—'

'I hope the baby himself realises he's supposed to fit,' said Jill mockingly.

'Oh of course at first he'll be just a little baby like any other,' said Ella ecstatically, choosing to ignore this gibe. 'Rachel's *thrilled* at the idea of having a baby in the house, incidentally, though of course we haven't said much yet; we don't want to raise her hopes too much—But by and by, as he grows up with us he will become one of us—won't he?'

'Ella,' said Ivor quickly, laughing, 'You've made your point but I'd leave it at that for now if I were you. You're in danger, my girl, of arguing yourself from one side right over onto the other!'

'In fact,' put in Willie, with less good temper, 'You've just done so.'

The months went by and Ella and Ivor's baby was born. They fetched it from the nursing home that very next day. It was a boy and they called him Simeon. His own mother had not even wanted to see him. She was in any case—Ivor told Willie

—engaged to a suitable young man, had been since before she'd gone to Israel on a Youth Aliyah holiday. This 'unfortunate episode' in Israel had just been an aberration, and her fiancé was still prepared to marry her—provided she got rid of 'her little abortion'. 'His own words, I understand,' said Ivor, grinning sourly. 'Delightful, isn't it? Such humanity, such charity.'

Willie reflected that she must be a crummy girl to want to marry such a man, however suitable and Jewish, and then that she didn't sound the sort of person who, at any age, would take in a foreign child in need of a home. He was surprised to find himself thinking that. Was that really, now and forever, his criterion of a basically good person as opposed to a basically callous one? He supposed, on reflection, that it was. He wondered briefly what the baby's unknown Israeli father had been like, and then told himself that such speculations were just idle and irrelevant to the present and future.

At first, as Ella had predicted, Simeon was just a baby like any other, though, it seemed to Willie, rather more fractious than many. Every time they went there to Sunday lunch Simeon seemed to be crying. Ivor laughed, and said that babies always picked the most inconvenient times to yell— weekends, or six in the evening when their fathers were coming home: even at a month or two they sensed competition and knew they had to assert themselves! Ella said seriously that of course babies were not so content on the bottle as they were on their mother's milk (she had fed Rachel herself). In a few months, she said, Simeon would be much more settled. The only person who seemed worried by his nerve-racking crying was Rachel, who, as predicted, doted on him and hung anxiously over his crib crooning to him to 'cheer him up'.

Then, for quite a long time, Willie and Jill hardly saw Ella and her family, because they themselves moved to Edinburgh. Jill had been offered a rather good post there, better than any she could have expected in London, and Willie was quite happy to move there too: in his particular social work field he was in a seller's market. They still came to London occasionally, but just for the odd night or two, and, rather than sitting in Ivor and Ella's little house in Finchley, they preferred to take the pair of them out to the theatre: Ella in particular looked, these days, as if she could do with an evening out now and then. She wasn't that young any more, of course—Willie realised with a small shock of surprise— and Ivor murmured to Jill that Ella was feeling the strain a bit, having a toddler again at her age: it would be better, of course, when Simeon was over the Terrible Twos.

Ivor and Ella invited them to stay at the next New Year— Jewish New Year—but Jill couldn't take the time off then. Then Willie and Jill invited the others up for Christmas, and at first they said they'd come, but then Ivor wrote apologetic- ally to say that Ella really felt it would be too much of an up- heaval, with two children, and anyway they really liked their children to have Christmas at home. It was, said Jill to Willie, the usual situation: people with children just grew apart from those without. Children were so damn circumscribing, and, far from 'enriching life', seemed to impoverish it—at least from the standpoint of outsiders. One child had been alright —and Rachel had always been an easy, accommodating child —but with two the rot had evidently set in. That was how Jill put it.

So they didn't see anything of Simeon till the following September, when he was two-and-a-half. They stayed with Ivor and Ella for a long weekend on their way back from a trip to Italy. The house was smaller than Willie had remembered—their own flat in Edinburgh was rather spacious —and it seemed uncomfortably full of plastic bricks, which crushed underfoot, and little cars with their wheels missing. Willie found it irritating, and muttered to Jill that he couldn't see why Simeon couldn't be taught to pick his things up sometimes, as Rachel had been.

'They like it like this,' said Jill. 'Ella and Ivor, I mean. Ella's revelling in it. She feels like a real mother at last—ground down. Smiling sweetly and saying "isn't it chaos?" Lots of women are like that, I've noticed. It's masochistic—or self-glorifying.'

Willie felt that she was right in general, but he wasn't certain about this particular case. There was an exhausted shrillness about Ella which he didn't remember in her before, and she seemed to pick on Rachel much more than she had before—and much more than Rachel, who was a good, stolid little girl, deserved. It was, he thought with sudden insight, as if Ella had taken a private vow never to let Simeon exasperate her, so she used Rachel as an outlet instead. Rachel herself didn't seem very happy, and no wonder.

Simeon was beautiful to look at, though (of course) nothing like either Ella or Ivor. Ella was black-haired but pale-skinned, Ivor fattish and fairish. Simeon had an aureol of black curls—very curly—and a sallow skin which occasionally made strangers wonder if he were Greek or Italian. He had a high-bridged nose, and a short upper lip in contrast to Ella's long one. His eyes were dark, like Rachel's and Ella's but, unlike theirs, were not soft and expressive but opaque and shiny like two pebbles, or like the glass eyes of a panda; they were curiously expressionless, even when he was screaming in one of his still-frequent tantrums.

Jill said privately to Willie that she thought his biological father must have been an oriental Jew, an immigrant from one of the North African countries.

'He's off again,' said Willie, cocking his ear to distant, furious bellows. He added, not entirely meaning it: 'I'd belt him when he did that, if he were mine.'

'Oh, I don't know,' said Jill with unusual tolerance. 'He's still very young, isn't he? I daresay one mustn't expect too much.'

Ella said the same thing next day, more sharply, when—after a teatime entirely devoted to forestalling Simeon's needs, placating him and humouring him to stop him knocking

things over on purpose—Willie had remarked drily that
Simeon was an unusually demanding child, wasn't he?

'They're *all* demanding at this age,' Ella snapped. 'You'd
know that if you had any of your own.' She looked, Willie
thought, white and old, and no wonder.

'Rachel wasn't,' he said with studied mildness.

'She was. She certainly was. You've forgotten.'

Well, perhaps he had forgotten. He had always forgotten
things quite easily. He looked across at Rachel, docilely drinking her tea, and smiled at her, but Rachel didn't smile back.
In fact she had been crying. Just before tea Simeon had got
at her knitting and had pulled it off the needles. Ella had told
him he was a naughty boy but, when Rachel had wailed 'Oh
Mu-um, why can't you stop him doing these things—' she had
snapped, much more sharply: 'Don't be so neurotic, Rachel.
He's only little. You can perfectly well pick the stitches up
again.' That—her mother's tone and not the knitting—was,
Willie thought, why Rachel had been crying. But it was true,
it *was* hard for him to remember what Rachel had been like
as a younger child. She was nine now. Suddenly Willie
recollected Ella at the same age, struggling across the station
platforms of Europe with her beret perched on her head and
her shoulders strained from the weight of a suitcase on one
arm and the responsibility of her small brother on the other.
Rachel, with her earnestness, her hyper-sensitivity and her
desperate desire to do the right thing, was really very like her
mother. He had never perceived it before.

The following summer they spent another few days in
London. Ivor met them at the airport. On the way out to
Finchley he mentioned to them, sounding faintly apologetic,
that Ella had got 'a bit depressed' and was on tranquillisers.
Rachel had failed her 11-plus—well, she was young to take
it of course—but she had also been refusing to go to school,
which was more worrying.

'Doesn't sound like my little niece,' said Willie, with an unaccustomed touch of sentiment. He found that, as he got older,

he rather liked using words like 'niece' or 'step-nephew'
(Johnny Prescott had provided a couple of these).

'No,' said Ivor, frowning. 'We were taken by surprise too.
But the local child-guidance clinic says—well, they say that in
these cases—school-refusal—it's not usually that the child dis-
likes school, as such, but that she doesn't want to leave her
mother for some reason—is worried about her mother, or feels
insecure for some reason. . .' His voice trailed off. Ivor wasn't
usually as inconclusive as this. 'Anyway,' he added, more
firmly, 'they've all been looking forward to you coming.
Rachel's made a banner to welcome you!'

To be such an honoured guest made Willie feel nervous.
The Prescotts had not gone in for such demonstrations and
he never knew quite how to accept them graciously. Nor,
judging from her expression, did Jill. Anyway, despite self-
conscious effort on all sides the visit did not seem to get off to
a particularly good start. The house was a mess—Willie had
never seen it in such a mess before. Ella seemed strung up and
talked too much, asking them questions without listening
properly to their answers. Jill said to Willie in their bedroom
that night that Ella seemed more as if she was on pep pills
than tranquillisers.

'You could ask her, couldn't you?' said Willie. 'Doctor's
privilege? Sister-in-lawly concern?'

'I could,' said Jill shortly, 'but I don't feel like it. Something
seems to be going on here and I'd rather not know too much
about it. We live too far off to be able to help, and I've a feeling
that any well-meant interference or even interest from us is
likely to upset an extremely precarious applecart. That's just
my view of course. I don't know anything about psychology
—not my field.'

The next day it became apparent that Simeon, now a
strikingly handsome three-and-a-half-year-old, had developed
in the last year from a nuisance to a menace. It seemed to
Willie, observing him sourly, that he was not just careless and
undisciplined in a childlike way but deliberately destructive.

When he crunched toys—even his own toys—underfoot, it was no accident. His movements were otherwise quite controlled: he knew what he was doing, that child, and he calculated his effects. He tore up a painting Rachel had just finished into methodical strips—and then quickly, just as Ella was about to remonstrate with him, tore up one of his own in a more babyish way, as if not fully understanding what he was doing. It was obvious to Willie that Simeon and Rachel, in spite of the difference in their ages, were now locked in covert warfare. He teased her as much as he could under the guise of being 'a naughty wee thing'—Ella's frequent fond phrase for him. Rachel bore it, but when her mother's back was turned she seized the opportunity to give Simeon a cross push. Simeon at once retaliated with a surprisingly vicious blow from someone his size, at which Rachel, who seemed to have gone to pieces in the last year, dissolved into tears. Then Ella would turn round and tell Rachel sharply not to be such a crybaby, at her age... This happened several times, till Willie could hardly keep his hands off Simeon.

That evening, in spite of what Jill had said to him about not interfering, he said to Ella in the kitchen:

'Young Simeon seems very jealous of Rachel, doesn't he?'

'*Oh* he is, poor lamb,' said Ella in an exhausted voice. 'Of course it *is* hard on him being so much younger than her, and she doesn't make enough allowances.'

'I don't see why it's so hard on him,' said Willie after a pause. 'After all, I was younger than you, and then later I was younger than Johnny and Mike Prescott—but I don't remember harbouring any such resentment about it.'

'Oh, I'm sure you did,' said Ella snappishly, beginning to wash up the children's tea. 'You just don't remember, that's all.'

Willie let it go at that, and the next day noticed that Simeon's supposed jealousy at his inferior position (*Inferior? That pampered brat?*) was invoked as a reason and an excuse for every outrage. He pulled the head off Rachel's eldest doll,

having first carefully fetched the doll from her room—
Jealousy. Of course. Jill also noticed, and pointed out silently
to Willie, that Simeon tried systematically to torment the cat,
who fortunately was better able to protect itself than Rachel
was. Oh yes, said Ella quite seriously, as if expecting them
just to nod understandingly, Simeon was dreadfully jealous
of Puss too.

'She's lost all sense of proportion,' said Willie furiously to
Jill when they were in bed that night.

'She never had all that much to start with... No, but
children do that to people. I told you so.' Jill sounded calm
and rather irritating.

'Not necessarily they don't, come off it! Rachel didn't...'

'Ella *thinks*,' said Jill after a long pause, 'that's what she's
treating Simeon exactly as she did Rachel at his age. I've
even heard her say so. But in fact she's not. Or, if she is, it
doesn't add up to the same thing. Simeon's so different from
Rachel. In practice, she's making allowances for Simeon the
whole damn time.'

'You don't need to tell me! It makes me mad—'

'It's as if,' Jill said after an even longer pause, 'at some level
she knows Simeon is utterly different from Rachel and always
will be, but she can't admit the fact. So she tries to cover up
by pretending it isn't so—which makes things still worse because Simeon gets so spoilt.'

'You can say that again! Well, I always did say that kids
are what you make 'em. Simeon's a hideous working example
of the fact.'

'I'm not so sure,' said Jill quickly. 'That isn't really what I
mean. Oh, Simeon is spoilt, I grant you. But—I don't think it's
all spoiling. I think he just *is* like that.'

It gave Willie an odd, rather unpleasant feeling to hear Jill
say that. He hadn't known she viewed people quite like that.
'You mean—biochemistry?' he hazarded, feeling foolish and
unmedical.

'Mm-hm. Biochemistry. Or whatever you like to call it. Inherited personality, anyway.'

In the morning Willie decided once again that he didn't really believe in inherited personality. Or not to the extent that Jill now appeared to, anyway. But he couldn't stand seeing Simeon get away with murder; it was becoming an obsession with him. So, feeling foolish but righteous, he dragged Ivor out for a walk on their own and then indicated to him what he thought of Simeon's behaviour. A less amiable man than Ivor would, he recognised, have resented this considerably: telling people they're children were spoilt was a deadly insult, like telling them they had no sex appeal. So he tried to clothe his criticisms in pseudo-professional terms, elaborately wondering if Ivor had read of some new research that had been done in America which seemed to indicate that the Anglo-Saxons in general tended not to expect enough of their children, and that this was bad for the children, who felt subtly patronised and insecure of the role and played up in consequence.

'Well I don't know,' said Ivor, knitting his brows, 'I sometimes think we've expected *too* much of Rachel this last couple of years and that's why she's in a bit of a state. . .'

This was so true in a way, while not being at all what Willie had meant, that he didn't know quite how to answer it. Nor was he at all sure if Ivor had got the real message. But he must have, because that evening in the kitchen, where he had carried some plates, Ella turned to him, eyes bright and angry, and said:

'I gather you've been telling Ivor you think Simeon's over-indulged.'

'Well—yes I have.'

'*I* see. From your marvellously extensive experience of parenthood and children, you have come to the conclusion that our Simeon doesn't behave quite like your ideal child.'

He said wearily—he felt weary, after three days in that house—'Oh Ella, come off it. I may have no children of my own, but I do know some and I'm not a complete idiot, you know. I can remember a bit too... When I was Simeon's age I was never allowed to behave like he does. Not remotely. It would have been out of the question. Why, I can remember being smacked just for wetting my pants, for not saying "Danke schön"—all sorts of minor things. Oh I know one doesn't smack a kid for that sort of thing now, but surely there's a reasonable mean—'

He broke off because he noticed that Ella looked as if she were going to cry. She turned away from him, biting her lips, saying:

'You've always said till now that you could hardly remember anything—about before we left Vienna, I mean.'

'Well I can,' he said awkwardly. He found he could—now. Memories, which had lain as hidden as old rubble under new turf, old ashes under stone slabs, seemed to have risen to the surface of his mind now, breaking its smoothness, causing him a deep, confused pain. For a moment he too wanted to cry. He left the kitchen.

The crisis was reached quite suddenly two days later. It was Saturday, and they were all taking the children to the Zoo. In the car on the way Simeon was reasonably good, once he had had an ice-cream bought for him; though of course he had to be separated from Rachel, as otherwise—said Ivor with a tolerant laugh—he would sit and pinch her. Jill scowled at Simeon behind his parent's back. She seemed, thought Willie apprehensively, to be disliking the child more and more—and he knew she hated the smell of ice-cream anyway.

But it was Willie himself who finally lost his temper with Simeon. They had been into Pets' Corner, where the children were allowed to fondle rabbits, guinea pigs and a goat under the benevolent eye of girl helpers. One of the guinea pigs had four babies—born three days ago, the helper said, but they looked surprisingly finished, furry and bewhiskered and already sniffing at blades of grass. Willie did not particularly like animals, but he did think these self-possessed babies rather appealing and was not surprised that the children lingered over them.

They moved on to the goats. The next thing he knew was that Simeon was back at the guinea pigs' enclosure and a girl was shouting at him. Willie reached him first. Simeon had one of the babies by the head and was systematically squeezing it between finger and thumb with scientific detachment till blood ran out of its eyes. It was squealing frantically—then suddenly ceased.

Willie did not afterwards remember taking any decision. He just found himself holding Simeon with one hand and hitting him hard and repeatedly with the other. As he delivered rhythmic, satisfying blows to Simeon's ears and Simeon's bare thighs he heard himself saying: 'You dirty little bastard. You loathsome, horrible little bastard. I'd like to kill you—'

It was Ivor, white with a multiplicity of unspoken emotions, who finally pulled the shrieking child from him.

'Willie how *could* you,' said Ella by and by, her lips trembling and tears running down her own face; 'How *could* you give way to your feelings so?'

A vague memory stirred in him of himself, saying to Ella about four years ago that he knew she couldn't help her *feelings* for God's sake, but that surely—Surely what? He could no longer remember what he had once consciously thought, what elaborate mental structure he had erected in order to ignore basic human truths. He felt oddly calm now, and relaxed, as if purged for good, by his open attack on Simeon, of all pretences and intellectual delusions.

Ella was saying, as she clutched the furiously sobbing Simeon to her: '... The *harm* you may have done...'

Willie's head jerked up:

'Harm?' he said derisively, 'What harm? To that embryo psychopath! It'll take a lot more than one beating to alter him —if anything ever does.' He agreed with Jill and her bio-chemistry now, one hundred per cent; he could feel her silently supporting him at his side. 'The harm's been done, Ella,' he went on, '—to all of you. It was done when you took him on, knowing nothing about his parents. It was done when you leaned over backwards to pretend he was just like a born child to you. He's ruined everything for you—all three of you. He doesn't belong with you. You don't know how to treat people like him—and he knows it. Good God, he despises You already! At three years old—he thinks you're soft; he knows you haven't tumbled to him. He's one of nature's Nazis—' He ranted on for several more minutes before finally falling silent.

The next day he and Jill left early for Edinburgh. What else could they do? His outbreak of home truths had created what would probably be a permanent rift. He quite saw that Ivor and Ella could not afford to believe him because they could not actually dump Simeon, now. He was 'theirs' for life. Their position seemed to him intolerable.

He felt profoundly depressed. It was not that he really regretted, even for a moment, beating Simeon or saying what he thought about him: Willie was not given to regretting actions, least of all decisive ones. But he felt deeply disorientated and not a little frightened by the loss of his own system of defences—his cherished belief that people were what their environment made them and that blood did not count. He found himself now believing, just as passionately as he had before held the opposing view, that blood *did* count, that genuine family ties counted, and that there was probably no one quite like your own relations.

For almost the first time in his life he felt immensely and vulnerably alone in the world. Jill was fine and she was his wife—but she wasn't his own kin, or even race, there were things she could never understand, and they hadn't had any children of their own to forge the most intimate link of all between them. Behind him lay sixty or seventy dead parents, grandparents, uncles, aunts, brothers and cousins—gone for good. Ahead lay a desolate, relationless, childless future, and isolated old age...

He would, after all, he decided humbly, have to make it up with Ella again, however much he had to crawl to her and tell half-lies to excuse his outburst. She was, simply, all he had.

8

The visitor

'SIT DOWN, DEAR, do sit down, you must be tired coming all
the way up here. Haven't you brought your—your machine
with you, though? ... Yes, you know what I mean surely? I
thought you'd bring it. The last person that came from the
wireless did. No, television—that's what he came from, but it's
all the same isn't it? ... I'll remember what the machine's
called in a minute. It's on the tip of my tongue.

I'll get you a nice cup of tea. Oh yes I will, dear, you can't
say No, I always get my visitors a cup of tea, no trouble at all,
I've got everything ready. What I say is, if you're lucky enough
to have the use of your legs at nearly ninety-three you ought
to use them oughtn't you? No use just sitting around letting
others wait on you. I wasn't brought up to it, anyway.

A tape-recorder! That's what it's called. Where's your tape-
recorder? ... That's it? You don't say. Gracious. Things get
smaller and smaller, don't they, I thought it was your hand-
bag. Well that must make things a lot easier for you, dear. I
was thinking, there now, there's this poor young girl coming
all the way out here on the Central Line with a heavy machine
to carry, I do hope she'll manage, girls aren't as strong today
as when I was a girl... Oh in a car. I see. Of course I never
learnt to drive. I would have liked to, I think—my father was
a coachman, you know, and owned his own cab later—but I
daresay that if I'd become used to driving everywhere like

you young people I shouldn't have the strong legs I still have now, should I?

... There we are, dear, everything's on the tray I think. Do you take sugar? No, I didn't think you would—you young people are always thinking of your figures—but I put it on the tray just in case. I don't take it myself—haven't since I was seventy-five. Doctor's orders. Yes, sugar diabetes. Tiresome, isn't it, but Nurse looks in twice a day now to give me my jabs. Of course, as I told her, I could perfectly well give them to myself—did for years—but I think she likes to do it herself, makes her feel useful. Poor thing, she's had a sad life I believe; her only daughter's in Australia, she told me, and she's not a woman with much *courage* for life, if you take my meaning— a bit of a moaner... She thinks too much. Yes. Well, anyway— you've got to have something, haven't you? When you're nearly ninety-three, I mean.

Do have a biscuit—if your diet allows it... Oh, you don't diet? Well isn't that nice! Now I want you to tell me something about yourself... You've come to interview *me?* Yes, I know dear, but it's a bit of nonsense, isn't it? I mean—what can I tell you that could interest people. I'm too old, dear. Once, now, I could have told you all sorts of things. Oh I had quite a lot of opinions in my time. Little-Miss-Knowall my mother used to call me. And at one time I gave talks to the Townswomen's Guilds on making Patchwork for Victory. In the War that was. Not the one my sons were in, of course, but the second one... But I really don't think much about talking these days, dear.

The patchwork, you said? Oh yes. Patchwork. Yes, I used to do a lot of patchwork once. We'd always done it at home, see —Mother and me and my sisters. All the bed covers and that, and for the Queen's Jubilee—Queen Victoria that would be, dear, you wouldn't remember her of course—Mother and Lily —that was my youngest sister—made a lovely cushion cover all in applicky work with God Bless Our Queen on it... No, I didn't work on it myself. I was grown up by that time and out

in service with a family in Brondesbury. Yes, seventeen I was
then—quick at figures, aren't you dear! I've always been
quick at figures myself. Anyway I was busy sewing my
trousseau then—on my afternoon's off, you know—because
the next year I got married... No, I don't recall the date.
Sometime in the July, it was, because that was when Bert—he
was my husband—had a week off. He was in the ironmongery
business—travelling he was then. A good job really... No, I've
never set much store by dates. After all, one day's much like
another, isn't it, when you come down to it; it's only thinking
it's a special day that makes it something. An anniversary
doesn't mean anything to my way of thinking. . . And anyway
there's only one date that should mean anything to me now,
isn't there, and I don't know when that is.

. . . Can't you guess what date I mean? . . . Well never mind,
dear, that's just my little joke. I'll tell you by and by.

. . . Oh, you were interested in the patchwork... What?
No, no, I've not got that cushion now. No, I've no idea where it
is, nor all those bed covers neither. Torn up for dusters long
ago, I reckon... A shame, you think? Well I don't know.
What's past using is past using, isn't it? We never set much
store by them ourselves anyway... Yes I did hear that some of
that sort of stuff fetches high prices now. The other person
from the wireless told me actually—from the television, I
mean. The young man who came before. He went on about
how valuable those quilts would have been today. Can't see it
myself. If you want the honest truth, dear, I think people are
a bit sentimental today—you know: soft. No offence meant
dear, of course—and none taken, I hope?

If you're really interested there's a few little pieces in that
bureau drawer there—yes, go ahead, have a look, I've no
secrets there! Just bits they are. Bits I did years ago when I
was first married and then later I used them as examples—
for my talk to the Guilds, you know. I never made them into
anything and it seems a bit late now, doesn't it?

Yes dear, I know some of 'em have still got their backing

papers on them. 'Templates' you call those—they're for keep-ing the patches in shape while you sew them in. Oh I used to cut the templates from any old paper—anything that was nice and stiff that was. Let's see... Yes, that's a bit of a laundry list, isn't it... Don't know where those come from, can't read that tiny print well these days—they look like a Temperance tract or something, don't they? ... Oh I forget, you wouldn't know about them, would you dear? In these days it's all sex isn't it, in the papers and that? Well in those days it was all religion and temperance. The one thing's as daft as the other, if you ask me. Just crazes—you know what I mean?

... That's a bit of my sister Dora's writing, can't see what. Must've been a letter from her I cut up. She didn't write no more after a while though. She was the one who went to Canada. Her husband was in the food business—great fat thing he was, too.

... Yes, that looks like a bit from a child's copybook, doesn't it? Nice thick paper them writing books from the Board School were, I used quite a lot of that... Yes, dear, a child learning to write. Yes, you can see the words, can't you.

... Oh I don't know dear. It might have been Jim's or there again it might have been Bill's. I really don't remember, dear. It doesn't signify, does it?—They've both been dead and gone so long.

Yes, Jim was my older boy... He was sent to the Front when he was eighteen and he Went almost at once. Bill was a year younger. He would have been nineteen when the War ended but he Went just before the Armistice. No dear, like I said, I don't recall the exact dates. And I didn't keep the telegrams or nothing. It's a very long time ago now, dear, anyway. And you get over things, you see. In the end.

Look—you know the 'In Memorials' people like to put in the newspaper? Well years ago there used to be ever such a lot from the War—a whole column of them on some dates, all those lads who went west on the Somme or in the other big battles. But there aren't today. You try looking in the paper regularly and you'll hardly see any from that War now—well, maybe one or two now and again, but hardly any. Well I mean, that just proves it, doesn't it? Nothing lasts forever, not even that. It all gets worn away in the end, dear, all the feeling, just like the old quilts.

No, we didn't have no more children after those two. We were building up the business, see. We had this shop out Hendon way. It's all houses there now, but it was like the country then. We used to stock all sorts of things for the farms. Bill hooks and plough shares and that. I bet you've never seen ploughing done with horses, have you? ... Oh, I see—abroad. Oh well, I wouldn't know about that. I wouldn't have minded going abroad, mind you, they say it's an interesting experience—but I'm a bit too old for them now. Experiences, I mean. Yes. Ninety-three next birthday. My mother was only seventy when she Went. But of course they had a hard life in those days—and they were ignorant too. I had a good education myself. I was always top of the class, though I say it myself. I sometimes think that's why I'm not sentimental, like some people are.

Yes, put those bits and pieces away again for me, would you dear. Don't know why I keep them, really, but as they've been there so long they might as well stay. You never know—my next visitor might be interested. Oh yes, I get a lot of visitors, I'm lucky that way. Mrs Lewisohn—she's the lady that runs the Welfare, quite young she is, about fifty I suppose—she says I'm quite spoiled! But what I really think, dear, is that people like to visit me because I keep up with the times. I mean—I don't dwell on the past, do I?

... You think your listeners would like it if I did! Goodness gracious. Well, you can't please everyone, that's what I always say. I'm afraid you'll have to make do with what you've got, dear. Perhaps you'll come and see me again some time? There's always my hundredth birthday to look forward to, isn't there! Unless that other date I mentioned comes up first.

It may well. I mean, I can't expect to go on living forever at my age, can I?

I think about that a lot. Most of the time, in fact. I think that these old people who just think about their next meal and what Nurse said are silly, don't you? I mean, we've all got to Go, haven't we? No sense in running away from it.

Just one thing, dear, before you go; how are you going to announce me? I mean, would it be 'Mrs Soames' or—? ... Well most people do call me Mrs Soames, yes, they have done for a long time. It's like that, you know, when everyone's younger than you. . . But what I wanted to say was, my name's Mary. Mary Soames. If you should want to call me by my full name, I mean.

. . . Yes. Yes I'd like that. No one's called me Mary for—oh, must be twenty years now. It'd make a nice change.

Well I expect you've guessed what that other date is? Must keep it in mind, mustn't I, even though I don't know when it'll be! No sense in running away from it. . .

. . . No. No, I'm not frightened of dying. Of course not. Never have been. What a peculiar idea. You'll have to get out of those sort of fancies you know, dear, they won't do you any good. As you get older yourself, I mean.

. . . There is just one thing that does worry me a bit. Shall I tell you? Well. Like I said, I'm very lucky to have a lot of visitors out here. And most of them have been sent by Mrs Lewisohn or have come like yourself from the television, so I know that's alright. But . . . well, the other day this young man called. . .

. . . I don't know where he was from. If I did, I wouldn't worry, would I? He did tell me but there was a car making a noise in the street and I didn't catch what he said. Why should he come to my door? I keep wondering.

. . . No, no not a thug, I should say, nor a spiv. . . Quite quiet spoken, really, and gentlemanly, only with the long hair like they have today and one of those coats that look like a hearth-rug turned back to front. They call them hippies, don't they? That's what Nurse said when I told her. But he was very polite and didn't want money or nothing...

He just said he'd come to pay me a little visit. Gave me a bit of a turn, it did.

... Well, I mean it was the way he said it. As if he knew I'd been waiting for him.

... Well of course I hadn't really, because I wasn't expecting him, was I? But he acted somehow as if I was. As if we'd had a date with one another.

He was very nice, I can't complain about anything... But he said he'd be back.

I keep wondering when.

9

Proof of survival

AT HOME, GEOFF Berry always got up before Mary and had breakfast on his own before taking her up a cup of coffee. He had always been an early waker, and the habit had grown with the years. He had a job, now, to stay patiently in bed as late as seven, even on Sundays; whereas Mary, always bad at getting up in the morning, showed no signs of improving with the years. Not that Geoff minded. It was to him all part of what he vaguely regarded—with only a tinge of irony—as Mary's creative personality. No reasonable person, he thought, should expect someone like Mary—Mary with her writing and her lecturing and all her other gifts—to have the same humdrum virtues as himself. And in any case, as she said, since her writing and lecturing rarely required her to be up and about first thing in the morning, where would the virtue have been? Mary was both too rational and too original to pay any attention to other people's concepts of 'wifely duty': indeed the very phrase had become one of those little, permanent jokes which had sustained them during the twenty-odd years they had been together. Fortunately, of course (they had accustomed themselves to thinking of it in these terms) they had never had any children. If they had had, then he supposed Mary would have had to get up in the morning. Well, a lot of things would have been very different—

On holiday abroad, though, Mary did make the effort and

rise with Geoff, because the sort of small French hotel they frequented (from both taste and economy) was not the sort with spare staff for carrying trays up to bedrooms. Not for them the false simplicity of places misleadingly called Auberge de Something-or-other, with a tempting *menu gastronomique* at twenty-five francs and a log fire in the bar. They specialised, rather, in the quieter of the places in the Routier guide—the lorry drivers' list, as Mary was fond of explaining to friends—and in small commercial travellers' hotels right on roads, too unpicturesque for tourists. They also made use of café-restaurants with rooms-to-let in remote villages, places they had discovered for themselves over the years and which were never in any guide because the lavatory would usually be out in the yard. Actually, in the last two or three years, Geoff hadn't been quite so keen on these. He entirely agreed with Mary in principle, of course, that the food in these little places was often marvellous value for money and that that was what really counted, but—well, anyway, they'd had a bit of an argument about it before setting out this year, and although Mary had stuck to her guns in principle, in practice there had been no earth closets this spring. It was all very well for her: she was always so healthy and, for her age, as slim as a girl; she couldn't (he supposed) be expected to understand what it was like to have minor, niggling middle-aged ailments—backache these days after long drives in their little Morris convertible, sudden cramps and pins and needles in the night, this early morning waking, catarrh, piles. . .

She came down the stairs to breakfast with him now, looking neat as a college girl in her navy blue slacks (as he called them) with her still-dark hair drawn neatly back into its pins, and slightly short-tempered as she always was till she had had her coffee. She did darken her hair in front, of course, now. He knew that, though he had never said anything about it to her. Not that she had hidden the bottle of root-tint away from him particularly, but—well, he felt, without expressing it, that she wouldn't like anyone else to know. Oh, not from the vanity of a good-looking woman trying to cheat age, but from that other vanity: the sensitivity of a woman who has always prided herself on *not* fussing about her age or her appearance and on *not* burdening her life with all the artifacts of gross femininity. Ultra-feminine women, with their plethora of bottles and creams and hair-appointments and little rose-patterned plastic make-up capes, were physically repellent to her, she always said. Rose-patterned plastic was another tiny, permanent joke between them, a cipher for everything they regarded as Not Us.

The table where they had eaten cutlets and chips and salad the night before was now set with bowls, and their used table napkins were knotted beside these. The fat young girl who had served them the night before brought coffee and milk in chipped china jugs. 'Could you get us any croissants, do you think?' asked Mary charmingly in her beautiful, fluent French. Uncertainly, the child agreed to go up the street for them. As she left on heavy legs, Mary said to Geoff:

'When we're staying in a town for once, it's nice to have fresh croissants. Otherwise they'd have given us last night's bread, you know. But this is quite a nice little place, don't you think?'

'Mm. They're generous with the coffee. And I like places that give one bowls to drink it in. I thought last night's meat was a bit tough, though.'

'Oh well... This isn't really a foody area, you know. Here in the Lozère we're in one of the poorest parts of France. Subsistence hill-farming, mostly.'

'Oh yes?' said Geoff politely—and then wondered momentarily why she always spoke as if she was far more familiar with France than he was, when they'd been coming abroad together nearly every year for goodness knows how long. But in a way it was true; she *did* know more about France than he did, because she read more and because (he supposed) she used her writer's eyes. His French, too, remained obstinately on the pedestrian language-course level: he wasn't, he was forced to conclude, gifted at languages; in fact there was something about talking in a foreign tongue which made him feel a cross between a fool, a con-man and an actor—and he'd never enjoyed acting, either. Mary could somehow throw herself into a French personality in a way that he knew he never, never would—but then there was her background. That must count for quite a lot, he always told himself.

Mary Randon. He remembered first being introduced to her, at a party someone long-forgotten had been giving for (of all things!) the Festival of Britain. People did things like that then. She had been standing rather tensely against a wall, feeling (as he had later come to realise) angry at being cut down to a size less than her own by this crowd of mediocre people. What tedious, fallow years those post-war years had been— hardly any foreign travel, nothing nice to eat in London, no cafés, nowhere to go but the French pub or that abortive 'Partisan' in Greek Street; no new literature or drama, just that windy, neo-classical Christopher Fry stuff and bloody ballet; no CND—and the ghastly bourgeoisie everywhere paranoid about Russian politics and American culture and hell-bent on 'getting back to pre-war standards', which meant putting their babies down for public schools and dressing for dinner and installing electric bells in their houses to summon the servants who would soon, they thought, be available again... He remembered, in a sudden warm image, Mary saying all that to him after that party, volubly and furiously, in a dire Lyons Corner House where he had taken her for a bite to eat—and how he had never quite thought of it in that coherent way before, but suddenly saw that she was right, so right! 'Of course,' she had said self-deprecatingly. 'I have a big advantage. I was brought up partly abroad. It does help to give one a perspective on England.'

It wasn't, he discovered much later, actually true. Or rather, it wasn't true in strict fact—her childhood experience in France had really been limited to a few holidays with distant cousins before the War cut them off. But in another, perhaps more essential sense, her whole upbringing (he came to understand) had been subject to an un-English influence. She was a descendant of Eugene Randon, the French writer and anarchist who tried to assassinate the Emperor Louis-Philippe in the late 1860s with a neatly hurled bomb which failed to explode. He was arrested, tried, condemned—and then escaped during the Commune and made his way to England, where he embellished literary life for the next thirty years with his bright, black eye, his malicious wit and his Zola-esque novels which he had great difficulty in publishing because they were too outspoken for the circulating libraries. Bilingual journalist, scrounger, gambler and friend of Meredith, Wells and Bennett, he finally took a common-law wife (another, the ancestor of Mary's distant cousins, had been abandoned in France) and produced Mary's father. The literary ability skipped that generation but reappeared (like the unorthodoxy, come to that) in Mary, her parents' only child and Eugene Randon's only English descendant. Her father had died in the 1930s while she was still a child, and Mary had grown up with the portrait of long-dead grandfather Randon in the dining-room as the nearest thing to a father-figure. She had told Geoff how his famous black eyes had seemed to watch her when she stole water biscuits and oranges from the sideboard in the dull, quiet hours after school, but she had felt that he was sardonically amused by the theft rather than disapproving. She had felt much more akin to him, she said, than she had to her toiling, widowed mother: she had known even at the age of ten that she was different and like him.

Not that Geoff had heard all that at once that first quiet, sedately surreptitious evening; (Mary had still been living with her Roman Catholic husband then, whom she appeared to have married in a fit of untypical absent-mindedness in 1945). But he remembered asking her about her unusual name (she had never, even then, used her husband's surname, any-where) and she had said offhandedly: 'Oh—Eugene Randon.

The revolutionary novelist, you know.' He hadn't known, actually, but had gone to the library to look it up next day.

In retrospect, Eugene Randon seemed to have stood like a brass or stone figure, a patron anti-saint, over their pairing, smiling sardonically down at them. Well, you could have a worse totem—though Mary had come to suspect, as she had admitted laughingly only the other month—that in life he had been a sort of psychopath, a real bastard, and not just the swaggering, gifted adventurer of popular myth. But then she knew a lot more about him now. For the past three years she had been working on a biography of him. There hadn't been a proper study done for over twenty years, and other papers had come to light in the meantime. Not that Mary was certain she was going to publish everything she had come across. There was a whole unpublished manuscript on demonic possession which was important—in fact really an editing job on its own, she said. But there were also a lot of odd letters written from London to Paris in the 1880s which had come to light after an old Randon cousin (one of the French line) had died in the 1950s. They were letters to a doctor known to have been interested in Mesmerism and to various other unidentified people. They were extremely short and allusive and it was difficult to make out what they were about. Mary was, as far as she knew, the only person to have access to them, and she had puzzled and puzzled over them but still could not decide (she had told Geoff) how important they were and what they really meant. She rather suspected that they were evidence of some sexual aberration. The most plausible explanation (though it didn't entirely fit) was that Random, who was a known libertine, had been procuring under-age girls from Paris either for himself or for someone else, and that the hypnotism had been used to this end. There was, she had said off-handedly to Geoff, a lot of that—procuring—about at the time, particularly in England: look at the Bradlaugh-Besant case. But she wasn't sure and couldn't prove anything. All the likely lines of enquiry she had tried to follow up had run into sand. The trail seemed to be extinct; the other names involved (the envelopes, with addresses, were lost) remained mere names and, she said, she hesitated to muck-rake on such slight evidence. It might all be one of Randon's practical jokes anyway—she wouldn't even be surprised if he had done it deliberately, to get future biographers snuffling after a false trail! In any case, she said, there were too many biographers today who thought that by grubbing around in the most intimate details of a writer's life they were finding something more important, more 'true', than the works which made him great—look at all that dust-raising about Hardy and Tryphena Sparks; as if it really made any difference to anything.

Geoff, who was accustomed to being told to 'look' at things with which he was quite unfamiliar, thought she was probably right, but he also thought that she wanted to protect the public image of Eugene Randon to some extent. It was as if she thought it was alright for *her* to know everything about him —she was his family—but why should others be allowed to pry into absolutely everything? He didn't say this to her because she might take it as a criticism of her literary integrity. She was working very hard on this biography now and was getting, he thought, a bit obsessed by it. Just a bit, of course. Even on this holiday she had not got away from the subject— on the contrary; the point of coming to the chilly, infertile, remote Lozère was that Randon had finally died there. His ancestors had come from there; the Randon was a small river in the region. After a lifetime in cities and nearly thirty years in exile from his native land, he returned to France (his crime had long-since been amnestied) and to the Lozère. Alone without his English 'wife', he had rented a house for the winter in the foothills of the Massif Central, and there, working on a last novel, he had died, apparently of a heart attack. It was not quite unexpected: he had high blood pressure and all his associates in England had been against his going to spend the winter alone in such a place—but when had Eugene Randon ever consulted anyone but himself?

Mary had come to believe that he must have had some premonition of his death—a theory which she admitted to Geoff rather shamefacedly, since it was so contrary to her usual rationality. The only really odd thing, she said, was that very shortly before his death he appeared to have burnt his entire unfinished manuscript, though ten days earlier he had been writing to his publishers in London with news of its progress. He had described it (in quotes) as 'a Gothick Romance'—though, as the genuine article had been out of fashion for at least two generations by then, that may have been just another of his jokes.

Anyway the last manuscript was gone: no trace had ever been found of it. 'Wouldn't it be wonderful,' Geoff said to Mary, 'if you found it.'

'Oh—' she shrugged and folded up her napkin, '*all* biographers have fantasies about lost manuscripts or letters being still in existence somewhere, waiting to be found. But practically all the "lost" things must be, simply, destroyed. No trace left at all.'

Destroyed. But, as a scientist, he knew that very few things are ever totally destroyed. Even papers burnt on a kitchen stove become a fine, indestructible ash, which flies out on the smoke and is borne over hill and dale on winds. Somewhere, up on those desolate limestone plateaux, those sheep *causses* over which they had driven for miles the day before, somewhere over the grass yellowed by the winter snows or among the rocks and scrubby thorns, that fine deposit must still be nesting, ungatherable but *there*, just as the traces of Roman terracing still were there after nearly two thousand years of neglect and soil erosion. But he did not attempt to convey this vision to Mary, it was not the sort of thing that appealed to her. She liked letters, dates, proof.

As they finished their breakfast he eased his back against the chair and felt relieved that they did not have to go far today. Most of their stops were for one night only: France was a large country, the Morris was a small car and Mary, at any rate, loved journeying for its own sake. She really enjoyed moving on, finding a new place or re-finding a half-remembered one each night. Her pleasure in this was so evident that he never had the heart to plead for a static holiday all in one. place. That would have seemed a pointless waste of time to her, and like being one of those moribund couples of their age who vegetated for a statutory fortnight in Majorca or the Lake District. But now they were going to stay in this tiny, incidental hill-town for two nights anyway, because they were going to spend today visiting the village where Randon had died. This town was near enough, they had said to one another on driving into it the night before: the hotel, with old men in the bar and a high dormer overlooking the cobbled main street, seemed to be their sort of place.

The day, when they set out in the car again, was chilly. Spring was coming late to that part. Even in the valleys the bare branches were only lightly dusted with green, and they had seen traces of snow still lying, like sheeps' wool only whiter, under banks along the mountain roads. It had looked odd, that snow, like something there in the wrong season, a spectral snow almost, for the sky yesterday afternoon had been high and blue and the winter-bleached grass gave a mis-leading impression of land scorched by a fierce sun. Yet it had been cold up there; in spite of the bright light they had been glad of their thick coats. Now this morning the clouds were right down again, the distances blotted out, the twisting mountain road damp and treacherous.

'What month was it Randon died?' Geoff asked to break the silence: 'January?'

'Yes. January. One can imagine what it's like up there then, can't one... You know, Geoff, I can hardly believe I'm really going to see the house he died in at last!'

She was leaning forward eagerly, her eyes shining. He loved her—and envied her unflagging enthusiasm for life.

The house, when they eventually found it in the afternoon,

was a bit of a disappointment. Or so Geoff felt. Perhaps Mary
had been better prepared for it. He had, he now realised,
vaguely supposed that Random would have rented himself
some ruined castle tower or medieval farmhouse—something that belonged to the landscape, since he seemed to have
come back here to this desolate region as a return to his
deepest origins. But when they located the house beyond all
doubt (having driven past it twice already) it was nothing
more nor less than a late nineteenth century villa set in-
congruously on the edge of a farming settlement, right on the
road. Above its high wall and locked, rusting iron gate, the
grey pebble-dash with its symmetric windows rose up, un-
compromisingly out of place. Over the top of the wall the
cracked and dirty glass of a porch-top was visible. All the
shutters were closed and the place looked as if it had been
unlived in for several years, but it would take more than the
frosts and winds of a couple of winters before its essential
structure began to subside.

'It's like a bloody fortress,' said Mary, having walked all
round it. 'That gate *is* the only way in. A great French
bourgeois castle. Wonder who built it.'

'It is a bit strange, isn't it,' he said, 'that Randon should have
chosen such a house. When he always said how much he hated
the middle classes, I mean.'

Mary shrugged. 'Not necessarily,' she said brusquely. 'He
wanted a house with water laid on inside—most of the houses
round here didn't have that then, and I bet lots of them still
don't. There's a bit about that in a letter he wrote... He was
getting old by this time, don't forget. I expect he wanted an
indoor loo. Like you.'

Choosing to ignore this gibe, since Mary seemed to be in a
funny, edgey mood, he said carefully: 'It would look very
different on a fine day...' Trying to imagine the splendid
mountain views that were still there, somewhere behind the
drizzling cloud. The wet dripped from laurels pressing round
the house walls, and a cracked gutter had left a spreading

damp stain, green with vegetation, on the stucco at the side.

'It wouldn't,' said Mary obstinately. 'It would always look like this. It's a place to die in and that's all. It might almost have been built for that.'

There was a tiny Epicerie in the hamlet. The worn woman inside it knew nothing of the villa's history. It had, she said, belonged to different owners over the years and was now the property of a gentleman in Mende, but he hardly ever came. She did not think anyone in the village had a key. Sometimes it was rented for a few weeks by summer visitors, but it hadn't been for the last two years. 'It wasn't in any case,' she said in a sudden burst of confidence, '*jolie* inside, by all accounts. The furniture wasn't much—just old beds upstairs and deck chairs downstairs. No proper cupboards or anything. Pity. It must have been a nice house once,' she said dimly.

'Do many people come here in the summer?' Geoff asked, rather to encourage the woman than to satisfy any curiosity he felt, and she said Sometimes—people who wanted a rest, like. And it was healthier than the town, wasn't it? But of course there wasn't that much for people to do up here.

A herd of cows passed in the mist, dropping a dank sludge onto the already muddied and pot-holed road. The woman seemed to tire of the conversation and made as if to return to her kitchen. No, she'd never heard tell of a writer dying in the villa. No, she didn't think there was anyone in the hamlet now whose memory went back before 1900—people had moved away, several of the farms were deserted now. No, she didn't know the name of the gentleman from Mende. They would know at the Mairie, she supposed—but that was at another village.

When they had photographed the house and got back into his car, Geoff said:

'Do you want to go and look for this Mairie?'

She seemed about to say yes, but then changed her mind:

'Not really. I mean—what's the point? It's obvious we shan't find anything here. It's all too long ago—and too irrelevant, really, to the rest of Randon's life. I suppose I'd get a copy of his death-certificate at the Mairie but what's the point? I know all the formal details from the letters his Paris agent sent to London. The agent was called down here, you see—Oh come on. There's no point. Let's go.'

Sensing her depression, he avoided the topic of Randon for the rest of the day. They drank more than usual in the bar before supper, and had a decent bottle with supper—because it was a fresh trout from one of those local, swollen streams—and then sat for a while in a stupor with coffee and books they had been trying to read all the holiday, before making their way up the spiral staircase, past the one cavernous roaring water-closet to their high bedroom behind the dormer. It was glacial; the weather seemed to have got even colder. They piled their coats and jerseys onto the inadequate bed-quilt and soon slept, but in the night Geoff found himself awake again—and Mary sobbing.

'Darling—whatever is it?' He tried to draw her to him, but she wouldn't be drawn. A sudden memory came to him—something he had blotted out for a dozen years or more: Mary weeping inconsolably like this and turning from him in their bed at home, Mary saying that they could never have a child, just like they could never be properly married, and that her life seemed to be going nowhere, making no biological progress, just turning round on its axis, arrested at one stage. . .

In the intervening years this image of Mary helpless, Mary frustrated and a failure, had been so heavily overlaid with that of Mary the success, Mary the fulfilled and ageless career woman, that it seemed almost indecent to recall it, even in the privacy of his own mind. He asked:

'Is it—something I can do anything about?'

'You? Of course not,' she said woundingly. She felt in his pyjama-pocket for his hanky to blow her own nose, and then said more quietly: 'Oh—it's just that awful house.'

'Where Randon died?'

'Mm. I was so—disappointed, Geoff.'

Carefully, aware of the risk (always present at such moments) of turning her emotion against himself, he said:

'I know what you mean.'

'I—I had the idea I might find something there. Oh, not a manuscript or anything obvious like that. But—a feeling, a sort of *recognition*—I don't know how to describe it. I thought that the place would say something to me, that going there would mean something... But it was just—nothing.'

Again he said, pitying profoundly and secretly the terrible emptiness of her life, filled only with a name and a shadow:

'I know what you mean.'

'It sounds silly,' she went on, rapidly scrubbing her eyes; 'it sounds silly and of course I don't really believe in this sort of thing at all—but I've felt that something important was going to *happen* on this trip. Something meaningful. And I thought it would happen there, at Randon's house. And there was just—nothing there at all. It really is as if the place just did get itself built as a house for him to die in, and once it had fulfilled that function its purpose was over, and that's why it's empty now with old deck chairs in it...'

'What *sort* of meaningful?' he asked cautiously. 'Something to do with Randon himself?'

'I don't know. No. No—something to do with me. Meaningful to *me*—to my life.'

In the silence that followed she added, with apparent inconsequentiality:

'He was reading books on the supernatural when he died, you know—Randon, I mean. Books on all sorts of related subjects: thought-transference, predestination, spirits, demonic possession, vampires, buying souls—necrophilia, even ... Well, perhaps that was for his Gothick Romance.'

'Perhaps,' said Geoff uncertainly. For some reason, the subject now filled him with an extreme distaste.

'Funny the way he got keen on all that sort of stuff late in life,' she mused, sounding happier now and more at peace as the tears dried on her cheeks.

'Very funny,' he agreed grimly. It took him a long time to fall asleep again.

They were down early the following morning. As they sat waiting for their coffee, the postman came in.

'Wouldn't it be funny,' said Mary frivolously, 'if there was a letter for us.'

'Extremely funny,' agreed Geoff. 'Considering that no one knows we're here and we didn't know beforehand where we were going to stay.'

The postman, after sorting out a couple of envelopes, glanced at them.

'Excuse me, *m'sieur-dame*—perhaps this letter is for you. Name of Randon?'

'Yes—give it to me,' said Mary after a barely perceptible pause. Her face, Geoff saw, looked odd, but her voice was steady. As she took the thin French envelope in her hand he rose to look at it also. It bore a French stamp and was clearly and correctly addressed to *Mary Louise Randon, chez l'Hotel de Poste, Meynac, par St Chely d'Apcher, Lozère.*

'It's his handwriting,' Mary whispered, although the postman had gone out again, leaving the door swinging behind him.

'Whose—?'

'Randon's, of course.'

'Are you *sure?*'

'Of course I'm sure. I know it like my own. I've been reading letters in it for the last three years.' She thrust the envelope into his hand as if it burnt her fingers with some demonic fire which over seventy years had not quenched. 'For God's sake, Geoff—get rid of it.'

'Get rid of it?' He could hardly believe she meant it. Wasn't this the momentous supernatural occurrence for which she had been keyed up? 'Well—if that's what you really want—'

'I do want.' She got up and stood there for a moment as if her legs would hardly support her. She said: 'I'm going upstairs again. You have your coffee. But don't come up till you've got rid of—it.'

She went, and he heard her pounding up the spiral stairs as if someone were coming after her. The fat girl brought him coffee and he drank some, eyeing the innocuous white envelope with its fresh, clear ink. Could Mary be mistaken about the handwriting? That was certainly possible, in her present overwrought state—but in any case *who*—? How—? After a brief debate with himself on the virtue of not reading other people's letters versus the virtue of courage, courage and curiosity won and he slit open the envelope.

What he had expected to find—what unimaginable message from beyond death and time—he did not know. What he actually found was a sheet of blank paper. He held it up to the light and examined both sides. Though it appeared old, unlike the envelope, it was perfectly clean. There was no trace on it of any communication either present or past, no erasure, no invisible ink—he passed his hand over its surface. There were the faintest pressure marks here and there, probably from writing on another sheet that had once lain on top of it. But you could not really say, even stretching the point, that this particular sheet could ever have contained a decipherable message.

He hesitated with it between his fingers for some time. Then, with sudden decision, he took out his own pen and wrote on the paper in his clear Italic hand: *Randon—get stuffed and leave her in peace. We don't want you. You are a bore.*

He replaced it in the envelope, and re-addressed it to Monsieur Eugene Randon at the villa they had visited the day before. Then he went out to buy some Sellotape to reseal the envelope and a fresh stamp. He doubted, on reflection, whether supernatural communications really need pay the standard postage rate, but he wasn't taking any chances.

... She couldn't have sent it to herself. Could she?

When he got upstairs again their cases were packed. Mary was sitting on the bed with a set face perseveringly tearing wads of paper into small bits.

'What on earth are you doing?' he asked—though already, with a sense of lightness in his stomach, he knew.

'I'm tearing up my notes. All of them.'

'Your Randon notes?'

'Yes.' What others are there? her tone seemed to say.

After a moment he said:

'Shall I help you?'

They sat side by side tearing. It took quite a long time before all the bits were small enough to satisfy Mary.

'No one's ever going to piece this lot together,' he said.

'I must be *sure*,' she said tensely.

He felt tremendously glad now that her obsession with the biography had extended to bringing all the files with her on this trip. Given time to reflect and get back home, she would never, he thought, have found the courage to destroy three years' work at a stroke like this. Three years? A lifetime, more like. For if the word 'possession' had any serious meaning, Randon had possessed her life from its earliest days. He felt a new, daunting fear as to whether even this grand gesture of wholesale destruction would be exorcism enough against all the years which had gone before. Well he must simply hope— and pray. Yes, pray, for she would not.

'Where are you going to put all this,' he asked. 'The waste paper basket? It won't hold half of it.'

'No. No that won't do. I thought of the loo.'

He considered. It was the hole-in-a-flat-stand sort, with no S-bend to block:

'Well, some of it could go there. Such are the uses of flush loos. I'll help you.'

When they had pulled the chain six times, waiting each time in between for the tank to fill, he said:

'That's enough or we *will* block it—and the people here

must be wondering what on earth we're doing. I suggest we wrap the rest of this up in a sheet of newspaper and dump it in some ditch as we go along.'

'Or scatter it to the winds,' she said, with a tremulous smile.

'Or scatter it to the winds! Rather fun.'

They put on their coats. In his mind he saw the great, desolate uplands, empty of everything but rocks and sheep, with the tiny scraps of paper fluttering in the air, settling into crevices like a faint trace of snow lying there, parched by suns and beaten by rain till they disintegrated into a fine, fine indestructible dust, becoming one with the soil, dissolving into it with a last, disintegrating ink hieroglyph visible till it, too, perished—the name Randon.

10

Heraclitus

They told me, Heraclitus, they told me you were dead:
They brought me bitter news to hear, and bitter tears to shed ..

HUMPHREY HAD NEVER been much good at English Literature
at school (nor at most school subjects, come to that) but one
or two things had stuck in his mind. He had no idea who
wrote the Heraclitus couplet, who said it, or who Heraclitus
had been, but for nearly twenty years now Heraclitus had
been, for him, a fellow called Ashley who had been with him
on National Service in Cyprus in 1951.

In fact he and Ashley had first met at the Officer Cadet
School near Aldershot. It had been quite obvious that Ashley
was officer material; his WOSB was only a formality. He had
done the minimum period in the ranks and, at that, had made
good use of his time (according to him and to others who had
been with him) concocting an elaborate trap for a bastard of
a Sergeant. Humphrey, on the other hand, had been a private
for almost a year, in Germany, before being sent home for a
WOSB, and he had had a feeling, most of the time at Cadet
School that *that* was just a formality—or a new and more
subtle method of cowing him—and that at the end of the ten
weeks he would find himself back again at Luneberg Heath
with just a lance-corporal's stripe to look forward to—if he
was lucky.

But in the end the whole mob passed out as officers, bar one bloody-minded little intellectual called Werner who went through the course and then turned a commission down— Humphrey had hated *him*. Ashley said that they usually passed everyone they could, particularly those they hoicked back from overseas to look at, because otherwise it would have looked like a waste of public money. 'You see, boy,' he would say, in imitation of the Colonel's clipped 1940 style, 'they *can't* ship you all the way back to Dusseldorf again, with your sloppy socks and your gig-lamps and all, they wouldn't have the face to. You do see that, don't you ol' boy? Chin up! I'm awf'ly sorry.'

And Humphrey, who, after a fortnight of being very wary of Ashley, had now settled down happily in the privileged role of Ashley's stooge, Ashley's feed and mascot, would glow with pleasure beneath his ritualistic indignation.

Ashley was two years older than Humphrey and three years older than a lot of the others. He'd been to Oxford and got his degree before being called up. When Humphrey wondered why, since this was a bit unusual, Ashley had said, laughing, that he had hoped in this way to put off the evil hour of call-up indefinitely, but 'fate had outwitted him'. 'I played my old widowed ma for all I was worth,' he explained. 'I practically dressed her up poor but respectable in a shawl and brought her to the War Office with me, playing "My Jimmy has gone to live in a tent" on the harmonica as an accompaniment.' (He really could play the harmonica.) 'But they were unmoved. These men have hearts of stone!'

Humphrey would have been a tiny bit shocked at the idea of Ashley 'using' his widowed mother in this way, had he believed for a moment that Ashley meant it. But in his heart he was sure that someone so cut out to be a soldier as Ashley had never seriously contemplated trying to get out of it. Anyway he'd seen Ashley's mother, who came down for the passing-out parade, and though she might be widowed as Ashley said she actually looked rather more *divorced*,

Humphrey decided. She was very slim, with the same good looks as her son, and wore a silk dress and a tiny fur cape and thin-heeled shoes like a mannequin, as they were still called. She had plucked eyebrows like a mannequin too, and could easily, thought Humphrey, have passed for thirty-nine, though Ashley (who was unreticent about these things) said she was forty-seven.

Humphrey's own mother was forty-seven, as it happened, but he hadn't encouraged either her or his father to come down for the parade. When he thought about it, knowing how proud they were of him, he felt a bit of a beast. It was true, what he had written to them—that it was a helluver long way to come from Scarborough for one afternoon, that lots of fellows' people weren't coming, that anyway he would get some leave before being sent overseas again—but he still felt a bit of a beast because the real reasons he didn't want them to come were known only to him. He loved his parents dearly —his mother often said, embarrassing him, what an affection- ate little boy he had been—but when he thought of her fat, red face, her pulpy hands in which the gold wedding ring lay embedded, and of Dad's new dentures which didn't fit properly so that he used to take the bottom one out surrep- titiously after tea—well, when he thought of that, he just didn't want them down there for the parade. Not with people like Ashley's mother anyway. They would be too impressed, too vulnerably proud of him, to sweatily eager to please— too like himself, in fact, when he had first come two months before. They had never learnt, and never would now, what he was just learning with dawning assurance from Ashley—the need to treat life as a bit of a joke. Well, of course it never had been much of a joke to Mum and Dad. They had worked so hard, mainly for him and (to a lesser extent) for his elder sister, had made so many sacrifices so that he could go to St Pelagius with its striped blazers rather than to the council school. He couldn't, he knew, ever expect them now to see things as Ashley did, who had had so much handed to him on

a plate—looks, wit, courage, brains, sex-appeal, enough
money, a romantic name, a home in Buckinghamshire, three
years at Oxford. . .

Humphrey was really surprised to learn, on the last evening
before they left for Cyprus, that Ashley hadn't actually been
to public school. He'd have put him down unhesitatingly as
—well, perhaps not an old Etonian, exactly, but an old
Malburian, say, or an old Wellingtonian. But apparently
Ashley had just been to a local grammar school, and not even
one which tried to be like a public school. St Pelagius wasn't
really a public school, of course, being only day, but at least
it was just like one in other ways. It wasn't till several months
later, in Cyprus, that Ashley, with gently snide innuendo,
made Humphrey understand that to be a minor public schoolboy was not an occasion for credit. That made Humphrey feel
still more awkward toward his parents, thinking how pleased
and humble they'd been when he got into St Pelagius, and
how willing they'd been to pay for him to have coaching in
Greek and Latin. But fortunately by that time he was very far
from them, driving under the remorselessly blue roof of
Cyprus, bumpety-bump over the unmade hill roads in the
drophead Morris Minor Ashley had bought cheap from a
lieutenant in the Engineers who was going home. The cicadas
screamed their song in the cypresses and Ashley sang too,
in a loud and tuneful baritone: 'Eskimo Nell', 'Hey-ho
Gethusalem', hits from *Oklahoma* and *Kiss Me Kate*, and
occasionally, in a mood of half-mocking nostalgia for the
Oxford of which he often talked, 'The Eton Boating Song'.

Ashley's Oxford, however, had not been all rowing and
chaps. He had had—as he by and by confided to Humphrey
—a 'wonderful woman' there. The word 'woman' conveyed
to Humphrey a picture of a full-bodied personage on the far
side of thirty: one of those Older Women, perhaps, that the
young princes and bloods used to have affairs with in the
rather sexy historical novels he had used to get out of the
Scarborough Public Library when he was fifteen. But Ashley

soon made him understand that his 'woman' had been a girl of
his own age—'but marvellously mature and adult with it, of
course—not one of those cock-teasing undergraduates from
LMH or Somerville, all T. S. Eliot and expecting to be taken
out for nothing'. She had been a nurse at the Radcliffe
hospital, and consequently knew about men's bodies. Her name
was Joyce. Ashley used a special tone whenever he mentioned
her, and Humphrey grasped that Joyce was the one thing in
Ashley's life which was not to be treated as a bit of a joke.
Humphrey half-suspected that Ashley was piling it on a bit,
as if he had felt that, after all, he needed *one* sacred object in
his life in order to throw the rest into light relief . . . but
perhaps that was because Humphrey had never been in love
himself yet. Anyway he was still impressed by what he was
told of Joyce, who had apparently had long black hair and a
special way of getting out of her roll-on which was very
moving really—not vulgar, but intensely stimulating—and
rather regretted his own earlier, far cruder confidences to
Ashley on the subject of tarts in Dusseldorf. That was the one
aspect of life on which he reckoned to be that much more
experienced than Ashley, and he had made the most of it—
till Ashley, blast him, had scooped everything by coming up
with Joyce, who rated as love *and* sex. (Most girls didn't, in
those days.) Oh, you couldn't get the better of Ashley!
Fortunately Humphrey didn't really want to: he had never
minded looking up to people. Perhaps, he sometimes thought
happily, that was why most people, even pretty marvellous
ones like Ashley, seemed quite to like him.

One night, when they had been drinking in Nicosia,
Ashley brought a photo of Joyce out of his wallet and showed
it to Humphrey. To Humphrey's mild disappointment, she
looked much the same as anyone else: in fact she bore a
distinct resemblance to a girl who had used to work on the
make-up counter in Scarborough Boots and wore a lot of the
merchandise on her face. But of course you couldn't tell much
from a photo. At the last Commem. Ball, she and Ashley had

danced all night beneath Magdalen tower and then made love
in a punt as dawn broke... Humphrey thought of a rhyme
about punts in that direction, but of course it wouldn't have
been appropriate. Not to Joyce. He felt provincial, unsophisti-
cated and rather drab, but hopefully reflected that he himself
possibly had all this to come. Perhaps a girl way out on the
Yorkshire moors, one day when he had learnt to drive too and
bought something secondhand, and it wasn't windy and larks
were singing...

'Shall you marry Joyce?' he asked.

Ashley brushed this aside. They might, of course, 'decide
to conform' for practical reasons—and Ashley seemed to
indicate, without saying so, that he would do the deciding—
but essentially their Experience had been complete and
perfect in itself. Nothing could take away from that.
Humphrey saw the logic of this, and therefore tried to repress
a slight sense of shock and disillusion when, on their next
evening in Nicosia, Ashley picked up a fat, squishy bar girl
and went off with her, leaving Humphrey to sit in the Morris
half the night getting both cold and sober. Of course, as
Ashley nonchalantly explained the next day, if a man had
become accustomed to getting it regularly, he had to go on;
repression was unhealthy. Humphrey agreed in principle, of
course—though when he remembered squeamishly some of
his early experiences in Germany with the sort of tarts who
frequented Other Ranks (he'd dolled them up a bit in his
reminiscences, of course) he couldn't help thinking that avoiding repression was sometimes a bit unhealthy too, indeed
could be positively disgusting.

Quite soon, Ashley was made a first-lieutenant. The men
liked him a lot: he was upper class, but without being wet
the way quite a lot of the young officers were. Humphrey
thanked God that he himself wasn't wet either—a touch of a
northern accent helped there—but he couldn't help knowing
that the men didn't regard him in the same light as they did
Ashley. One day he asked Ashley if he'd ever thought of sign-

ing on as a regular, since the life obviously suited him so well? Ashley treated this as a huge joke, saying the Army might have his body for the moment but he damn well wasn't going to sell it his soul. Yet Humphrey noticed that several times in the months that followed Ashley referred to the matter, as if, after all, he was playing with the idea in his mind.

They had a quiet time on the whole—just regular patrolling work, showing the flag and moving dubious-looking characters on: the Enosis troubles hadn't really got going in '51, though they were simmering. One night, near the end of Humphrey's time, they were driving back to camp in the Morris when shots were fired in the dark behind them, as if they had barely scraped through an ambush. Ashley accelerated like mad—and the next thing they were over the edge of the unfenced road and crashing down a steep slope of rock, furze and asphodel. They came to rest with the front of the car buckled against a rock. Humphrey, who had clung to the open side, was unhurt, but Ashley had a nasty cut on the head from the top of the windscreen and was knocked out too. Humphrey spent what seemed like hours, first cradling his friend in his lap among the scratchy, pungent vegetation and sharp flints, and then trying to lead him up the slope to the road with a field dressing held to the wound, while Ashley raved and waved his arms around and seemed to think Humphrey was someone else entirely. Humphrey was at his wits' end when a group of anxious, perspiring, volubly helpful Cypriots arrived out of the cicada-singing darkness, guns shouldered. They had, one explained, been out hunting rabbits by lantern light when they had seen the car pass and heard it crash. They gave Humphrey and Ashley a lift back to their camp. Ashley was off sick for several days and afterwards remembered nothing about the accident itself, though, when Humphrey told him about it, he swore that it must have been a spur-of-the-moment attempt on them, and that the men, being Greeks, must have lost their nerve afterwards.

It was soon after that, when Ashley's scar was still a noticeable pink gash across his sunburnt forehead ('Quite stylish, don't you think?—I shall say it's a momento of my gangster days')—that Humphrey's time in the army came to an end. On his last night he and a lot of the fellows had a big beer-up in the Mess, and Ashley had done 'Eskimo Nell' with all the variations, standing on the table. Earlier, Humphrey had done 'Our Albert', very northern, which was *his* party-piece and always went down well but wasn't, of course, in the same class. Reeling back to their quarters at last, when the unnaturally opulent stars of the Mediterranean were already retreating before tomorrow, he and Ashley had had their arms round each others' shoulders and Humphrey had felt a yearning tenderness in his bowels which, till now, he had only felt rarely and fleetingly in the company of girls. He minded very much leaving his friend and was only sustained by the thought that in another year—unless Ashley did decide to sign on—the two of them would probably both be in London. Ashley had talked vaguely of going into copy-writing: Humphrey wasn't absolutely certain what that was, but it sounded creative and up Ashley's street and his degree should come in useful. He himself was going into insurance; an uncle of his had managed to get an opening for him with a London firm. At least, he consoled himself, it was a way of escaping from the north.

Six months later, as a lonely young man living in a room in Willesden, he had been glad enough to come across, on the tube another ex-National Serviceman from the same unit in Cyprus whom he had never known well nor particularly liked. At Humphrey's suggestion they got off to have a drink together in a pub in the Kilburn High Road which turned out dirty and comfortless. The other man would only drink tomato-juice, which was partly why (Humphrey now remembered) he had never liked him. In answer to Humphrey's eager questions, he gave desultory news of one or two people: someone had got caught by a Greek girl and had had to marry her, someone else had had his foot blown off by a homemade

Turkish bomb. Just as he was leaving Humphrey—he didn't want a second tomato-juice, he said, and anyway his mother would be expecting him—he said:

'Oh, by the way—I did hear that that chap you were friendly with, you know—whats-his-name—had got killed out on a patrol.'

'Not—not Ashley Hamilton?'

'Was that his name? Yes—Hamilton, that's it, I'm sure. He was a friend of yours, wasn't he?'

'Yes. Yes, he was.' The dirty floor of the pub slid about before Humphrey's eyes. He did not trust himself to look at the other man. He felt—he suddenly knew—as he would have if he'd been told his mother was dead, and far, far worse than if his sister had died. He said after a moment:

'How did it happen?'

'Dunno. Bullet through the head, I think. Dunno, though. The chap I heard it from had heard it from someone else... I say, gosh, have I given you a shock? You do look pale, shouldn't have drunk that stuff so quickly.'

In the long winter alone that followed, Humphrey, going from Willesden to Holborn and back every day in his new charcoal grey suit, thought often of Ashley with great grief. It must have been true what the other man had told him for otherwise Ashley would certainly have looked him up on getting demobbed and he never did.

Gradually, as time wore on, his sorrow for his lost friend was—no, not exactly assuaged, since nothing could assuage it, but somehow transformed. He ceased to rage inwardly at wasteful, cruel fate, and began instead to find comfort in solemn words, in converting Ashley in memory from an individual into an archetype. Half remembered literary scraps, suppressed and unvalued till now, came to his aid: *'They shall grow not old as we that are left grow old'* ... *'Those whom the Gods love, die young'*... And, most apt and most moving to him of all: *'They told me, Heraclitus, they told me you were dead...'* Something about the construction of that

sentence bothered him. By and by he realised: of course, it
was in the vocative! Addressed, presumably, to a Heraclitus
who after all had returned—or to a vain dream of him? If he
could remember the rest of the poem he would know. But he
couldn't, nor did a rather desultory search in the public
library turn it up. Knowing no one to ask, he eventually let it
go. But he did not forget Ashley, who still walked with him to
the tube on quiet, chilly mornings, livening the grey air, or
accompanied him in gay spirit on luminous summer evenings
when he slipped round to the local—he'd made one or two
friends in the neighbourhood now, though of course no one to
touch Ashley.

Five years later, when he met the girl whom he presently
married and whose name, by a lovely coincidence, was Joyce,
he did not mention to her that *other* Joyce whom he had known
only by proxy (she might not have understood, and she was a
little bit sensitive about the other girls he had known). But he
did, one sympathetic evening, tell her about Ashley, who was
dead, and say how much he would like to call a son after him
one day. Joyce, eyeing her solitaire diamond happily, agreed.
She wasn't usually difficult about things, which was partly
why Humphrey liked her. That, and her big, soft breasts.
Anyway, he was absolutely sick of living on his own and
several of his mates had recently got married. He could, he
told himself, do a lot worse.

Quite often, over the next fifteen years, he told himself the
same thing: things could have been a lot worse, he and Joyce
could have been a lot more unlucky. They had a nice house—
well, quite a nice house—in Carshalton, near Croydon, which
they were lucky to have bought before prices went up. It
could have been more convenient for public transport, but
then, as Joyce always said, if it had been it wouldn't have been
in such a nice area. *She* didn't have to get to town every
morning. His job was alright—and he'd never expected more of
it than that, had he? It made him a bit angry, to see how some

youngsters had things handed to them on a plate—he voted Conservative now, like Joyce—and he reckoned that if all these new universities had been around when he was eighteen, he'd have managed to get to one instead of square-bashing and life might have turned out very different. Still, it was no use crying over spilt milk and he didn't make a practice of it. He and Joyce were comfortably off, considering.

The only real piece of undeniable bad luck had been Carol, their little girl. Well—little; she was fourteen now, but, as the specialist at Great Ormond Street had said, her mental age was more like six. Joyce had insisted on taking her there, wouldn't believe the man at the local clinic or the one they'd gone to privately, but in the end all the specialists had said exactly the same: subnormal but not severely so, IQ about 50, should be able to do simple repetitive work but would probably never be able to lead an independent life. It had grieved them terribly—taken them years to accept it—though of course (they realised now) they should have been prepared for it from her birth: Joyce allowed to go on in labour for days and then that idiotic young hospital doctor not wanting to disturb the consultant in the middle of the night... It made Humphrey see red, even now, to think about it, so on the whole he managed not to. Joyce should have had a caesarian after the first day. He felt that the dopey old GP they had had then, plus the hospital registrar, had robbed him of the normal, bright little kiddie Carol should have been—just as a stray sniper's bullet in Cyprus had robbed him as abruptly of the dearest friend he had ever had. Sometimes he thought, rather guiltily, that if he had understood earlier the full implications of Carol's 'backwardness' he would not have let Joyce get away as she had with declaring that she could never face it again. He would have *insisted* that they try for another baby—with a private doctor, of course, and no expense spared, he wasn't a bastard. Had he done so, he might even have got his son. His Ashley.

Too late now. Joyce was forty, as he was, and anyway the

idea was unthinkable. They didn't even *know* anyone with babies any more. They were a middle-aged couple with a daughter who, even if she wasn't ever going to be a grown up really, was at any rate turning into a facsimile of one. When Joyce, who kept thinking she was starting the change and seemed to imagine that she had a right to be temperamental and demanding in consequence, used to go on at him playfully to take her out more often, to get more 'with it' and wear wider ties and heavier shoes, he turned sourly from her. He was middle aged, wasn't he? No one was going to push him around these days. The long future did not hold many enticing promises for him, but at least he wasn't going to be nagged or wheedled into 'keeping up' with anyone or anything. Being just himself, and bugger ambition or false hopes, was one luxury at least which his declining years might afford him.

Because of his prevailing frame of mind he very nearly didn't take Joyce out on their anniversary at all that year. She'd been dropping arch hints for weeks, and he was getting thoroughly needled about it. But at the last minute he relented: after all, they always *did* go out for the anniversary, and poor old Joyce probably needed the break, what with Carol and everything. But it was too late to get tickets for the comedy hit Joyce had wanted to see, and instead they'd gone to some smart, with-it thing which had sounded risqué from the advertisements but which turned out just boring and dirty the way so many things were these days. In the second interval, when he was indulging in some mutterings about going home now, and Joyce was insisting in a bright, disappointed voice that they 'ought' to stay to the end, the broad-shouldered man in the seat in front of him suddenly swung round and said:

'Good God—Humphrey! It is you, isn't it? Remember me? —No, I can see you don't, I've put on weight. Ashley Hamilton's the name.'

He had put on weight but not all that much—in fact not as

much as Humphrey himself. The reason Humphrey started and blushed and hesitated and would hardly believe it even when Ashley repeated his name a second time and spoke of Cyprus, was that Ashley had long hair. Well—not that long, Humphrey had to admit, by today's standards, but it definitely wasn't a short back and sides or anything like it, and, in addition to luxuriant side-whiskers, Ashley had a heavy moustache which had come out lighter than his hair the way moustaches do. All this foliage had altered his appearance entirely.

Thinking about it afterwards, Humphrey realised that you could say, in a sense, that by changing Ashley had remained true to himself: he had always been rather a natty dresser, off duty—his line in 1951 had been suede shoes, Humphrey remembered, and silk scarves at the neck. His present hair and moustache were, like his expensive-looking suede jacket which was worryingly half-way between a suit-jacket and an overcoat, just a 1970s version of natty dressing. But Humphrey only worked this out afterwards: at the time it gave him a shock—almost as much of a shock as finding Ashley alive at all. He himself still had substantially the same style in hair and clothes—well, modified a bit of course, but discreetly, not showily—as he had had twenty years before, and so did most of the men of his own age that he knew. Somehow (though he realised afterwards this was daft) Ashley's transformation into a swinging Londoner seemed almost a betrayal, and this confused sense of betrayal coloured his first pleasure at re-meeting, even while he was rising and shaking hands and exclaiming:

'But I thought—I heard—' (*They told me you were dead*)

When he finally managed to get it out—it seemed rather an indecent thing to say—Ashley threw back his head and laughed so much that people round about turned to stare. Well, he had always liked laughing a lot.

'Whoever told you that was dreaming,' he said at last. 'Wishful-thinking, anyway!'

'He wasn't absolutely certain of the name, as far as I remember. Only I thought—' He did not add what he had thought. Ashley must have lost his address. He was saying now:
'It was probably that other Hamilton in our unit. You know —weedy little character. *You* know. Oh no, wait a tick, maybe he only came out after you went home... Yes. I can see him getting killed. No sense of self-preservation.'

A warm relief and confidence was spreading over Humphrey, like when you wake from a long, bad dream and realise that it was only a dream after all and could never have been true. For of course Ashley was not the sort to get killed —he could see that now. Of course. They stood beaming at each other, and then Humphrey recollected himself and introduced Joyce. Her eyes nearly popped out of her head when she understood who it was. Ever since she had known Humphrey, Ashley had been a sort of myth to her, like Christ, or the Unknown Soldier.

Ashley in turn introduced the rather beautiful girl with long red hair who was sitting silently at his side. Humphrey supposed she must be his wife, but registered that she was called Barbara: in any case she was far too young to have been the original, legendary Joyce, who must now—he thought with another odd sense of betrayal—be forty herself, or more, and perhaps the mother of teenage children.

Ashley asked if they were enjoying the show and Humphrey said 'Not much'—quickly, before Joyce could shame him by pretending to be enjoying it because she thought it was smart: she tended to do things like that. And Ashley said he knew the guy who'd put up most of the money for it, and it was amazing what phoney stuff people would pay to see, wasn't it, but he'd put the odd few hundred into it himself, just for fun, so he wasn't complaining. And then the house lights went down and the third act started and Humphrey spent most of it wondering what overtures it would be best for him to make about seeing Ashley again.

But when it was over Ashley, in his old, warm decisive way, asked them to join him and Barbara for a drink at a little place near by where they were meeting up with friends. And Humphrey was just about to accept, recklessly, though he had only a pound or so in his wallet and also there was young Carol—but Joyce said loudly:

'Oh, I'm frightfully sorry, Mr Hamilton. We would have *loved* to—perhaps we can fix it up for another time—but tonight I'm afraid we have to be getting home. The baby-sitter you know!'

Humphrey could have killed her. He couldn't bear that she should show so nakedly how much they would have loved to join Ashley and his friends, and saying that about the baby-sitter was the last straw. Of course Carol couldn't be left alone in the house and they had gone on over the years using the inappropriate term 'baby-sitter' for the neighbour who used to sit with her—but Joyce didn't have to go *saying* it, did she, to someone like Ashley who, if he did have children, certainly had a Nanny or at any rate a French au pair... At least Ashley wouldn't know that this 'baby-sitter' was in fact sitting-in for a fourteen-year-old girl: to explain about that now would have been the ultimate humiliation. There would be another opportunity. A sympathetic tête-à-tête in a pub some day after work, with no wives present...

'Ah, the eternal baby-sitter! I quite understand,' Ashley was saying to Joyce, almost too readily as if he had not really expected them to join him anyway. 'Well—never mind. We must be pushing along. Super to have run into you again...' Humphrey's heart died within him. He was about to speak, to say—anything to retain Ashley another moment, to force this diguised figure with the moustache and the unfamiliar vocabulary to recognise the old, indissoluble links that bound him to Humphrey. But before Humphrey could think of anything, Ashley—who had always been sensitive to other people's moods—turned back:

'Hey, I've just remembered, I'm giving a party next week-

end. At my place down at Marlow. Why don't you two come?'
He stood beaming almost accusingly at them until (as Joyce
said afterwards) she wanted to say 'Because you haven't asked
us yet!' Finally seeming to recollect himself he got a card out
of his wallet:

'Here you are—here's an invite all ready for you. Don't
bother to RSVP, of course: I'll take it you're coming. Map of
how to reach us through uncharted Injun territory on the back
of the card. Bless you! Bye—'

During the next week Humphrey worried a bit about what
he was going to wear for the party. He felt a fool doing so—
like a bloody woman—but he went on turning over the
problem in his mind. He did not possess any clothes remotely
like what Ashley had been wearing at the theatre. Parties—
the office party, for instance—normally meant a dark suit, but
he somehow felt this would be inappropriate to Marlow on a
Saturday night. Something more casual, then? But that, for
years, had meant his good tweed jacket and a silk scarf folded
inside an open-necked shirt the way Asley used to. . . That was
the trouble. He realised now that he had actually copied that
style originally from Ashley. It had become part of him, as his
memories were part of him. But now that he had seen Ashley
again, looking so different, he suddenly realised that it would
not do at all. He would never wear a scarf that way again.
In the end he decided to wear his dark suit after all, with a
new and rather noticeable tie which he bought at the Civil
Service Stores and which Joyce immediately said was vulgar.

Joyce too was having trouble with her clothes. She had
been for some time, actually. Years ago Humphrey, in a sentimental moment, had told her that he liked her shape in a
certain tight-fitting pinkish number of hers described by her,
with a certain unconscious aptitude, as a 'sheath dress', and
consequently she had gone on buying the same sort of dress
ever since. It was like the way she had gone on for years calling yobbos 'Teddy boys', and alluding to his hi-fi equipment

as 'the radiogram' because her parents had had one and she didn't understand the difference. About five years ago, when skirts had gone short and Humphrey had begun to notice how middle-aged she was looking in her eternal refined-sexy-lady get up, he had one day, in a mood of untypical savagery, told her to take a look about her and cut six inches off her hems, for God's sake. She had done so, but had gone on buying the same sort of tight dresses and wearing the same stiletto-heeled shoes. The result had been unbearably vulgar, and eventually he had told her that too. This criticism seemed really to have wounded Joyce, and he had felt guilty about it ever since. She had gone on strike at this point, refusing to take any further notice of his tastes and saying that men had no taste anyway. But 'vulgar' had become a loaded word between them, and she had used it sometimes, with innuendo, to get her own back on him.

Anyway, knowing that her current party outfit was a shot-silk effort with a sort of bunched up bosom effect that reminded him of his mother, he told her to get herself a new dress and treat it as an early birthday present. A long one, he suggested. He wasn't quite sure himself what he had in mind. Barbara in the theatre had been wearing something long: he had a vague impression of formless black butter-muslin... Well of course he didn't quite expect Joyce to come up with anything like that, but—

Two days before the party Joyce paraded for him in a long, tight pink and white striped dress with frilled sleeves and a stand-up collar over a low-cut bosom that vaguely reminded him of Nell Gwynn. Not bad. Not bad at all. He even began to look forward to Saturday.

They drove out to Marlow under a lowering summer evening sky. They had started early—in fact Joyce insisted it was too early and that they would be the first to arrive—but the Thames Valley towns were choked with traffic. Time ticked away. The invitation said nine o'clock but it was approaching ten and almost dark by the time they reached the area shown on the map and plunged into what seemed to be a densely wooded and curiously remote region. Roads twisted and turned, never bisecting one another where you thought they should. Shadowed drives led off to presumed houses that were invisible and seemed to have neither names nor numbers. Humphrey was sweating hard and they were barely on speaking terms by the time that, by accident, they found the place.

It seemed huge. Parked cars lined a gravel drive. There was a floodlit fish-pool. Light streamed under a porch, from the front door, which stood open, and music streamed too, strident and unmuffled. The whole effect reminded Humphrey a bit of the youth club in Carshalton that had been closed after all that fuss in the local paper about drugs and teenage sex. But of course out here at Marlow there weren't so many neighbours to disturb.

There were people everywhere and yet nobody seemed to see them. They stood uncertainly for what felt like ages in the hall, till Humphrey said loudly 'Come on—let's look for him'— and then suddenly Ashley himself appeared. He had on the sort of loose overshirt with little bits of mirror-glass embedded in the embroidery down the front which Humphrey had some-times seen on negroes in Brixton or girls in the West End. Well one couldn't possibly have predicted *that*. Not that they need have worried, however, about what either of them was going to wear. Everything seemed to be represented here, from jeans to dinner jackets, and Humphrey had just caught sight of two girls with grimed bare feet.

'Hallo there!' said Ashley loudly. 'Super to see you. Bar's on the left.' He at once passed on to another room.

'I don't believe,' said Joyce after a pause, with a tiny, irritating giggle, 'that he's recognised us.'

'Of course he has,' Humphrey snapped back. 'He's just busy with all his guests, that's all.' But the horrid knowledge that she was right, and that the whole thing might just possibly be a ghastly mistake, was implanted in him.

By the bar, when they eventually found it, was a very noisy young woman of about twenty-eight who seemed to think she owned the place. She was laughing her head off with a lot of men and wore the sort of garish floral garment with a plunging hemline and platform-soled shoes that stirred in Humphrey vague memories of wartime films. A string of what were very clearly green plastic beads dangled over her equally dangling bosoms. She was extravagantly and absurdly made up, with an orange cupid's bow painted on top of her own wide lips, and virulent green eye-shadow to match her beads. Eyeing her sourly, Humphrey reckoned that he preferred colourless lips and black butter-muslin: it was more sexy really. If you weren't a tart of fifty why try to look like one? He was disconcerted when the creature suddenly swooped on him and Joyce, asking them effusively if they'd got what they wanted to drink. Fortunately there seemed plenty of that.

'How *vulgar*,' Joyce muttered in his ear, after the girl had moved on and they heard her braying fishwife laugh on the other side of the room. He couldn't disagree. Still, a 'character' like that, whom everyone could laugh at on the quiet, was quite fun at a party.

'Marvellous, isn't she?' said a man standing next to them who must have heard Joyce too. He was thin and very tall, but with round, stooping shoulders and a generally unhealthy air. He didn't sound as if he was laughing at the tarty girl, or not entirely, but Humphrey thought perhaps his was just a very dry type of humour.

'What does she do in life, do you know?' Humphrey asked. 'When she's not playing the clown like that, I mean.' He had decided to enjoy this party after all and was glad to talk to the stranger.

'PR of course,' said the man, looking surprised. 'Don't we all? Cindy's one of Strontium Cane's brighter sparks.' (Could he really have said Strontium?) 'She's doing very well, actually, so I'm told—Waldorf tights, Culton's canned fruit, Vagex—all big accounts... You know the girl with the green twat?'

'Eh?'

'On the escalators. *You* know. Anyway, that's Cindy. So I'm told.'

'You mean that's her in one of those ads on the tube?' said Joyce, 'Fancy. Quite famous!' Her party manner made it difficult for Humphrey to tell if she was being spiteful. He hoped she was. She could be, sometimes.

'No, no,' said the man with rather obvious patience. 'She handles the account. You know—the big public relations bit. With Scrotum Keen.' (Could it really be Scrotum either?) 'Very swinging lady, our Cindy.'

'Well I'm very surprised in that case,' said Joyce, 'that she looks so *obvious*. I mean, I'd have thought a person with such an important job would have been a bit more careful about her make-up and her clothes.' (No, damn her, she wasn't being spiteful, just truthful.) 'It looks awful and gives people quite the wrong impression, I'm sure.'

Although Humphrey agreed with Joyce he wished she'd shut up. Something in the way the man was now looking at them both—sort of smirky and knowing, with raised eyebrows—was making him suspect that in fact Cindy was doing it on purpose: looking like something off the sleazy end of Dusseldorf a generation ago must be a new In thing. But surely no True Woman (Humphrey had for years tended to use the words to himself with capital letters) could want to be like that? He remembered the 'wonderful woman' in Oxford and thought that Cindy could be very little to Ashley's taste. Perhaps (though it seemed unlikely too) she was a friend of Barbara's... To change the topic of conversation, he said loudly and warmly to the thin man:

'Marvellous place old Ashley's got here, hasn't he? We haven't been here before.'

'You like it?' The man raised his eyebrows again. 'Hmm. Bosky suburbia isn't much in my line, I'm afraid—'

Bloody little sneerer, thought Humphrey: probably jealous. He didn't know what bosky meant, but he said firmly.

'Well I like it. I quite envy him.'

'Mmm. Well I wouldn't envy Ashley myself much, at the moment...'

'Oh. Why?' said Humphrey aggressively. The creep was obviously longing to tell him.

'You hadn't heard? Poor old bugger's been out of work for the last five months. Whatsits dumped him. He's been made one of our *re*-dundant rising young executives of forty-plus—pretty plus in his case, I should imagine.'

Humphrey said stolidly, as if he didn't entirely believe the man';

'Well be that as it may, for someone out of work he seems to be keeping things going pretty well.'

'Perhaps his wife's got money?' suggested Joyce in a sympathetic undertone.

'Oh Madam provides, certainly,' agreed the man absent-mindedly. He was looking around him now. Failing apparently to see whoever he was looking for in the thickening crowd—more people seemed to be arriving every minute—he turned reluctantly back to them and said, smoothing his sparse, unhealthy hair:

'Yes. Old Ash. Huh! He's not a bad picker. Trouble is, that's the way marriages go west, isn't it? When wives get too much the upper hand, I mean. That's exactly what happened with Ash and Patty Shat.' (But it surely couldn't have been Shat?) The room was noisy, the man talked between his teeth: Humphrey leant forward—

'Sorry—didn't quite catch. Who?'

'Biddy Snatch,' the man said—or appeared to say—distinctly and irritably, though it didn't sound any more likely. '*You* know. The musical comedy piece. Orpington man's Judy Garland. She's...' Humphrey had never heard of her, but Joyce seemed to have and began to look quite excited. She had a thing about actresses being glamorous. Goodness knows why. Their lot always sounded hard to Humphrey, particularly now all this poncing around in the

nude had come in, and anyway he was still worrying over
whether the man's last phrase (drowned by Joyce) had been
'Ashley's ex'. And did he mean, if so, that Ashley's present
marriage was in danger of breaking up? Certainly they hadn't
seen Barbara yet this evening.

'You admire Paddy then?' the man was saying to Joyce.
'Can't say I did much, in the days when she was still humble
enough for me to know her. Bit sentimental for my jaded
tastes. The sort of breathless girl who's always the lay of the
last minstrel, if you know what I mean...' Joyce obviously
didn't, but Humphrey did because that was one of the oldest
jokes in the book, wasn't it? In fact he rather thought he'd first
heard it used by Ashley twenty years ago. It had seemed
witty then, but really, this little creep, with his crumpled suede
shoes, his green-stained teeth and his cynical, knowing talk
like a bad imitation of Ashley himself...

Joyce, who seemed (he registered nervously) suddenly to
have decided to enjoy herself too—or perhaps it was the drink
—was saying to the creep:

'Listen to that music in there! It quite makes me want to
get on the parquet myself.' It was just the sort of phrase
which made Humphrey curl up and wish she'd take evening
classes in modern slang instead of flower arrangement, but the
creep didn't seem to notice. He said:

'Oh they've got the lot going in there. A pop group, strobes
—the lot. But then Ash has never been noted for his discrim-
ination, has he? Oh it's alright in its way, I suppose...' He
stared moodily about him.

'I'd love to dance,' said Joyce to Humphrey.

'Oh would you?' said the creep unexpectedly, as if he
thought she could only be addressing him. 'Come on then—
before it gets any fuller.'

'It *is* getting packed isn't it?' said Joyce with a pleased
laugh. Basically, she just liked parties, in a way that Humphrey
didn't.

'Old Ash will ask everyone he comes across,' the creep was

saying with lofty tolerance. 'Particularly at the moment because he's feeling ve-ry insecure. Ve-ry tensionful. What with one thing and another.'

Joyce went on grinning inanely, but the man's veiled rudeness almost took Humphrey's breath away. Why the creep might have *known* that Ashley had run into them last week in a theatre.

'Just a minute,' he said as they were moving away. He laid a hand on the man's arm:

'I'm going to look for Barbara,' he said gruffly. He wasn't just going to stand there like a lemon while Joyce was led off, was he?

'Who?' said the man, wrinkling his forehead.

'Barbara. You know. *Barbara.*' He almost shouted. 'Ashley's wife.'

'Ashley's wife—? Oh, you've got the wrong name. Anyway you've met her. We were just talking about her. Cindy. Yes. . . I'd be mighty surprised if Barbara were here too, ol' boy. Ashley doesn't share that one around much.'

And he was gone into the crowd with a sudden spurt of energy as if to stop Humphrey asking any more questions. Joyce was gone too, clinging determinedly to him. Brave Joyce! She was going to dance, come what might.

Humphrey felt as if he had been slapped in the face with a wet fish. *Cindy.* He could hear her raucous, self-advertising tone, her incessant laugh now, from where he stood alone. Cindy the obvious smutty, good-time piece (however fashionably packaged), a bit of a joke to one and all—It was incomprehensible. He wondered momentarily if she and Ashley had any children, but dismissed the thought. That painted clown with a baby would be ludicrous, obscene. . . In spite of everything, he supposed, feeling awkward and humble, motherhood was still a bit sacred to him. He had a sudden image of Joyce, years ago, cow-eyed and gentle with the warm, pink, still-apparently-perfect Carol in her arms. That was good and right and sweet, no matter what came after.

Beside Joyce, even with all her obtuseness and her irritating
ways, women like Cindy were muck, the sort that destroyed
a man...

He shook himself. He was getting morbid. Better have
another drink.

... And why had the creep said 'Ol' boy'? Obviously the
phrase wasn't natural to him. The only possible explanation
was that he'd been making fun of Humphrey. Obviously.

Humphrey had another drink, and another, since there was
no one there to watch him, standing grimly by the bar-table
surveying the gibbering hordes. It was after that that in his
memory the rest of the evening disintegrated, splitting into a
series of isolated and incoherent pictures, each loaded with
embarrassment.

He was making a half-hearted and dutiful attempt to locate
Joyce—though she was certainly the last person he wanted to
talk to. Through a back lobby, he walked into a room with no
one in it but three men sitting round in big, puffy armchairs,
apparently discussing something. There were filing cabinets.
This must be Ashley's study, though there was no sign of him.
As he hesitated at the door, trying to assess the atmosphere of
privacy and thinking that, if these fellows were even half-way
friendly, he would rather join them than the shrieking mob in
the main rooms, one of them looked up, stared at him, and
then said pointedly:

'Were you looking for the lavatory? It's the other door, on
the right.'

He hadn't been, and resented such blatant rudeness, but—

'Thank you,' he said coldly, and withdrew. He heard them
laughing when he had shut the door. Bastards. For want of
anything better to do he did go into the cloakroom, which was
a very swish affair carpeted in midnight blue, with a shower
room beyond. Over the seat, as he relieved himself, he read
a decorated notice:

You hold my future in your hand.

One of Cindy's tender thoughts, no doubt. No *thank* you, mate.

He glanced into the room where the dancing was going on —a howling cavern crossed by sliding bars of red and ultra-violet light which assaulted his eyes. No hope of finding Joyce in such a place. He retreated thankfully to the bar. Later he was talking to a very sun-dried woman in a tight black dress that looked wet. The sort of dress which Ashley, years ago, would have described as 'somebody poured her into it and forgot to say "when" '. Good old Ashley, he must go and find him in a minute and have a proper chat about the old days. . .

He seemed to be getting on fine with the wet-woman, who was being awfully responsive and enthusiastic about every-thing he said. He felt very gratified—till some chance remark of his made her toothy smile falter:

'I don't understand,' she said. 'I thought you were an accountant.'

'Me? No, no—I'm in insurance.' He was about to go on and tell her about it, since she seemed an intelligent sort of woman, but she had already turned to another woman standing by and was saying coldly:

'He isn't him, after all.'

'Aren't who?' said Humphrey desperately.

'Not Ashley's marvellous new accountant. We thought you must be.'

She stared at him crossly as if he had deliberately misled her, and shortly afterwards moved away.

Later again, beginning to get vaguely worried about Joyce by now (she must surely have run out of conversation with the creep?) he went on a further hunt and found himself again in a quiet side-lobby. Again he opened a door at random and found himself in the room with heavily-padded armchairs, but this time, as if it were a different night altogether, the men were gone and in their places were four youngsters. One, a boy of about fourteen sitting on the arm of a chair, seemed to be fully dressed in a t-shirt and jeans. Another boy, younger, was stripped to the waist, and there were two girls—

'Did you want something?' asked the elder boy in very much the same insulting tone that one of the men had employed earlier. But Humphrey stood staring. One of the girls, a well-developed young woman, was sitting demurely in the chair facing him in a t-shirt, wedge-heeled sandals and nothing else but a pair of tiny, transparent bikini panties. The other, who was slimmer, had on a floor-length skirt but nothing on her upper half at all. Her half-developed breasts were just like Carol's. But then Carol was—mercifully—backward in that way as well as in others. This girl was probably no more than eleven or twelve.

'What the hell d'you think you're all doing?' Humphrey asked angrily.

Four pairs of clear young eyes gazed at him in amused contempt. Only the youngest made a half-hearted gesture toward putting an arm across those small, pointed buds, but then took it away again and giggled at him. Discarded clothing lay around on the floor. Cards lay on a coffee table.

'If it comes to that,' said the biggest boy, 'what are *you* doing, pushing in here?'

'I'm looking for my wife, as it happens. And I don't like the look of what's going on here and I'm sure your parents wouldn't either.'

The children laughed.

'We're just playing strip-poker, of course,' said the boy in a laconic, throw-away tone that suddenly reminded Humphrey of the young Ashley. 'Want to join in? You look as if you could afford to lose a layer or two of that business gent's outfitting.' The girls tittered appreciatively, and Humphrey felt himself beginning to lose his temper.

'You've got a bloody nerve, young man. If I was your father I'd take you home right now—*and* send those little girls home to their mothers.' 'Little' was hardly perhaps the word, but he dared use no other. He averted his eyes. He avoided seeing

much of Carol undressed these days and had stopped bathing
her, even though she herself did not understand why.

Roars of laughter.

'Well you couldn't send Jason and me home,' said the elder
boy, 'We're home already.'

'You Ashley's boys?' But already he knew they must be.

'Yeah,' said the big boy. 'Going to tell our Daddy of us, are
you? He'll think it's a great joke. Strip poker's his and Cindy's
favourite game. Everyone'll play it at the end of the party,
anyway.'

'He isn't *my* Daddy,' added the younger boy inconsequenti-
ally, in what seemed to Humphrey a cissified, camp voice.
'He's my wicked step-father!'

'You Cindy's son?' said Humphrey belligerently.

'No fear! She won't have kids—thinks it'll spoil her tits or
something. My mama's Paddy Shast.' Untypically, it seemed,
there was a hint of pride in his unbroken voice.

'Well you all ought to be ashamed of yourselves,' said
Humphrey with ineffectual force. 'It's downright dirty and—
and childish.' They all laughed again at this, not the belly-
laughs Humphrey remembered from his own youth, but
twitteringly, as if even humour could not disturb their essential
cold-blooded composure.

'Go on, piss off,' said the big boy aimably. 'Stop staring at
the girls, you dirty old man, you!'

Defeated, Humphrey shut the door quickly on their giggles.
Only kids, he told himself firmly. Just silly kids who didn't
know what they were saying.

As if he was caught in some repetitive time circuit from
which he could not escape, he once again moved on to the
cloakroom. This time the inner door leading to the shower
room was shut. Splashing, and the sound of shrieks and
laughter came from within. He hoped that it was just some
more kids up to their tricks, but without much conviction.

On his way back to the bar again he saw the thin man
leaning against a doorway on his own, glass in hand. His

cadaverous body was now so stooped that the area between his chest and his pelvis was positively concave. There was no sign of Joyce. Humphrey approached him, wondering in passing how he kept his trousers up.

'Seen my wife, by any chance?' He hoped his tone was casual rather than anxious.

'Should I have?' said the man disagreeably, raising an eyebrow.

'Well you were dancing with her,' said Humphrey crossly. There was really nothing clever about being so unhelpful and in a minute he might tell the man so.

'Oh—that. Yes. Little Miss Muffet outfit with a lot of Ladies' Corsetry defences under it?'

Humphrey nodded, hypnotised by the accuracy of this description—and a moment later could have kicked the man, and himself as well. How the hell—?

'Last seen in the kitchen,' said the man, shutting his eyes as if to close the conversation.

'Could you tell me where that is, please?' said Humphrey gruffly.

'Oh for God's sake—' The man opened his eyes again wearily and tried to focus them on Humphrey. 'If it was *my* wife,' he said at last, 'I wouldn't be in any hurry to find her. I'd be only too eager to *lose* her. I think it was jolly dee of me to take her off you in the first place. I expect someone else is lumbered with her by now. Why don't you relax. Just cool it, man—as I expect the nauseating young would say.' And he closed his eyes again, like an eccentric character in *Alice in Wonderland* preparing to go to sleep.

Humphrey stood over him for a moment, breathing heavily. 'You're lucky,' he said at last. 'I don't hit drunks. You've had a lucky escape, I can tell you.'

Not unpleased with this remark, he turned smartly through a doorway—and bumped into a solid paunch under soft cotton. 'Watch it!' said Ashley's voice good-naturedly. He was carrying a clutch of glasses in one hand and had a cigar clamped between his teeth. His forehead was beaded with sweat and so were his whiskers.

'Can I take some of those for you?' said Humphrey, and did so.

'Jolly dee of you, ol' boy.' Humphrey could not bear the thought that the obviously joke military accent in which Ashley made the remark was a take-off of himself again. He said, amost pleading now:

'Ashley. Don't you know who I am?'

Ashley peered at him with deliberation, then beamed.

'Humphrey! Course I know you. Super to see you again. Glad you could make it.' He was solemnly shaking hands now.

'Actually,' said Humphrey awkwardly, 'I think we must be pushing off quite soon. I was just looking for—'

'Already?' said Ashley, sounding genuinely hurt, 'but you've only just come. Don't you like it here?'

'Of course I do! But we came hours ago, actually. And I think Joyce is maybe getting a bit—er—tired—'

'Who?'

'Joyce. My wife. You know, you—'

'That's what I thought you said. Mmm. I knew a girl called Joyce once. Great girl. Had the dirtiest mind of any woman I've met—bar Cindy!' His loud, public laugh made heads turn towards him, smiling indulgently. Good old Ashley, everyone still loved him. But oh, these people, those childen; oh Ashley . . . Something inside Humphrey bled and bled.

'Actually,' he said in a lower tone, hoping wildly at this last moment to break through Ashley's public shell, to make some sort of real contact with him again: 'Actually I'm a bit worried about Joyce. I last saw her going off to dance with a—a very offensive character indeed. I only hope he hasn't been rude to her. . .'

'Somebody been rude?' said Ashley in vague concern, as if he was a bit deaf. 'I am sorry. Can you point him out?' Humphrey indicated the frog-footman, still apparently asleep against the door-jamb. Ashley said cheerfully:

'Ah-ha! Moulton Spurgeon. Ve-ry clever lad, that, as I expect you've discovered. Handles a lot of big accounts— Wettex, Sheldons—'

Desperately, Humphrey said:

'I don't care how clever he is. I think he's a creep and he was bloody insolent to me.'

Ashley gazed at him with a concern that Humphrey was not sure was real or assumed.

'Insolent? Was he now? Well, well.' He laid a heavy arm over Humphrey's shoulders, dropping ash down his back. 'You don't want to take things to heart so much,' he said in a brotherly voice, as if some faint memory of his relationship with Humphrey twenty years ago had stirred in him after all: 'Sure, Moult's a schmuck, but it isn't altogether his fault, you know. He's had a down on life ever since one of his kids turned out a mongol. He handles the publicity for one of those charities, actually—you know, sob-stuff and let's-keep-'em-all-alive-for-eighty-years—but it doesn't make him feel any better about it. After all, it's very hard on a clever guy like him having a drooling imbecile about the place.' And he suddenly made a drooling imbecile face, distorting his mouth and casting up his eyes. Ashley had always had a gift for mimicry.

The hall spun. For a moment Humphrey thought he already *had* knocked Ashley down and that Ashley was writhing at his feet, a spongey mass of over-fed matter rapidly deflating like a balloon. But an instant later he knew he would never hit Ashley because Ashley wouldn't understand if he did. Ashley would never understand anything now.

At last he said, glaring at Ashley, breathing with difficulty as if through a constricting pain in his chest:

'Well all I can say is—I'd rather have my girl than your kids. *Any* day. *Any*where. Even if she is a drooling imbecile.'

Ashley blinked, puzzled.

'Sure old son,' he said soothingly. 'Sure baby. We all prefer our own imbeciles, don't we? Any day. I understand. . . Why don't you go home now?'

'I shall,' said Humphrey. He turned towards the room where the dancing was, and, braving the appalling assault on his ear-drums, pushed his way determinedly round the sides, between and over entwined couples. He trod on an arm or two on purpose. At the far end was another door leading to a short passage, and beyond that was a large kitchen full of machines. It was empty except for a man morosely eating Gentleman's Relish out of the pot.

'Seen a woman in a long pink, striped dress?' said Humphrey determinedly. The man did not answer but simply jerked with his teaspoon toward the other door. Humphrey crossed the kitchen, opened the door—and found Joyce sitting neatly on a chair beside a spin-dryer, sobbing into a paper towel. The rest of the roll stood on the floor beside her. Her face was bloated. She must have been there ages. Humphrey knelt beside her.

'Why on earth didn't you come to find me?' he said gently. She clutched at his hands.

'I was frightened to come out again. Anyway I thought you'd be cross. You always say you hate me to cling to you at parties...' She wailed and buried her head in his shoulder.

'What happened to you? Go on,' he coaxed, 'tell Uncle.' He hadn't said that to her for—oh, years and years.

'That awful man—'

'The one in the kitchen?' He clenched his fists.

'No, no, not him. He just came into the kitchen while I was there, so I came in here. No, the *other* man—the one I was dancing with.'

'Did he,' said Humphrey very gently, 'say something to you about idiot children?' But Joyce just stared at him in surprise.

'No—why should he have? No, he—he—he-took-me-into-the-garden-and-put-his-hand-up-my-skirt,' she ended in a rush.

After a short pause during which neither of them knew what to say, Humphrey asked mildly:

'Why did you go into the garden with him?'

'I—I didn't realise what he meant. He said we could dance

out there and I thought—I thought it looked romantic. With the lights in the trees and everything.'

Humphrey went on holding her hands and wondered if what the man had done to her had been all that had upset her. She might be a chaste wife, but after all she *was* a wife, not an untouched girl. Wasn't it a bit ridiculous—though rather sweet and reassuring—that she should be so upset just by a crude physical approach.

Suddenly she raised her head:

'It wasn't just—what he did,' she said. 'It was—what he said, too. What he called me. Mostly that. Oh Humph!' She was crying again, freely in his arms, and though he tried to get out of her what the man had actually said, she never told him.

They drove home slowly. The sprawling Thames Valley towns, which a few hours before had seemed choked with traffic as if permanently, lay almost empty and full of moon-light, so that Humphrey half-expected to see a horse-drawn vehicle clattering through their ancient centres. The clouds had lifted, the yellow moon lay heavy and dusty-looking on the tops of the black trees. It was a night to believe in cider from home-picked apples, in white-armed young girls lying innocently in stubble fields, their simple faces to that moon, and in Harvest Homes before the First World War. Or perhaps during that War, with young officers driving roadsters at a daring forty mph down to Maidenhead on empty, dusty roads a few days before going back to death beneath a field of poppies... Young officers like Ashley, who had not survived and who were therefore forever unchanged. Time had lent romance even to their more ignoble exploits. It could lend romance to anything.

In a mood of sentiment as warm and forgiving as that mild, muggy luminous night, he eventually pulled the car into a lay-by and switched off the engine. 'What are you doing?' asked Joyce with a little giggle. For answer he took her in his arms.

Someone else had desired her: they were not so old after all.

At the back of his mind the substantial shadow, the mocking, approving or exhortatory ghost which had accompanied his thoughts and actions for the last twenty years, gave a knowing twitch. Ashley knew all about parking in a lay-by under the full moon: it was just his sort of thing. Not really meaning much, but stylish and romantic—like a Strauss waltz, or a theme from *Kiss Me Kate*...

... Or it had been just his sort of thing. Now, of course, it would be a sweaty grope up someone else's wife on the dark floor of a packed lounge, with the hideous and inappropriate music of the young thundering in his poor old ears. Poor old Ashley...

The shadow-puppet shivered and dwindled—dwindled to a dark speck like an insect on the retina of his consciousness, and then was no more.

11

The night driver or an alternative life

THE TAXI-DRIVER CALLED one Sunday morning in what must have been early autumn, several years ago. I know it was that time of year because it was a month or two after we had come back from a trip to Russia mainly paid for by E's paper. (He was a staffman on *The Warden* then.)

We weren't expecting anyone and I wasn't terribly pleased when the bell rang because I thought it would probably be a neighbour wanting us to do something for the anti-motorway lobby-group, or local children after jumble—somebody *wanting* something, anyway, just when you're not in the mood to give it. Sunday mornings are like that. So I was a bit forbidding when I opened the door, and it took me a few moments to realise that the taxi-driver actually had something to give us.

It was a letter from Russia. We were rather excited. Naturally we assumed the letter would contain some message too risky to send by ordinary post—a smuggled manuscript, or even word of a planned escape. Something like that would have been quite a scoop for E. (He's one of that generation of bright boys who did the Russian Course for their National Service in the 'fifties.) He remembered that when Anatoli Kusnetsov defected to the West his vital contact was a journalist of similar vintage on the *Telegraph*. But it turned out that the letter was just from a teacher in Tashkent to whom we had given our address but not, apparently, our surname. It seemed that he believed a letter with just our first names on it would never reach us in the ordinary way, and so had entrusted it to the next Londoner he met at the Tashkent Anglo-Soviet Friendship League. This was a bit disappointing—though of course we were glad to get the letter because one is always glad to get letters from the other side of the moon. I almost wrote 'from the other side of time', since Russia, even though I've now been there more than once, seems to be so fundamentally alien, so distant, exotic and strange under its disguise of being real, that I almost believe time runs differently there as it was once supposed to in fairyland: I think whole years pass there, while merely months go by here—or else, abruptly, time sticks there for a while, arrested in one groove, one season, with no progress or change... Needless to say E, who fancies himself as a kremlinologist, thinks this fantasy perfectly idiotic. He likes theories to be more formalised and consistent than that.

The man was obviously hoping to be invited in, so we did. Anyway it isn't everyone, even if they are a taxi-driver, who is prepared to spend their Sunday morning driving half way across London to do a favour to two strangers. He came readily and drank a cup of Nescafé while I made vague gestures of clearing the breakfast away. I'm not at my best first thing in the morning after the one good sleep of the week, and he must have noticed this because he hoped he hadn't disturbed us too early and remarked sympathetically that, to him, it was quite a different time of day because he was a night worker. He had been driving all night—Saturday, he said, was his heaviest night of the week—and was only now on his way home to New Cross. There he'd go to bed till four or five in the afternoon, then have his Sunday dinner which the wife would have ready, bit of a play with the kids, and then off to pick up the cab again from his mate who used it during the day. Except when it was being serviced, he said, Sunday mornings, like now, was the only time neither of them was ever on the job. Otherwise, day or night, the cab was pretty well always in use. Lots of drivers went shares on a taxi and did that, he said in answer to a question, amiably surprised we shouldn't have known this simple fact of life. Since a taxi was an expensive item that was the way to get your money's worth out of it.

He didn't mind talking about himself; in fact he enjoyed it. He was a well-built man, compact and muscular, with short, curly, slightly greying hair and fine side-whiskers. I'm not much good at guessing ages, and he could have been anything between thirty-five and close on fifty. What I did notice was an air of conscious health, robustness and, yes, a kind of exuberance about him. His eyes were brown and bright. You felt that he enjoyed life and, unlike many people who do, was very much aware of doing so. It was almost as if it was a matter of pride with him.

Inevitably we talked about our Russian contact, who was also the only point of contact between us, and the taxi-driver —his name was Harry Pizzey—said that since meeting Mihail Alexandreov last month he himself had tried Galsworthy and had been reading through the books with real enjoyment. I did not catch E's eye. An enthusiasm for Galsworthy, coupled with the mistaken belief that he was an important English writer, had, I remembered, been one of this Mihail Alexandreov's more typically and depressingly Russian characteristics. But if Harry Pizzey, thus recommended to Galsworthy, really was reading him with enjoyment, who were we to sneer? I thought he was a little proud of enjoying Galsworthy, but that the enjoyment itself was perfectly genuine. You couldn't help liking him, E and I agreed afterwards. Although he seemed rather self-centred, there is nothing wrong with self-centredness if it makes you behave in a deliberately open, friendly, hearty way towards others, careful of your own image. To be aware of the passing of your own life and to take an ingenuous pleasure in the use you put it to, is surely better—as I said subsequently to E—than

hurrying blind through the years in a cloud of over-activity,
occasionally indulging in a bout of frustration and neurosis
about some supposedly wasted opportunity.

I thought that Harry Pizzey's job probably suited him well.
I couldn't see him working in an office, and as an owner-
driver—still more, a night driver—he must feel free and in
charge of his own life, even though he wasn't really. He was
probably the sort who chats up his fares, trying out on them
his own newest opinions—on Galsworthy, or high-rise flats or
decimal currency—collecting from them interesting gobbets
of information which he would, in turn, pass on to other fares.
('An MP I had in my cab the other day—Cabinet Minister he
was, actually, though I didn't let on I'd recognised him—said
to me. . .') Anyway he displayed interest on hearing E was a
journalist, and I could see him storing up various remarks E
made on Russia as good provision for future conversations.
He didn't read *The Warden* himself, he said—didn't have the
time now to devote to a serious newspaper, unfortunately.
You couldn't fit everything in and there were other things in
life besides news. At one time he'd read the old *News
Chronicle*, but he couldn't stick *The Mail*, now, which his
wife had—he reckoned it was a woman's paper, if I would
excuse the term, no insult intended! The *Evening News* was
more in his line, as he followed the horses a bit—though he
never betted these days.

So he wasn't a Party Member then. Most of the English like
him, and of his sort of age, whom you meet in the Soviet
Union, are. Or they have once been, and, like people who have
escaped from a profession or a marriage but still feel a
contrary, nostalgic yearning towards it, they can't resist an
opportunity to visit what was once, to them, the holy place.
But Harry Pizzey said readily, in response to our politely leading questions, that he hadn't visited Russia out of any
particular yen for the régime but simply out of interest: he
liked to see different ways of life. Once, he said, if someone
had said to him 'How'd you like a trip to Russia, Harry?', he'd

have turned up his nose—thought it wasn't his sort of thing. But now, he said, he was readier to get interested in all kinds of things that hadn't interested him once, and to take things more as he found them. There were more things in Heaven and Earth and so forth. He laughed, as if at some private pleasure. He had a very attractive laugh. In fact I realised— thinking about it afterwards—that it was his attractive and magnetic personality which imparted a glow to what he said, transforming the commonplace. In the same way, in one's own life, an inner awareness and conscious delight can transform the standard events of existence into something personal and spectacular. I even wondered idly—and I don't think I'm making this up in retrospective knowledge—if Harry Pizzey was a recent convert to some religion of salvation and charity which now dominated his life, and that the quotation about Heaven and Earth (which he probably didn't know comes from *Hamlet* because lots of people don't) was partly a reference to this.

From Russia, we passed by a natural transition to other countries: Roumania, Tunisia, Israel, Turkey—surprisingly, Harry had been to them all in the last half-dozen years: a pretty total, as E remarked jocularly and jealously, for a family man who didn't travel as part of his job. (E is intensely competitive, even in situations where competition is obviously inappropriate.) Yes, said Harry with pride, and he'd taken some of the family with him each time, too. Not the two youngest—they'd stayed with their Nan, so far. But Paul, the big lad, had come with them all over the shop. And next year they were thinking of taking the whole family. The nippers would be three and five, then, and he believed in starting them off young. The wife was saying they might play safe and make it Spain, but he thought that sounded a bit ordinary. He wanted to make it Greece—if she could overcome her fears about the Greeks, that was. You had to be prepared to overcome things, he reckoned, genially.

Obediently we asked what particular fears the Greeks held

for Mrs Pizzey. I thought it unlikely that—unless she were
Greek herself?—she had an obsession about the Colonels,
and I was right. What had happened, Harry explained, was
that, six years ago this winter, on their first ever trip abroad,
he, his wife and Paul had been on the *Theodosis*.

Of course E registered the name at once. The *Theodosis*
—I remembered as soon as he began to tell me—had
been a Greek cruise ship which had engine trouble in the
Mediterranean, had drifted off course and rammed a reef, and
then had failed to cope with the emergency that followed.
Over a number of confused and wasted hours the ship had
gradually filled with water and eventually sank. Over a
hundred passengers had been lost, either left on the ship when
it finally went down, or struggling to reach the small boats
from which, it turned out, the basic provisions of water,
blankets and first-aid had been pilfered anyway. There had
been many allegations afterwards of negligence, dishonesty,
panic and drunkenness on the part of the crew, and a big
public enquiry. Of course, we remembered it well.

Harry Pizzey retailed to us some of the already-familiar
stories—the Captain and the first mate shouting contradictory
orders and coming to blows, the steward sent round to assure
passengers there was no need for alarm at a moment when
some of the crew were already trying to lower boats at the
other end of the ship. Later, there were still uglier scenes.
'When I was already in a boat with Paul,' said Harry, 'I saw
one seaman—cook or something—elbowing a woman with a
kid in her arms out of the way and scrambling in himself. I
knocked him sideways, I can tell you, and got the woman in
myself. And then they cast that boat off without warning—
and it was only half full.' He had certainly told the story over
many times, to journalists and others, but repetition had not
dimmed it and never would.

'I was in this boat,' he went on, 'with Paul, who was six
then. When the boat hit the water we were in the bows and
we got soaked—everyone got pretty wet because the ship was

listing badly by that time and so the boat landed in the sea half-sideways. And it was a roughish sea. People say the Mediterranean doesn't get that rough, even in winter, but it isn't true—I know. Well, like I said, that boat was only half full, and I was the only grown man in it—naturally, most of the British passengers unlike the crew let the women get into the boats first. I'd only got in because I had Paul in my arms. He kept on asking where his Mum was—' He paused dramatically. 'Well, I couldn't answer that one. Rita and I'd been separated in the crowd. I didn't know what boat she was on—if she was on one. In fact I spent the rest of the night—seven hours it was, till we were picked up by a French ship—thinking she was drowned. And meanwhile she was spending the night in another boat thinking Paul and me was drowned.' He paused, and this time I thought it was not a calculated effect but genuine, a gap for experience which was forever inexpressible.

'I reckon it was worse for her,' he went on. 'I mean, I had Paul. And rubbing him and breathing into his neck to keep him warm kept me going, like. I was alright—I've got a good constitution. But he was so young and he'd got soaked too, right through his little anorak. I took it off him and wrapped him in mine. I kept from getting chilled to death myself with keeping going at him—and at all the others. Jollying 'em along, like. Making 'em sing and wave their arms about and tell stories and so on. Luckily I'd read *The Cruel Sea*. . . And in the night one woman up the far end of the boat *did* die of exposure, even so.'

So that was it. This was the change that had come over his life, the sudden revelation—not a religious conversion but a confrontation with mortality so naked that nothing would ever be the same again. For ever afterwards time would have for him a new proportion, a different perspective and point of reference. We were looked at one of the Saved.

We asked him if he felt like this about it? He readily agreed he did, as if pleased we had got the point. It had changed his whole way of looking at things, he said. Before It happened he'd gone around life half-awake, he reckoned now. Oh, he'd enjoyed things, he supposed, in a way. But he'd been a moaner, fussed about trifles, really bothered if he thought someone had done him down—cut in on him in the cab, for instance, or snapped up a fare that should have been his. And he'd used to worry about money too: although the cab business was a good one and he and his mate had done well, he was always thinking about security and so forth—that was why he and Rita had had only the one child. Well It had changed all that. As soon as they were all home and dry again (he laughed) he and Rita had decided to go in for another child, and in the end they'd had two more. And they'd decided life was for living, not for piling up possessions—they'd stopped putting their money into things like new furniture and fitted carpets, and had decided to go in for experiences instead. Hence all the foreign travel. And, yes, they had been on a ship again!—to Turkey, that had been. He'd insisted on it. You couldn't afford to limit your life, he said, by silly prejudices and ideas that you couldn't do this or that. He'd realised now that you could do almost anything, if you wanted to. It was just a matter of wanting. To read Dickens, for instance, or to learn how to skate or to read the Russian alphabet—he'd done all of those things recently.

'In fact, You only live once,' said E self-consciously. Being very clever, he is always a bit embarrassed by simple truths, as if he secretly thinks that to very clever people they should not apply. But Harry wasn't at all embarrassed and didn't seem to recognise the phrase as a cliché. He said very earnestly that that wasn't quite it, actually. On the contrary, the way it seemed to him, it was as if he *had* lived twice—once before It happened and once after. That had been like a second chance for him, such as most people don't get, and that was why he was so aware he must make the most of it. In fact, he said, even more earnestly but with a slight laugh to show that we didn't need to follow his fantasy this far if we didn't want to, he almost felt as if he were on an alternative loop of time.

'A loop?' I said, since he seemed to want me to.

Yes. Like in science fiction. I don't read science fiction and nor does E, but E nodded sagaciously as he knows about science fiction anyway. E knows a lot *about* things.

Well then, said Harry, E would know what he meant. Like in Asimov. He felt as if, on one loop of time—or perhaps branch would be a better word, since what happened happened and there was no way back again—Harry Pizzey had been a goner. That was the branch he had very nearly taken the night It happened. But Someone or Something or even just chance had switched the points. What he was on now was the alternative branch—the other loop—which swung out into a different circuit.

And suppose, I said, he had never gone on the *Theodosis* at all?

Ah, he said, in that case he'd never have come to the place where the lines forked, would he? He'd just have gone on on the same old track, without dying but without swinging out into a new life either. Pleased to have made the metaphor work so neatly, he sat back and smiled at us.

E said that there was a very entertaining book which might interest him—it was (to express it shortly) about alternative loops of time in history: what would have happened if Drouot's cart had stuck and so the French Revolution had been averted, for instance? Harry took out a notebook and carefully wrote down the name of it, though he said that he thought he'd have to read up some straight history before he'd appreciate the book properly. History was something he'd planned to tackle that winter, anyway.

E said that he was inclined to think that loop *was* a better word than branch, actually, since in the end we all die anyway —reach the same terminus, that is. Death is Waterloo! (We all laughed at this.) Therefore, said E, the alternative branches were genuine loops, curving off separately but finally all joining up again. If you could see them from some vantage point beyond space and time you would see them winding their separate ways, perhaps through quite different landscapes. Though, equally, certain features might be common to several of them. Several different loops might all have to cross the same great river, for instance, at different points—that would be a metaphor for personal crisis, he supposed. And if you didn't climb up onto a plateau in one place you would have to do it in another. Or there might be a dangerous bend and tunnel on one line and not on another, but the other might have a precipice which the rails had to negotiate... He stopped there and didn't enlarge on the last point. I, too, thought it would not have been tactful to do so.

Harry laughed and shook his head thoughtfully, and said he'd never pushed the idea quite as far as that. Perhaps he felt a little confused by the concept of not just two Harrys— a dead one and a live one—but other, further, alternative Harrys who had forked off at yet other branchings and were pursuing other, unknowable, hypothetical lives. After all, it was his own, very precious existence we were talking about. It wasn't just an intellectual game for him as it was for E.

He went soon after that, I think. We thanked him again for bringing the letter from Mihail Alexandreov (we'd all forgotten about him by now, which seems to support E's theory that Russians are irrelevant to almost everything). We also said how nice it had been to meet each other, which it had. We saw Harry to his taxi. He told us to take note of his licence number and look out for it whenever we were hailing a taxi, because the odds were one or the other of us would hail him one day. He was, we saw, the sort of man who can't bear to leave anyone without making noises about how much he'd like to see them again, but I thought he meant it too in our case. I did note down the licence number in my mind and it stayed there, because I have a good mnemonic system for things like that.

I thought about him several times over the weeks and

months that followed, and for quite a long time whenever I did take a taxi I got into the habit of glancing at its number as soon as I got in. But gradually the habit wore out, and, as time went by, we all but forgot Harry Pizzey.

In time, the landscape of our own life changed, slightly but perceptibly, darkening a little. The frame through which I saw the passage of days, of years, shifted somewhat. The angle of vision was altered.

Quite recently, I picked up a taxi in Fleet Street. I was tired and on the way to being late for a doctor's appointment, otherwise I wouldn't have done so. I sat back 'for safety and comfort', as the notice tells you to, and thought that safety and comfort should be so easily acquired... We were almost at Wimpole Street before I realised why the number on the back of the partition, which my eyes had been meaninglessly reading and re-reading, was familiar.

I looked then at the driver's back, but of course it was daytime so it wouldn't be Harry Pizzey anyway. In any case he and his mate might have sold this taxi by now and bought a new one. Or would they, in that case, have kept the same number?

I was feeling low and not particularly like striking up a conversation, but when I got out and paid the driver (fat and lugubrious, with glasses) I felt I had to ask, and I did.

Now if this were a ghost story, or a science fiction story, I would have had a very odd reply. The taxi-driver would have stared at me, and then said, in the manner of cabbies in stories:

'Lord love you, dear, this cab's never driven at night—never has been. I've heard of ghostly coachmen or riders, now, but never ghost-taxi-drivers. S'against union rules!'

Or, if the point needed to be made slightly more explicit, the taxi-driver would have given me an almost frightened look and said:

'Now it's very odd you should say that, dear, very odd indeed. I did have a mate called Harry Pizzey and in fact he and me was going to go into business together—me driving days, him driving nights. We'd got it all set up—and then he went down in that Greek cruise ship that was wrecked. 'Bout seven years now, that was.'

Or, to make the story a little more subtle—the alternatives get quite copious when you start thinking of them, branching and branching—he might have said:

'Yes—poor Harry Pizzey. You didn't know, then? He was killed in an accident several months ago. A lorry ran slap into him on the North Circular' or 'He was killed by lightning'—or even, 'He was drowned on his summer holiday. . . Well, what I always say is, if your number comes up then it comes up, doesn't it? You can't escape it.'

In fact, he didn't say any of these things. But, on reflection, I find what he did say almost as unnerving in its implications. Possibly rather more.

He said, staring at me rather rudely:

'You a friend of Harry's then? Because, if so, I don't want to say anything you wouldn't want to hear.'

'No. . . No, I'm not. I mean I only met him once. I just wondered . . . What might I not want to hear?' Everything about the man's tone and bearing implied that, whatever he said, he wanted to tell me things, if only to get his own back on Harry for some wrong. He was pleased to have been asked by a total stranger, the oddness of it didn't strike him.

'Well I suppose it doesn't matter,' he said quickly. 'Harry's not working with me any more. Not for the present, anyway.'

'Oh?'

'No. He's turned a bit funny, you see. . . You a friend of his missis?'

'No, I've never met her.'

'Oh well, in that case—' he became more confiding: 'Harry's not been well. Depressed. Not able to work.'

'*Really?*' But almost at once I realised that it was not, after all, amazing but quite possible, even predictable. To be alive to the sum total of potential happiness is also to be endlessly

vulnerable to potential pain, and unable to hide from it behind
platitudes and reservations.

As if he saw what I was thinking, the man said resentfully
—he half-suspected his partner of malingering:

'The doctor calls it manic-depression. Moodiness—going
from one extreme to the other. *I* wouldn't know. I always
thought he was quite normal—bit of a jolly type, even. But
now he just sits and cries all day like a baby. In the middle of
the kitchen. It's disgusting, actually.'

'How awful for him. . .'

'Awful for his missis, you mean, she's at her wits' end. . .
And it's hard on her after all the trouble she had with him just
before—him wanting to throw up the job and go and live in
India and stuff like that. . .'

'Did he? I didn't know that.'

'Didn't you?' The man was clearly having difficulty in sizing
me up, and I suddenly realised, from the half-hostile, half-
intimate way he was looking at me, that he thought I must
have been a lady-friend of Harry's—just the sort of arty type
who *would* encourage a man to go to India. 'Then I'd better
not say too much about that, had I?' he said, as if there was a
lot more he would have liked to have told me about the way
in which Harry's quest for experience had developed.

'Well, I'm extremely sorry,' I said briskly, trying to dispel
his murkier illusions. 'It seems very sad, I hope the doctors
manage to treat him successfully. They can do wonders today
with drugs, I believe.' I believe, I believe, I must believe. . .
'He seemed to us such an energetic person with so many good
ideas. As I say, my husband and I only met him once but we
had a most interesting talk with him—mainly about that
shipwreck he was in.'

'Oh—that,' said the driver irritably. 'Well I reckon that was
the cause of it all, myself.'

'Really? But he seemed to have come out of it so well. He
talked about it as if it had been a blessing to him.'

'Ah, but it affected his nerves, didn't it?' said the man,

tolerant of my foolish optimism. 'Bound to have, an experience
like that. Made him restless and excitable, you see. After that,
he couldn't settle down.'

'I see. . .'

'Oh, I'm *sorry* for him and all that,' said the man untruth-
fully, 'and I know they say mental cases can't help themselves
—but what he's doing now is driving his wife potty. He ought
to think of her, instead of himself all the time.'

I shivered, for it was cold. The wind blew pieces of grit
bowling along the ground. A pigeon had been crushed in the
road, hours before. All that remained of it was a whitish smear
from which all the blood had been pressed away, and the
feathers of one wing, still splayed out. I thought of Harry
sitting upright on a hard chair surrounded by space, aghast
at the pain of a world he could not, after all compass or
control.

'What—what does he do, exactly? Apart from cry. . .'

'He sits there,' said the man with deep disgust, 'saying that
he ought to be dead—that he ought to have been drowned in
that shipwreck and that it was a mistake he wasn't. Bloody
fool. You'd think he'd be thankful, wouldn't you? I know *I*
would be.'

But would you? I thought, looking at the fat, resentful face.
Perhaps being one of the Saved, living on extra time, is not
so easy after all, and Harry was bright enough to realise it
and to feel the crushing responsibility of his own good fortune.

I paid the driver, who drove off without a backward glance,
perhaps embarrassed after all by his own confidences. Almost
at once the taxi merged indistinguishably with the other
traffic, as if it and its inmate had only materialised temporarily
out of it to give me a message—like the motorbike riders in
Cocteau's film, impassive and grimly commonplace. With a
heavy heart and uncertain feet I turned towards the door in
Wimpole Street, wondering if Harry Pizzey's responsibiliy
would ever be mine.

12

Mother Russia

NATASHA HAD ALWAYS known that Russia awaited her and that this was her private and peculiar destiny. It was confusing, but on the whole irrelevant, that Ian had got there first.

Ian was her step-brother and really nothing to do with her or Russia, she had always felt, but it was typical that he should finally reach Russia before she did because superiority had been the keynote of his relationship with her ever since they met. She remembered clearly her first sight of him, although everything before that was remembered differently, with nostalgia yet without precision, like an unmistakable scent which cannot be recalled when it is not actually there, or like the lingering yet unnamable atmosphere of a dream. But her meeting with Ian was quite prosaic and clear-cut in her memory, though not specially interesting. He had been a public schoolboy in large grey flannels and an aloof manner which the grown-ups told one another was 'shyness' but which she, at seven, knew perfectly well was straightforward dislike. Why should he like her? He was a boy, he was twice her age, and he was used to having his divorced father to himself. Why should he like the strange new mother with a foreign accent his father had brought home from the Liberation of Paris, still less that 'mother's' own small, inferior girl child? Obediently shaking his hot red hand she had known they would never be more than enemies, but in fact he had always been more or less civil to her and she did not think he even knew now that he disliked her. Ian's emotions today were so overlaid with years of education and conditioning, restraint, prejudice and professional ambition, that they had probably ceased to trouble him altogether. The idea that what people *felt*, in their essential selves, was necessarily important to them, was surely (she thought) fallacious? With people like Ian feelings simply did not count.

But in any case, quite early, he had won. His father's second wife, Natasha's mother, did not survive her transplantation. Brought over from Paris in 1946, equipped with a new name, a ration book, and new Utility clothes as suitable to life in an English commuter's village, she obstinately refused to thrive. At first, thought Natasha, it had seemed to work. She had laughed a lot, rather nervously, with Father's friends 'in for drinks', had learnt English, had bicycled about the Sussex lanes with Natasha on a fairy-cycle behind her, had darned Ian's matted grey wool socks in the holidays, had even made some gestures toward resuming 'her' painting, relic of her Parisian existence—as if her past and her present could be synthesised into a coherent whole. But the gestures had faltered, like the English and like her new-found, tentative friendships with other mothers on bicycles, and she had turned away again. She had been, thought Natasha, like one of those out of the ordinary plants you send for from a special nursery somewhere near Milton Keynes and put into the garden at the right time with just the right sort of potting compost. At first the plant seems to put down roots and grow, but after a few months you find it wilting. You water it more, with different things, and erect little screens to give it more shade—or less—but it's no good, its leaves curl and drop. One day when the thing is obviously sick you are trying to stake it to give it support and suddenly the whole stem is there in your hands, unattached to the earth. You see that the few shallow tentacles it had put into the ground have rotted away entirely and the wonder is that the thing still managed to give any semblance of life at all: it is fit only for the rubbish dump.

Thus, Maria Vasilievna, when, one desultory autumn day in 1951, she went out on her bicycle and did not come back. Bicycle and woman disappeared, and it was two weeks before both were found, deeply sunk in the ooze under twenty feet of water on a long-abandoned stone quarry. She must have had quite a job, the police said, to drag and shove her machine across banks and tree-stumps and through the thick undergrowth to reach the wooded lip of that hidden chasm, the only place to drown yourself for twenty miles around. At first people were surprised and said surely it must have been an accident?—or 'foul play'—telling one another that she had seemed quite cheerful, or at any rate not really what you'd call *depressed*... Pointing out to one another her attempts at painting, the kindness of her husband and dutifulness of her step-son, her love for little Natasha (safe at boarding school when the tragedy occurred: how fortunate!) But later, going through her belongings, they found other evidences: a diary, abruptly broken-off, one or two letters addressed to people in Paris but never posted; and then they became thoughtful, with a note of shocked regret in their voices combined, in one or two cases, with a querulous insistence that they couldn't possibly have known, could they?

As for Natasha, exiled at her boarding school like someone doggedly serving a long prison sentence for a crime of which she knew nothing, the intimations of her mother's solitary end only reached her gradually, by hints and half truths and then, quite soon, by a baffling fiction that it was all old history now anyway, wasn't it? But she thought, looking back, that she herself had known the plant was dying for some time, and that therefore 'the shock' which the grown-ups seemed anxious to 'spare' her was different for her anyway. With hindsight, she became convinced that her own exile to boarding school, which she knew had caused Maria Vasilievna pain as well as herself, had all been part of Maria's preparation for her own dying—the gradual breaking of the links. She also thought that when, the following holidays, her step-father and Ian made efforts to be particularly kind and forbearing with her, that was because they knew they had won and felt guilty. Step-father too? Yes. For he had brought Maria Vasilievna home like a trophy from foreign parts, war booty like the shoulder badges from the Italian he had taken prisoner and the revolver from the dead German. He had tried to subdue her to his way of life. There had been a contest there, just as much as between Ian and his step-sister—and just as unspoken. Now father and son were both, in their own ways, victors. They were very sorry, of course, but took particular care to explain to Natasha that the fatal event had been 'no one's fault'—least of all their. Perhaps they were both afraid she might think differently.

Of course long, long before her fatal transplantation to the loamy soil of Sussex, Maria Vasilievna had been transplanted already. As a small child in 1918 she had been carried across the southern border of Russia away from the revolutionary armies and onto a rocking ship that brought them from Odessa to Marseilles. Paris received them. Vasily, her father, found a job in a gymnasium, her mother joined the crush of well-born Russian ladies who came down to giving language lessons, often to students whose interest in the Russian language stemmed from their enthusiasm for the new regime. But the flat they found in an unpretentious quarter was not so unlike the first floor sitting rooms in their dear, former house off the Nevsky Prospect, and they had their ikons and quite a bit of jewellery and, of course, many old friends in the same boat. Hadn't they, the Petersburgers, always looked to the West and spoken excellent French and deplored the general backwardness of Russian life? Now that backwardness was behind them forever. They missed it greatly, more than they could admit, but they survived. Life was possible, even gay. Maria grew up speaking French at school and Russian at home, reverencing Voltaire and Danton in the class and the memory of the Czar with her parents. She grew up as a foreign flower, a faintly exotic hybrid, a congenital expatriate. No wonder, thought Natasha, the second, more total transplantation had proved lethal to her.

In such romantically objective terms Natasha had come, through the years, to think of her dead parent. In the same way she did not think of her as 'Mama' but as Maria Vasilievna, a young woman of (now) much the same age as herself. And this fellow woman, so near to herself and yet so unknowable, had become a fixed point of reference for her, a mute accompanying presence in her life, just as, for Maria Vasilievna, Russia, the unreachable motherland, had been a fixed point. As Natasha had been abruptly cut off, in childhood, from her early life with her mother, so had Maria herself been cut off young from her native roots. As Natasha now husbanded her memories of her mother and a handful of keepsakes (resented but respected during her adolescence by the surrounding grown-ups) Maria had husbanded the heritage of a lost country and a lost life, as represented by the ikons, wooden dolls, sepia photos and bits of lace and embroidery that garnished the Paris flat where she grew up.

Into that flat and that collection of meaningful objects Natasha had been born the year the Germans marched into Poland. She had been given her Russian name in loyalty to the grandparents who were by then dead and to a language which Maria herself was using less and less in daily life. And there, during the Occupation, Natasha had passed her earliest years, living behind the grey shutters in a miniature Russian world which was already at one remove in space and time from reality. So that, when the War ended and she and her mother moved to England and later Maria died, this world-within-a-world became doubly inaccessible to Natasha. In the bleak winter dormitory, among girls spitting gobbets of peppermint toothpaste into basins and talking of preps and bells and people who were going to be simply *furious*, she thought not so much of her mother as of that Russia she had known only through Maria Vasilievna and had now lost, it seemed forever. Sometimes she grew quite faint with a forlorn, illicit nostalgia—for a country where the snow fell all the year round, even on the fields of wheat, as in one of those glass balls, and which was, like the interior of a glass ball, tiny and out of reach. Far off, behind the glass of another's memory, little figures moved, wore uniforms, drove in troikas, walked in forests, gazed on fields of sunflowers (still under the whirling, perpetual, painless snow)—but she herself could never reach them now.

Slowly, through the empty years, she grew up. School at last ended and she became a person again, of sorts. She shared a flat in London with two other girls, studied domestic science, and eventually she met a serious young man who introduced her to Tolstoy and Dostoyevski and Turgenev. The tiny, whirling snowball expanded, became more complicated: the flakes ceased to fall at every season and she learnt that Russia has a short but warm summer and that in Petersburg where Maria Vasilievna was born there are nights in June when the sun never sets. The serious young man, who was studying architecture, gave her books as Christmas presents with pictures of ikons and onion-domed churches and innumerable kremlins, and she bought others for herself with photographs of men in baggy suits playing chess in public gardens. She learnt names and a new alphabet. By and by she really did know more about Russia, in an unassuming way, than most do who have never been there. She bought a Russian cookery book and made borsht and blinis and Easter cheese-cakes in the shapes of crosses. And eventually, in her Russian obsession, she turned away from the serious young man and he from her, because he was so English and was devoted to his parents in Guildford, and wasn't really interested in Russia at all, she decided, but only in Literature and Art.

Her obsession did not pass but gradually she incorporated it into her life. It did not dominate her days but it was there.

People who got to know her—and she tended to know people for a couple of years and then drift away from them or they from her—came to understand that she just 'had' Russia as a theme in her life, as some people have string quartets or pot-holing, or as her stepbrother Ian had his stamp-collection and his preoccupation with doing the right thing. He had gone into the diplomatic service, and talked in terms of postings and ladders and suitable people to marry. His fortunate future wife, it was understood, must be someone of the right 'background' who would 'know how to talk to people'. Not, of course, a vague, dreamy girl who drifted through a series of not very well paid domestic science jobs, a succession of flats and cottages on short leases, and abortive, uncommitted affairs with people who were vaguely arty.

Just as most of Ian's friends assumed that he would find the appropriate suitable girl in good time, so most of Natasha's assumed that she would visit Russia at the first opportunity. But the years went by and neither of these things happened. Perhaps the few girls whom Ian thought totally suitable turned out to be mysteriously unimpressed by him; at any rate in his late thirties he was still unmarried. Nor did Natasha seem in any hurry to see Russia with her own eyes. She always said she couldn't afford it, and her friends thought it was because she couldn't organise herself into doing it. But really it was because she knew it was not yet time.

Then Ian was posted to Moscow for a three year tour of duty, and for Natasha, it seemed, the time had come.

That Christmas Ian wrote to her on the inside of a crested British Embassy card: 'Greetings and all that and why don't you come out and see me? Now's your chance. This flat's quite a good size—and a palace, of course, by Russian standards—and I've got the usual maid and chauffeur and so forth. Can't say much else in the place's favour, but I daresay you might find it interesting.'

He had, unknown to Natasha, written approximately the same thing to a number of people, not really expecting any of them to take up his offer, so when he received her letter of acceptance his reply was less enthusiastic: '... Come by all means, if you like, though not, for God's sake, till the spring, which means effectively not till about June, I gather. The winter is unspeakable, my car is laid up at the moment because the dammed Russian anti-freeze in it has frozen and my chauffeur just doesn't seem to care. The people here are inefficient beyond belief...' He complained for half a page more, and ended: 'Anyway, if you are coming nonetheless, let me know when in good time, as summers here are apt to get busy, I gather. Incidentally, if you could buy me some sock suspenders and send them out I should be most grateful. They seem to be one of the many things Russian shopkeepers have never heard of.'

She sent six pairs of suspenders, in six different colours, and a letter of a few lines saying she would fly to Moscow on 15 June. She never put more than a minimum of words on paper if she could help it. She was aware that it had been Maria Vasilievna's diary and unsent letters which had given her away after her death, exposing her pain helplessly to people who didn't care and who, because they lived, were eternally superior to her. To commit thoughts to paper—any thoughts—was evidently to lay oneself open.

A knowledgeable acquaintance to whom she showed Ian's letter said:

'Journalists and diplomats who are sent to Russia always complain non-stop. They get totally neurotic and expend so much energy on hating the place that they've no time to cause trouble. I think they're picked in the first place as the kind of people who'll hate Russia anyway. It would be a security risk to send people who are natural Slavophiles.'

'I thought it would be difficult to get to Russia,' she said. 'People talk as if it is—as if the iron curtain was actually there and you had to climb over it, in the ice and snow... But I just showed the Consulate Ian's letter. People said that I might have my visa refused because of my mother. But the Consulate didn't seem a bit interested.'

'Oh they're not worried today about the descendents of people who left at the Revolution,' said the knowledgeable acquaintance. 'That's all old history in Russia now. You'll find it a different country from the one your mother left, Natasha. Hydro-electric stations, great blocks of flats in the cities—'

'I know,' she said. But she did not entirely believe it. A country the size of Russia could not be changed that easily.

But there were still five months to elapse before 15 June, and in the course of them her acquaintance became a friend and then a lover and then the one person she wanted to spend the rest of her life with. He was of Polish origin and worked for the BBC. Unfortunately he had a nice wife and two little boys in Bromley whom he loved and had no intention of leaving. He was quite fair: he had made his situation clear to her from the start.

She had loved, and even been loved, several times before, but it had never been like this and, as she was over thirty now, she strongly suspected that it never would be again. She couldn't have what she wanted and that was that. It wasn't a question, she felt, of being 'blinded by love' but of seeing only too clearly what the unpromising future held—or rather, did not hold. By the time June came she had begun to live in a world where she started and wept whenever the 'phone rang, and where the initials of his name surged at her from posters on the Underground. But by then she had given up answering the 'phone, and so he rang in vain.

'It's a good thing you're off to Russia soon,' he had said at their last meeting, attempting with the clumsiness of the essentially selfish to 'put himself in her place'.

'Don't be stupid, Stefan,' she had said implacably. 'How can going to Russia, or to anywhere, change anything?'

'I just meant that I think this trip will be important to you. I feel it will be. Let me see your hand... No, the right one...

Yes, look: there's a change here. It's clearly marked. A whole change of being—of—of condition, one might almost say.'

She did not yet know what he meant.

The plane came down over the chains of light that were Moscow. 'Look,' said her garrulous neighbour, 'you can see the red star on the Kremlin.' He seemed excited, although he claimed he had flown into Moscow more times than he could count. She thought, heart sinking with the plane: It's no good. Stefan was right: it'll just be a great city like any other... But then they were down, and it wasn't quite like anywhere else, all the same.

On the far side of the interminable Customs Ian was waiting for her, in a hall like a Victorian railway waiting room with a huge, dusty but twinkling chandelier, as if those chains of lights seen from the air had resolved themselves together in one big cluster. He seemed cross, but she remembered that it was late at night and that he had always hated being kept up. His regular bedtime had been one of several little manias he had developed while still in his twenties.

He also seemed disappointed to hear that the Customs had not eventually shown much interest in her one suitcase and her paperback copy of *Oblomov*. Some people, he informed her with something close to pride, like a person expatiating on the unique badness of his local laundry or of the telephone service, were searched from top to toe and had perfectly innocuous things like cameras and binoculars taken away from them.

'Well I haven't got any binoculars, you see,' she said. 'And my camera looks so unimportant.' She wasn't sure why she had brought the camera, for which she had not bought any film. Inwardly she giggled. Ian was so exactly like he'd always been only more so, and, in the context, this was reassuring and even made her feel momentarily light-hearted.

Ian's large black car was meanwhile carrying them through the darkness, presumably towards the centre of Moscow but in fact going in circles. It drove what seemed to be back and forth, describing great arcs and abrupt U-turns, now with tall modern blocks on either side of it as if they were already in the centre, now out again crossing what appeared to be darkened plains without a house in view. Gesturing at the solid back of the chauffeur, she asked:

'Has he lost his way?'

'Sergei? Oh Lord no. (He speaks English, by the way.) No—this is the way one has to drive around this confounded city. We turned onto the ring road a while ago and had to go right round it to get to a place where Sergei could make a turn, and then come back again the same distance, and all this just to turn onto the boulevard we need. You spend your life in Moscow driving twice as far as you should just because there are hardly any left-hand turns.'

'It sounds quite a good system, in a way,' she said. 'Safe, I mean. . .'

'Nonsense. Totally unnecessary. One wastes hours perpetually going all the way round the Kremlin and back. Look—we're going to do it now.'

She leant forward, and saw medieval domes like black paper cut-outs against the light summer sky. The red star glowed low like some dying heavenly body. It was as familiar to her as a picture in a book known from childhood, and yet strange because it was situated, not far back in her childhood, but *here*, outside their large, closed car, with Ian sitting beside her.

'Sergei can bring you down here tomorrow to have a look round,' he said. 'I'll have to go into the office of course, but the car's at your disposal and Sergei has nothing else to do.' His tone was faintly contemptuous but the solid back, in spite of understanding English, did not move. She felt intimidated by it and did not want to be alone with it yet.

'Couldn't I walk down to the Kremlin on my own?' she said. 'I mean, your flat is fairly central, isn't it? Am I allowed to go around on my own?'

'Oh of course if you want to walk no one'll stop you,' he said grudgingly. 'But for heavens' sake do make use of Sergei as a guide while you're here. He has very little to do for me.' She thought: he speaks deliberately loudly when he wants Sergei to hear. He doesn't like him. Why? As if belatedly answering this unspoken question once they were at the block where Ian lived and going up in the lift, Ian said:

'Oh, I expect you realise—Sergei's main function, like all servants attached to foreign residents, is to report back on me. So be careful what you say in front of him. Or to him.'

'Really?' She thought of the heavy face, seen briefly in the lamplight only when Sergei lifted her case out of the car and politely wished her good night. The dark chauffeur's jacket and equally dark slicked-back hair seemed entirely Western but something about the face had not fitted and she realised now in the lift what it was: with its broad nostrils and faintly crumpled, ageless look it was basically a Mongolian face. It did not come from Europe at all but from far over the other side of the world where Ghengis Khan's hordes had risen and where Russia went on, and on, to the Pacific shore.

Rather to her surprise, she slept at once, and deeply, in the small room to which Ian showed her. He himself, she discovered next morning, had a large bedroom opening off the living room of the flat, and also a separate study. There was a large kitchen too, and another room beyond that. It was really a family flat, he explained to her, which his post 'carried'. People on the same 'rung of the ladder' as himself, with two and even three children, had exactly the same accommodation.

'Are there a lot of foreign families in this block?'

'All foreign. This and two other blocks are the only places in Moscow where foreigners are allowed to live. And wired accordingly.'

After a minute or two she realised what he meant, and after that couldn't think of anything to say because of the unseen listener who would be taking it all down. Presently, for the

listener's benefit rather than for Ian's, she said in an artificially
social voice.

'The furniture's very nice, anyway. I like that rug.'

'All Finnish. They don't furnish foreigners' blocks with
Russian-made stuff, of course—it would be too bad an
advertisement.' Evidently it was 'unwise' remarks you were
supposed to refrain from, not rude ones: those, the unseen
listener had to swallow. Indeed, after she'd been there for
several days Natasha became convinced that Ian went out of
his way to be rude when he thought he was being overheard,
rather than at other times. Clearly Stefan had been right
about the neurosis of foreigners living in Moscow, and she
came to think that it was really quite clever of the foreign
office to post Ian there. With his natural talents for suspicion,
caution and resentment, he fitted there beautifully.

In view of his generally unwelcoming air, she found the
efforts he made to entertain her in the following days
surprising and rather touching. He invited other Embassy staff
and their wives in to meet her, and they drank Scotch whisky
and ate American peanuts. Apparently there was one food
shop where you could get Western European branded goods,
paying for them in a special paper money which was issued
to foreign residents, and none of them ever shopped anywhere
else. The ones she met all seemed to have just come back
from Finland, or were going there next month, to buy tights,
or contraceptive pills, or to have a baby. It seemed that when
you were in Russia, Finland suddenly surged from obscurity
to symbolise the Western world of high-priced comfort.

But of course they weren't in Russia—not really. Ian's flat,
with its light oak furniture and gaily coloured modern rugs,
wasn't in Russia, and nor were any of the similar flats to which
she was kindly invited. She discovered by and by that most of
the wives seldom entered Russia at all. They drove everywhere, or were driven, in cars provided by their own govern-
ments, ignoring the metro stations that were like ornate
mausoleums and the routes of the packed, swaying trolley

cars. When they or their children were ill they went to the British Embassy surgery where the nurse dispensed calomine lotion and Gee's linctus. Many of them seemed to be going to Russian lessons, but it was hard to discover when they would need to use the language: the servants with which they were provided all spoke a European tongue.

She did not blame the wives: they had not asked to come here, why should they treat this barbaric, fusty yet oddly exotic place as anything but a backdrop to their lives, a library-shot of a multitude of granite buildings with only a few of them distinct and neatly labelled as in an instructive panorama: the Kremlin, Novo Devichy, GUM? But after a day or two she learnt that if she wanted to penetrate the backdrop herself and slide in between the stolid, two-dimensional crowds of people, she had to be on her own. And even then Russia wasn't always there. At times she walked and walked, seeking Russia, and could find nothing but traffic and tall cement and glass blocks from anywhere—as Stefan had warned her—and even the letters running round the tops of the buildings were no help because when she managed to decipher them they were simply slogans about the Party and the Glory of the Working Classes: flat, unreal proclamations on a flat picture. But at other times Russia was suddenly there all round her. It came abruptly and fleetingly, as in the oversweet smell of someone's scented soap or onion-and-vodka-laden breath as he brushed against her. Or completely and satisfyingly, as in the sight of a public flower bed untidily piled with flowers flourishing in the brief Russian summer. It came when she saw old women sweeping the streets of the capital with twig brooms, or a young girl with cheap earrings wheeling a pram in which lay a baby swaddled like an Easter egg in lace and ribbons. And it came once in GUM, the big department store that was like an Eastern bazaar selling poor-quality hand towels and plastic toys, when she saw fat, middle-aged couples in shoddy clothes queuing for glasses of champagne.

And she found Russia most of all in a small enclave of wooden houses built on sloping unpaved earth behind the People's Market: Ian told her there had been more of them but they were all being demolished. On the side of them which faced the boulevard trees grew high, right up in front of their windows, as if to screen the houses from the street and street from the houses, but behind there was space, and sunflowers and benches by open doors, and even chickens. 'They're all going,' said Ian. 'Probably just as well. They've got a family in each room and that shack over there by the wall of the Market is the communal lavatory.' He thought she regretted the houses' passing because they were 'picturesque' and was faintly scornful, on principle, of such a 'sentimental' approach to the complexities of the modern world. Natasha's hopelessly impractical attitude to life (as he had always seen it) made him feel, by contrast, hard-headed and pragmatic, a man without arty pretentions who knew how 'people' really lived, and he enjoyed feeling like that for once.

'You'll see plenty more old wooden houses when we go on the trip to Yaroslavl this weekend,' he said. 'There are villages all along that road. We can't *stop* in them of course, or the Militia will be onto us. But you'll get a good look. They are quaint, I agree.'

She did not attempt to explain that what attracted her to the old houses was not their 'quaintness' or remoteness from her own life, but a haunting air of familiarity about them. She seemed to know those houses, as if recognising them from some distant period of her own life.

'I wish we could go inside one,' she said.

He laughed loud and humourlessly at this preposterous suggestion. 'Not a chance of that! Not a chance—I'd be out on my ear... If you want to see inside an old Russian home why not go to Chekov's house? It's on the garden ring. I haven't had time to go there yet myself, but it's said to be quite interesting—lots of family letters and photos and so forth.'

She went to Chekov's house, which was like a stucco villa in a French provincial town. She liked it, but Russia wasn't there. Perhaps the Chekov's country house would have been better? She realised now for the first time how much the view which Maria Vasilievna had imparted to her had been of rural Russia and of antique date. Although born in westward-facing St Petersburg and into a Europeanised class, the Russia which Mari Vasilievna's family seemed to have carried with them to Paris had been something subtly other—more Eastern, harder now to trace. At any rate it was not the Russia of bearded Victorians in frock coats and letters home from Baden-Baden, that Natasha in her turn now sought.

She began to see Moscow not as a city like other cities but as a piece of Russian earth disguised under only a thin, cracked layer of tarmac and cement. The native soil kept bursting through: every boulevard had its fringe of rough grass and shaggy trees, and pavements degenerated into mud down side streets. And the people themselves, with their solid bodies and slow, deliberate walk, perpetually encumbered with string bags of vegetables, she saw as country-dwellers. Modern Moscow was an illusion, and a patchy one at that. The essential Russia was there and she was on its trail. It played hide and seek with her, just as the known sounds of familiar Russian words hid from her within the square, hard-to-decipher alphabet, but she could break the code when she tried.

Familiar Russian words? Yes. But why so familiar? Some, certainly, she had come across in her questing reading in recent years. But others, fragments and ends of sentences heard in the streets and in shops, she could not recall having met before, yet she knew them. Only gradually did it occur to her that, in her inaccessible infancy, Maria Vasilievna must have talked to her in Russian as well as French and that it was this first, forgotten language that was now returning to her.

On Saturday morning they set out for Zagorsk, fifty miles from Moscow. They were to see the famous complex of

churches there and then go on, via several other monasteries,
to stay the night at Yaroslavl. Ian made so much of the trouble
and fuss there had been in booking them into the Yaroslavl
hotel, and of the sheaves of papers they had to carry with
them to pacify the Militia at the control points, that she
began ungratefully to wish they were not going. In any case
an obscure dread had come over her. She felt as some people
did when taking an aeroplane, or as she had when she had
rung Stefan one night at Bromley and his wife had answered,
so friendly and unsuspecting. But it wasn't Stefan that was
making her stomach contract and her hands grow clammy this
morning. Stefan lay dead inside her like a baby that would
never be born but it wasn't that. . .

She discovered, after a little thought, that she was afraid
that something lay in wait for her on the road to Yaroslavl.
Some accident, some event, some person—what?

Then, as they drove out of Moscow, her fear receded. It
was still there, like a vulnerable point in her stomach, but it
was manageable. The cottages strung out along the road were
all that Ian had promised, their colours straight from the
child's paint-box, their eaves and dormer windows fretted
like lace. There were gardens full of flowers crammed behind
white paling fences, and ducks on ponds and geese walking
in lines and pumps by the road with long handles.

'That's their only water supply,' said Ian in a tone of
ritualistic indignation, as if he had some personal concern
with the fate of people condemned to carry pails of water all
their lives. 'And do you realise we're only about as far from
the centre of Moscow as Orpington is from London?'

Sergei remarked placidly, without turning his head, that the
water pipes were however coming. He indicated a deep
trench along the side of the road. He was more communicative
that morning than Natasha had so far known him. It seemed to
her that he had set out to enjoy this trip. Ian, who had gone to
the trouble to arrange it all, was by contrast a skeleton at the
feast, and talked steadily most of the way to Zagorsk about

the poverty and backwardness of the Russian countryside and the corruption of the local councils. When they reached Zagorsk he announced he had a headache and would stay in the car.

'I've seen the place before. Sergei can show you round—churches are really more his thing than mine anyway.' In an undertone he added as they were getting out of the car: 'Sergei goes to church. But don't let on I told you.'

In Sergei's near-silent company she walked through the massive medieval gates, gazed upwards at towering white walls, at gilded domes and silver domes and blue domes painted with stars. He knew the names of each of the churches and she had the feeling that, had he wanted to, he could have told her much more. At one moment two men with softly curling beards and swinging cassocks passed them at a brisk step.

'Surely those were priests?' she said.

'I think, yes.'

'I didn't realise they still had them here.'

'Why not?' Sergei spread his hands out in the gesture of a Russian indicating that everything is possible.

'But they're quite young. I mean, I thought the only priests left in Russia were old men. . .'

'There is a seminary here for young priests,' Sergei remarked. 'And one in Leningrad.' He smiled at her, a secretive smile, faintly self-satisfied. A few minutes later as they were passing down a side path in one of the more neglected parts of the monastery precinct, he pointed to a low building which did not seem to invite visitors:

'Look. I think that is where the priests are living.'

'Really?'

'Perhaps. I don't know. I think.'

They peered through a door leading to a staircase. The place seemed inhabited but, unlike the resplendent churches, was in poor repair. Lying nearby she noticed saucers of milk and water and an open tin of meat. A small cat slunk from under a bush and inspected the offerings, but took fright at their approach.

'I suppose the priests put that food there,' she said. Sergei did not answer. In her mind the priests and the cats merged into one another, an underlife going on behind the public façade, obscure, tenacious and inextinguishable. The half-open door, the pans of food, seemed like messages from the hidden world, if only she could decipher them. She felt frightened again, as she had when they had started from Moscow that morning, but elated too.

They drove on, and stopped in a grove of birch trees by the road to eat the picnic lunch which Ian had bought ready-packed at the foreigners' food shop. Sergei refused to share it, saying that he had already eaten that morning. He sat in the car and read a thick Russian magazine. Yet he was not, thought Natasha, politely absenting himself like a British servant 'knowing his place'. It was more as if he remained aloof from them on purpose—or on orders. Yet in other ways he was friendly enough. She wondered if he had a wife, one of the multitude of fat women in sleeveless dresses and dyed hair, and perhaps one self-effacing and well-conducted child in a cramped flatlet.

'Yes, he has a wife and family,' said Ian, 'but he never talks about them. I don't even know where he lives.'

'Where is he going to stay in Yaroslavl?' she asked. 'At our hotel—or a different one.'

'There *is* only one, apparently—or only one admitted to officially. I offered to put him up there but he says he'll drive back to Rostov and stay there. He's got a cousin there or something.'

'I wish we could stay with the cousin too!' There, in one of those wooden houses, behind the elaborate screens of looped lace and geraniums which closed the small windows to view, Russia was hiding from her. Sergei might have been able to lead her to it.

Ian looked at her as if she was mad.

'Good heavens, we'd never be able to do that. Sergei would never suggest it anyway. And in any case you've no idea how these people live. They may look quite Western and normal when you see them out and about, but they sleep together in winter with the pigs and the hens. They're all just *moujiks* really—just peasants. Even Sergei, though he is a Muscovite.'

She thought of saying: Since you've never been inside one of their homes how can you tell?—but there was really no point in baiting Ian.

'Hallo,' he was saying with a note of anxiety in his voice: 'What do *they* want?'

A yellow police car had drawn up beside Sergei in the car. A policeman got out and papers were examined.

'We'll stay here,' said Ian sharply. She thought of what Stefan had said about foreigners in Russia getting paranoid.

She heard his sigh of relief when the police car had driven off again. They walked over to Sergei.

'Just a check,' said Sergei soothingly. He had already gone back to his magazine.

'But why?' said Ian edgily. 'They knew we were coming along this road today. We've got permission—and they'd already seen us at the ring road check-point.'

'Yes,' said Sergei equably, 'but they told me we should not stop by the road.'

'Not stopped—? Oh really. How ridiculous. People do it all the time.'

'Of course.' Sergei shrugged as if the matter were quite unimportant but Ian pursued it.

'We've often done it before. Why didn't you tell me it was forbidden? Didn't *you* know either?'

'Yes. I know...' Sergei looked down and brushed the lapels of his jacket. 'But, as you see, the police did not really want us to go,' he said after a moment. 'They do not say to me "You must drive on now, this moment." They say "Stopping forbidden: for this point you have only a transit visa." And I say "Very sorry. Excuse me, please." And they say "That is OK" And then they go away again, quite happy.'

Ian snorted with disgust as they got into the car. 'Bloody nonsense,' he said to Natasha. 'If it'd been me in the car I'd have told the police not to be so damn silly. If we've a right to be on the road at all we've a right to stop by the side of it, and I'd have told them so...'

Yes, you would have, thought Natasha, but that is because you do not understand. Ian spoke more Russian than she did —but somewhere behind the scenes a game was being played, a whole secret life was being lived and Sergei was part of it and Ian wasn't. She felt a desire to keep close to Sergei. He was both her protector and, just possibly, her secret interpreter. Ian didn't count.

She sat in the front seat next to Sergei as they drove on toward Rostov. The countryside went on like a film going round and round in a projector: unhedged green expanses and straggling houses and duck ponds, silver birches and conifers and green expanses. Identical battered grey lorries each with an identical trailer drove along the same bit of road under an unchanging sky. Once or twice, among the houses, they passed derelict churches, unimportant ones which had not been rechristened museums. Their bluish domes were sprinkled not with stars but with crisp rust and their precincts were churned by the feet of cattle. And once, on a sunlit hill, there were flowers, and crosses and red stars interchangeably distributed.

'Oh look, a cemetery,' she said.

'Would you like to stop and look?' said Sergei softly.

'Oh yes... But isn't it "forbidden"?' She laughed, trying to make a joke of it, in spite of the sense of trepidation and impending significance which had suddenly come over her again. Sergei smiled his secretive smile.

'I am thinking not. Not seriously, anyway. Let us look.' He got out, walked round the car and opened the door for her. Getting out, she said to Ian: 'Are you staying here?' hoping he would, but he said grumpily, 'Might as well come, I suppose,' and followed them up the grassy path.

She wandered around for a while deciphering the Cyrillic inscriptions and looking with pity, disbelief and a vague squeamishness at the photos on small enamel plates which were set into many of the head stones. Faces, eyes, lips, stiff collars, neatly combed hair, the tops of Sunday dresses looked back at her, enamelled forever, daring her to think of corruption. She didn't like the photos: she was afraid of them. But the sunlit view was nice and so were the masses of flowers, both plastic and real. Ian sat on a bench and smoked, holding his ivory holder prissily.

'Look,' said Sergei softly to her. 'Look at the food.'

She looked, and on one grave pears and tomatoes lay, fresh but beginning to swell and burst under the sun. 'But why. . .' she asked.

'The fruit is for her—the woman buried there. You see, her relatives bring it. For her *dousha*—her spirit—to eat.'

'Goodness. Do people often do this? Even today?'

'Oh yes. Often. Often. See—over there is some bread.' It was true. A round loaf, fossilised by wind and sun, lay beside a fresh bunch of phlox.

'But do they really think,' she said seriously, 'that the dead need it?'

'Of course. The dead must eat—like all of us!' He sounded gay but it took her a moment to realise he must be joking, and even then she wasn't sure. In the heat he had taken off his jacket and rolled back the sleeves of his shiny white nylon shirt. He stood between her and the sun. His bare forearms were very hairy and she was afraid of him, as of the open-eyed people who sat under the earth and ate, but she also wanted him. Was this what lay waiting for her on the road to Yarosalvl, had been waiting all the time? Weak but luxuriant she stared at his chest: like most Russians, in spite of his dark suit he did not wear a tie.

'Come', he said, just touching her arm. For a wild moment

she thought he meant: Come with me—but of course he just meant 'Come, let's go back to the car.' She followed him and Ian back down the path to the road with a sense of shame.

I must be going sex-mad, she thought. I hardly know Sergei and anyway he's Ian's chauffeur. Ian would be furious. This has never happened to me before. I suppose it's because of Stefan... But it isn't even as if Sergei looks like Stefan or has the same accent... Is Sergei all part of some plan?

In the car, to make conversation, she asked Ian if he had seen the food on the graves. He hadn't. Over his shoulder, Sergei explained.

'Good lord, how primitive,' said Ian disgustedly.

In a priggish voice he had not used when he and she were standing together, Sergei said:

'In the country, people believe such things.' He tucked in his fleshy chin, put on a town-dweller's smile, patronising, almost like Ian's. But still secretive.

She did not speak for a while. A connection had suddenly clicked in her head and once again the sense of mingled dread and excitement had swept over her. The food ... lying under the bushes at Zagorsk or laid out in the cemetery—it was all one: unobtrusive evidences of the underlife, secret messages. A communion. And Sergei had shown it to her. Sergei knew.

When they came to Rostov, where two great kremlins project on spars of land into a lake the size of an inland sea, the sun was going down the sky and Ian was fussing to get on to Yaroslavl. 'We haven't got a permit to drive after dark. Sergei knows that perfectly well.'

'But does it really matter?' she said. 'I mean, if we find our-selves driving into Yaroslavl in the dark, so what? They can't stop us. There's nowhere else for us to go.' She felt mazed with the sun, the drive and the continued presence of Sergei. He, she was sure now, was for her the key. If anyone could open for her the Russia of Maria Vasilievna, that remote, private, semi-Eastern country, it would be Sergei.

'We can't stop long here,' Ian nagged. 'Anyway these

churches are falling to bits. Typical, of course. They look impressive, I grant you, from across the water but now we're here there's nothing much to *see*. Just some old merchants' houses round the market place and they're nothing special.'

'I thought I might go down to the lake and see if I can get a shot looking across the water at the other kremlin. It ought to be good with this sky...'

'It's much too dark already...' he said, but she got out clutching her camera to her like those paper permits they carried everywhere. This must, she realised, have been why she had brought it to Russia: it was, like Ian himself, part of her disguise as a tourist. Ian wasn't to know there was no film in it.

She walked down the unmade road to the lake. As she expected, by now, Sergei came gently after her. She felt a suffocating excitement. The old Russia was not dead: it had not died at Ekaterinburg in 1918 nor yet in Sussex in 1951. It lived on, and Sergei knew it and was her conspirator. Somewhere, in one of those wooden houses whose weak lamps were beginning to spill light onto the mud road, he had a cousin and would would spend the night, in Russia. Somewhere, in a similar village-like town on the face of the vast landscape, she too belonged. On an alternative circuit of time, in which the Revolution had never taken place, her real self was living—if only she could find it and fuse with it.

In the lake were moored dozens of rowing boats: the last of the sun made their sides glint yellow against the flat silver water, but over the sky above was spreading a huge shadow. The other kremlin was a grey silhouette on the far shore. Sergei came and stood beside her.

'You should stay here,' she said, not looking at him. 'I mean, it seems silly for you to drive us into Yaroslavl and then have to come back here. Can't my brother—can't Gaspodin Reynold drive to Yaroslavl?'

'He could, of course, but... I think I will accompany you. It is my work.' He smiled to himself. Ian would have said that

Sergei stuck close to them all the time in order to watch them.
Standing by the lake with him she felt it was rather that he
was her personal guide, the intermediary between her and
the hidden Russia, and for her sake could not risk abandoning
her. He understood her, yes—but was he really her ally? Was
he there to reveal Russia to her—or ultimately to keep it from
her? By the water she clenched her fists and wished, at first
silently then suddenly aloud:

'I wish I could stay here with you—at your cousin's house.
I wish you would show me things.'

For a moment she thought he was going to pretend he had
not heard her. He remained looking out over the oily water
and his face was impassive as is the face of someone who has,
in fact, understood but will not admit to having done so.
Then, as if making up his mind, he turned towards her.

'Another time,' he said quickly. 'Another time you will come
again. It will not be like it is now... There will be another
time.' He cast a look round but they were alone. Very quickly,
almost before she knew he was going to do it, he put his
hands over her breasts and kissed her on the mouth. As
quickly, he stepped back. A moment later he was the chauffeur
again strolling off towards the road looking with ostentatious
discreetness at his watch.

It was quite dark by the time they reached Yaroslavl. The
hotel had old, tiled floors and they seemed to be almost the
only guests. Alone in her room with two silk counterpaned
beds she hardly slept all night.

After breakfast the next morning a local Intourist guide
took them round depressingly battered churches, where Ian
became abruptly knowledgeable about frescoes, and past
fragments of medieval wall in between trolley bus lines. Then
Sergei and the car were waiting for them outside the hotel.
The weather had changed, the sky was overcast, and Sergei
seemed to have changed too. He smelt strongly of the tainted
perfume of Russian soap, and his Mongolian face wore the
shut expression of someone who regards himself as being on

duty and nothing more. As they took the same road back that they had taken the day before, and skirted Rostov without seeing the lake, the sense of a missed moment grew on her. There had been a chance—a point when she had begun to perceive a pattern, to break through the barriers of time and identity—and it had gone again. Then, as they drove toward Moscow and her depression increased she began to wonder if she had fantasied the whole thing anyway, attributing a cosmic significance to chance events. That moment by the lake when she had stood there waiting for Sergei to touch her and he had... He must have thought her a randy, decadent Westerner, just the sort he was supposed to report on to the KGB. Or else he thought she was unbalanced. Mad—

Perhaps, she thought, in a sudden bleak moment, a cold space between two other ideas, she *was* mad. Perhaps she had imagined the whole thing?

It was then that they passed the funeral. They heard chanting and the noise of brass instruments played at half the usual speed, and then the procession was there on the other side of the road: scores of people marching, threes and fours abreast in slow time, carrying real and plastic wreaths like the ones in the cemetery. Perhaps it was to that same cemetery they were going. There were girls in ankle socks, weeping, and old women of forty in scarves with cloths pressed to their faces, and a great noise of shuffling feet on the tarmac. Sergei slowed right down. A group of men in front carried an ikon held high like a banner. In the thick of the crowd came more men together, in suits like Sergei's, bearing an open bier, Natasha had a brief glimpse of a peaky, white face, its black hair half hidden in piled flowers: she couldn't tell if it were a young man or a middle-aged woman, but had the impression, even at that distance and from inside the car, of eyes not quite shut, of a withdrawn yet knowing presence of another order in the midst of this chanting, shuffling throng. As they drifted past the rain began to spot down, onto the wreaths and the summer dresses and the face bare to the sky.

'Wow, what a show,' said Ian. Even as she—and Sergei—
were both taciturn this morning, Ian seemed more ebullient,
as if to redress some pointless balance. 'Did you see the ikon?'
he asked after a minute, and then, as Sergei said nothing: 'So
much for the modern, progressive Soviet State, mm?'

How dare he, thought Natasha: Sergei will be furious. One
shouldn't say these things. That side is dark, secret... But
after a moment Ian went on, in the same bantering, almost
camp tone, addressing her, but loudly so that the chauffeur
would hear:

'Sergei doesn't like passing a funeral. He's really super-
stitious as hell. A mass of primitive beliefs.'

The rain began to fall heavily now. The perpetual lorries
in front—always the same lorry, it seemed, from its grey,
numbered rear—threw a fine, muddy spray back at their car.
Sergei would have to wash the whole thing as soon as they got
to Moscow. As they neared the first concrete suburbs and the
outer expanses of railway lines, her fear and tension grew. She
felt oppressed, more than ever, by a sense of impending fate.
It had not, after all, happened on the road to Yaroslavl. Sergei
had said 'There will be another time.' She had interpreted
this as meaning, mystically, that on another circuit of time he
and she would stand there together again, and that that time
things would all work out, coming clear like an intricate game
of cosmic Patience. But perhaps that time would never come,
or she would not be there when it did. Perhaps she had now
swung back onto a narrower loop of time, and Sergei was
powerless to save her. Their brief moment of contact was over
and she would travel downwards again, down into an ever-
darkening ever-narrowing spiral of exile and loneliness and
death, Maria Vasilievna's death and her own.

That night, in Ian's flat, she wrote a letter to Stefan, addressing it to the BBC in London. *'Is it possible,'* she asked, *'that
one might inherit memories, or the feeling of a way of life
known below the level of consciousness?'* Stefan's parents
were Poles, living in a Polish-speaking, eating and thinking

world in Kilburn; only by an earlier slip in the pattern did Stefan find himself with English as a native tongue and London as his native city: he ought, she thought, to know the answer to her questions.

'Could a person possibly be born into the wrong place and time and so be trying all their lives, without knowing it, to get back to where they ought to be? And do you think it would be possible for someone else—someone quite unconnected with them—to realise this and try to help them and then realise it is useless?'

She thought of telling him all about Sergei—but what was 'all about'? Anyway it seemed hard to put down on paper. She signed the letter sadly, affectionately, but then wrote as an afterthought beneath the signature:

'Could sexual attraction be just there as a metaphor for something else? Could one mistake for sexual feeling an emotion which is really about something quite different? Dying, for instance?'

The next day, on reflection, she did not post this letter, but left it on her writing pad. She was still waiting.

Three days later she and Ian took the night train to Leningrad. She was due to go home from there by boat, and Ian had arranged a long weekend off from the Embassy. She wished he had not. Sergei saw them off at the station, handing them both, with a flourish, miniature flasks of Russian cognac. But he did not look at her. She thought of the opening of *Anna Karenina* and of train wheels in the end going over and over that body, turning it into something other, translating it to another sphere, another condition.

Leningrad was the Petersburg of Maria Vasilievna's birth, but here she was not. Natasha tried telling herself that here, of all places, she should find the hidden, fabulous Russia of her borrowed memories, but it was not so. Leningrad, with its canals that looked like Venice and its classical facades that looked like Brighton, was a Western city: she quailed before it. Only one building seemed to strike in her mind a faint, flat chord, tantalising echo of an echo like the words on the lips of old women in the streets, and that was the cathedral by the canal where Alexandra II had been assassinated. But Ian, who waxed knowledgeable about Leningrad, far preferring it to Moscow, said that that cathedral was a perfectly dreadful example of Russian neo-Gothic, its onion domes a sham, every bit as phoney as St Pancras station, and once she'd seen what he meant the echoes vanished. Russia—her Russia and Maria Vasilievna's—had retreated again to a tiny, far-off scene in a glass bubble, forever out of reach. She had lost it, and had lost her chance.

Children were wheeled in prams in the Leningrad public gardens and men played chess under the trees, and she was dying.

On the night before she sailed Ian had managed to get tickets for the ballet. She did not especially want to see it, but she was grateful to him and felt apologetic in advance for what she was going to do to him. He wouldn't exactly *care*, she thought. But he would feel bad about it, and wonder if anyone would say he had failed in his duty to his step-sister. His career might even suffer, for a few months.

It was *Swan Lake* and, because they had had to queue for a taxi outside their hotel, and arrived late and had to stand up in the gallery till the first interval, Ian fumed silently. As she gazed down and down onto those foreshortened figures it was not the measured antics on stage which drew her eyes so much as the audience. So many of the women there seemed to have luxuriant heads of hair. That hair, and their billowing breasts, would break her fall. They were the real swans, unwontedly soft and scented for the occasion. When she fell—if she fell— the angular dancers on stage would, of course, just go on, like so many automata.

Not till the third act, when she had not after all fallen and they were sitting safely in their stalls, did it suddenly come to her that the jester-devil (or whatever he was) in *Swan Lake* had the face of the man-woman they had seen on the open bier. Androgenous, boney, dark-haired and a little scornful of everyone, he gyrated under the lights like a geometrical pun, his costume red-and-black, black-and-red. But she had seen him lying quiet with his knowing lids not quite closed, his face to the uneasy sky. Why had he returned to this manic turmoil?

Perhaps, then, *he* was her messenger and not Sergei at all? Too late, too late again: she could not plummet now from the high gallery, that moment too was passed. She went on sitting as the waves of clapping billowed round her and the figures were gone.

The next afternoon the ship carried her away. At the last moment, in the Customs shed, she suddenly felt desperate at the thought of leaving, but it was already too late, too late again. The decision, and now every decision, had been taken for her.

As if even he felt some anxiety for her, or some queasy intimation of what was about to happen, Ian kissed her good-bye with unaccustomed affection and stood for a long time at the barriers till at last the ship pulled away and he could wave and go. But perhaps he had just waited 'to see her off' because it was the thing to do. She did not know, and now never would. The thought that she would never, now, have to learn anything more, or struggle any more to suit her comprehension to the realities of her own badly fitting existence, gave her new strength. She kept her eyes on Ian's angular, jerky figure—as inconsequential and mannered as one of those figures on stage—till at last she saw him decide that she could no longer see him, and he dropped his arm and turned away with alacrity, the performance over.

Alone now, and a person to no one—just a name on a list, a new face among a whole ship of faces, new and blessedly meaningless to one another—she made her way quickly to the upper deck at the stern. It was windy there and, with the docks of Leningrad sinking behind them, most people had gone to their cabins to recover from Russia and to prepare a shipboard identity for themselves. A man in an anorak strolled by and looked at her as if he might speak, but all that was passed, past, there would be no more messengers now—she turned her eyes resolutely toward the water, tumbling like glacier mints from the ship's screw, and when she looked up again he had gone.

Out loud she said 'Maria Vasilievna' trying on the fresh, uncaring air the name that had lain unspoken for more than twenty years. It sounded surprisingly natural, and, though no one answered, she felt happier, more confident and confiding, free—

Free.

With joyful expectation and the certainty of ultimate fulfilment and fusion—a circle completed, a loop of time joined again to the intricate pattern in which all time was one—she climbed nimbly over the wooden side, glanced round once more to make sure she really was alone, and then let herself fall without hesitation into the stinging water of the Baltic. The gulls rose and wheeled.